## More Praise for Augusta Trobaugh

"Trobaugh streamlines her rich Southern style and creates a
narrative as delicate as a line drawing."
—*USA Today*

"Heroines are Trobaugh's forte, and she has
created a memorable one . . .[*Swan Place*] should be
on your must-read list."
—*The Newark Star-Ledger*

"Thank you, Augusta Trobaugh, for proving that love,
passion, redemption, and compassion continue to
flourish in Southern literature."
—*Spartanburg Herald-Journal*

"Family secrets, redemption, and the power of love are
Trobaugh's themes . . .[her] prose is deft and sweet . . .
A comforting read."
—*Booklist*

"Trobaugh's supreme skill is her command of character.
[She] manages to make her characters both
inspirational and down-to-earth."
—*Publishers Weekly*

**Augusta Trobaugh** is the author of the novels *Swan Place* and
*Sophie and the Rising Sun* (both available from Plume). She
earned a master's degree in English from the University of
Georgia, and has been awarded several grants from the Georgia Council for the Arts. She lives in Georgia.

**Visit AugustaTrobaugh.com**

# RIVER JORDAN

## A NOVEL

# AUGUSTA TROBAUGH

A PLUME BOOK

PLUME
Published by Penguin Group
Penguin Group (USA) Inc., 375 Hudson Street, New York, New York 10014, U.S.A.
Penguin Group (Canada), 10 Alcorn Avenue, Toronto, Ontario,
Canada M4V 3B2 (a division of Pearson Penguin Canada Inc.)
Penguin Books Ltd., 80 Strand, London WC2R 0RL, England
Penguin Ireland, 25 St. Stephen's Green, Dublin 2, Ireland
(a division of Penguin Books Ltd.)
Penguin Group (Australia), 250 Camberwell Road, Camberwell, Victoria 3124,
Australia (a division of Pearson Australia Group Pty. Ltd.)
Penguin Books India Pvt. Ltd., 11 Community Centre, Panchsheel Park,
New Delhi – 110 017, India
Penguin Books (NZ), cnr Airborne and Rosedale Roads,
Albany, Auckland 1310, New Zealand (a division of Pearson New Zealand Ltd.)
Penguin Books (South Africa) (Pty.) Ltd., 24 Sturdee Avenue,
Rosebank, Johannesburg 2196, South Africa

Penguin Books Ltd., Registered Offices: 80 Strand, London WC2R 0RL, England

Published by Plume, a member of Penguin Group (USA) Inc. Previously published in
a Dutton edition.

First Plume Printing, July 2005
10   9   8   7   6   5   4   3   2   1

℗ REGISTERED TRADEMARK—MARCA REGISTRADA

The Library of Congress has catalogued the Dutton edition as follows:

Trobaugh, Augusta.
River Jordan : a novel / by Augusta Trobaugh.
    p. cm.
ISBN 0-525-94755-8 (hc.)
ISBN 0-452-28660-3 (pbk.)
    1. African American women—Fiction. 2. Grandparent and child—Fiction.
3. Female friendship—Fiction. 4. Southern States—Fiction. 5. Stepfamilies—
Fiction. 6. Ex-convicts—Fiction. 7. Aged-women—Fiction. 8. Nurses—Fiction.
9. Girls—Fiction. I. Title.

PS3570.R585R58 2004
813'.54—dc22            2003056489

Printed in the United States of America
Original hardcover design by Eve L. Kirch

PUBLISHER'S NOTE
This is a work of fiction. Names, characters, places, and incidents are either the product
of the author's imagination or are used fictitiously, and any resemblance to actual per-
sons, living or dead, business establishments, events, or locales is entirely coincidental.

*For Dwight Abraham Hurless Crumbecker,*
*my father.*
*I was born late in your life,*
*and you died too soon. But I remember*
*our "conversations"—not the exact*
*words themselves, but exactly how*
*they lifted me on wings of thought.*
*Thank you, Daddy.*

# River Jordan

# PROLOGUE

*I* REMEMBER *exactly how long and dark the nights were for me when I was in prison, and I also remember how I used to try to lie real still and keep my eyes closed, so that sooner or later—usually later—I would be able to fall into a bit of sleep.*

*But there was one particular night when sleep didn't come. My parole hearing was only a few weeks away, and it was all I could think about. Lately, I'd become even more aware of the night sounds and the night silences, and I wondered what it would be like to sleep once again in a regular bed in a regular house and not hear keys jingling or the sad yelping of someone having a nightmare a few cells away. Not hear one woman call another woman's name in the dark.*

*I knew all the phantom sounds, as well—the ones that weren't real. Like hearing my cell door opening and some silent voice telling me that I could go. Be free. I knew for sure that was just a being-in-prison dream. And when I heard my sweet mama's voice, I knew it was just another homesick-dream.*

*But when I heard a man's voice that long, dark night—and it so close that he had to be right there in the cell with me—I*

1

*couldn't figure out what kind of a dream that could be! And why
on earth would I dream something like that at all? I certainly
wasn't interested in any man, not after what I'd gone through
with Earlie. And while I was trying to think what kind of a
dream sound it was, I heard it again.*

*"Pansy?"*

*Who on earth could that be? I was thinking. And just then,
I heard Lizzie, in the cell next to mine, snorting as she turned
over in her sleep.*

*"Pansy? Pansy Jordan?"*

*"Who is it?" I whispered. "Whutchu want? Whutchu doing
in here? And how'd you get in here at all?"*

*"Pansy? Who you talking to?" Lizzie's sleepy, scratchy voice.
But I didn't answer her. All I could think about was that if there
really was a man in my cell, I might not get paroled, because nobody would believe that I didn't invite him in! Didn't break all
the rules just to have him there. But how could any man get into
my cell anyway? Even if I wanted him there, which I certainly
did not!*

*"Whutchu want? Who are you?" I whispered again, this time
with what I hoped sounded like a growl in my voice.*

*"This is Jesus speaking to you."*

*Why, I was never so surprised in all my life! That voice was
deep and sweet, and the breath that came drifting across my cell
had a fragrance to it, like the perfume of blooming tea-olive and
something else—orange blossoms, maybe. And honeysuckle, the
way its aroma is sizzled out on a hot summer noontime. All so
sweet a perfume that I thought I might just faint from the beauty
of breathing it!*

*"Whutchu say?"*

*"Pansy? Who you talking to?" Lizzie called.*

"Nobody. Shut up, Lizzie!" And I listened again for the voice. Listened so hard that my ears seemed to grow, reach out for the sound.

"Pansy, this is Jesus."

"Go on with you!" I whispered. "You think I'm some fool who'd believe that?" I waited, with my heart hammering in my ears, and when I couldn't stand it any longer, I sat up and craned my neck to look all around the dark cell. A soft, wavering glow appeared in the far corner. A corner where no light should be. And while I watched, a hand appeared in the glow. A soft, bloodless hand with a nail hole in the very center of the palm.

Maybe it was just a dream. Or maybe it really was Jesus.

And then, all at once, I got things figured out. I laughed—a short, nervous laugh. "Oh! It's probably Lizzie you're looking for," I said simply. "She's right next door. You've just come visiting the wrong cell." Because everyone knew about Lizzie and her "personal Savior." So what would be so strange about Him coming to see her, in person? Lizzie talked to Jesus all the time, and she even said that sometimes, He talked right back to her. Maybe He was just visiting with her. Sure would take more than prison walls and iron bars to keep Him out, anyway.

"Lizzie?" I called. "I think there's somebody here looking for you."

"What?" Lizzie asked. But before I could say anything else, the voice came again.

"Lizzie is my child, but tonight, it's you I'm talking to, Pansy," and once again, the fragrance of the breath drifted sweetly across my cell.

"Me?" I asked.

"You," He said. "Get yourself washed clean in the River Jordan, Pansy, and come to Me." With those words, the glow and

3

*the voice and the fragrance and the image of the hand all disappeared. But for the briefest possible moment, I could see another something or someone in the last glimmer of the light. It was a big woman. Black woman. Smiling at me. Showing a gold tooth right in the middle of the smile. An angel? Yes, of course!*

*Lizzie called to me again. "Who was looking for me? What on earth are you talking about?"*

*"Nothing, Lizzie. And nobody. Just me having the strangest dream I ever had," I answered, rubbing my eyes and wondering what I had eaten that could make a dream like that! And what was all that about getting myself washed clean in the River Jordan? I'd certainly heard of such a river, because my mama dragged me to church every single Sunday when I was little. But where was it, I wondered. Then I remembered that I didn't need to wonder. After all, it was probably only a dream. Even the big, black woman angel was nothing more than a dream.*

*I sort of fell back on my cot with a huff that sent all of the air out of my lungs. Whoever heard of such a thing! Me a woman in prison for killing a man, and somebody like me dreams about getting a visit from Jesus Christ Himself? And one of His angels?*

*" 'Night, Pansy," Lizzie said. "Try not to dream no more, you hear? We got a long day tomorrow."*

*"Yes," I answered. But I stayed awake for the rest of that long, dark night, wondering what such a dream could possibly mean.*

*At breakfast the next morning, Lizzie clumped her metal tray down beside mine.*

*"Now tell me about that dream you was having last night," Lizzie said, putting a spoonful of sugar into her coffee.*

"Guess I forgot," I said. "Guess I forgot what all it was about." I didn't look into Lizzie's eyes, but just kept on drawing my spoon through the congealed grits on my plate. Lizzie stopped stirring her coffee and gave me a piercing glance.

"You didn't forget," she pronounced.

I was silent.

"Why don't you want to tell me?" Lizzie pressed. And I felt the ire rising up inside of me, so I decided to tell the truth. " 'Cause I know if I tell you, you'll go off on one of your tirades about Jesus being your personal savior and about trying to get me saved, and I just don't want to hear that."

"You dreamed about Jesus?" Lizzie's interest visibly heightened.

"Oh, Lord!" I muttered, because I knew that even though I'd tried hard not to get Lizzie started, I'd already done it. Already walked across a barnyard inside of myself and gone right along and stepped in something!

"You dreamed about Jesus?" Lizzie repeated.

"Yes!" I slapped my palm on the table and attracted the glances of several other women sitting near us. I looked around at the guard, who was studying me from across the room with a placid expression on her face.

"S-h-h-h!" Lizzie warned, and then she asked the very same question yet again. "You dreamed about Jesus?"

"I did that," I whispered. "And one of His angels too."

"Tell me about it," Lizzie urged, and I figured I'd already gone and said too much anyway, so I might as well walk right into Lizzie's Holy Ghost lair with my head held high!

"I dreamed Jesus came to my cell in the night. I figured it was you He was looking for, and He called you His Child, but He said he was talking to me. Just think of that! Him wanting this *old prisoner woman! Well, that's a dream, sure enough! And right after He left, I saw an angel."*

"I'm a prisoner woman too," Lizzie reminded me. "And I know for sure that He loves me. And maybe He's going to send an angel to help you."

*Here we go! I was thinking. Might as well lay it all out on the table, else I'll never have me any peace:* "He said for me to get myself washed clean in the River Jordan and go to Him, but I sure don't know what that means."

*Lizzie remained quiet, obviously thinking hard.*

"Well, whatever He said for you to do, you just go ahead and do it. That's all. You just do it and don't ask any questions," she advised.

"Where is the River Jordan anyway?" I asked.

"Blamed if I know. But what you gotta do right now is invite Jesus into your heart."

"What?" *I sputtered, but at the same time, I wasn't really surprised at all. It was only what Lizzie did all the time, going around and telling everybody to do that very same thing. Lizzie got some black eyes and missing teeth from some of the prisoners, but she just kept on doing it anyway. So I tried to speak real softly to Lizzie, whispering,* "Lizzie, He already came into my cell, I think. Or else I just dreamed it. So why do I have to ask Him to come into my heart?"

*Lizzie hesitated, and then she said,* "You just do, that's all. Just do it!"

*Something in Lizzie's pleading eyes put a pain in my stomach.*

*And I was thinking, why not just do it? Make her happy and keep me from having her pester me to death! But then another thought crowded into my mind: maybe it would help me get paroled! Maybe if I told the parole board that I had asked Jesus* to come into my heart, they would think more kindly of me. But I better not say nothing about that angel. Why, if I told them I saw an angel who was a big black woman, they'd think I'd lost my mind.

So I closed my eyes and whispered, "Come into my heart, Lord Jesus. And if You are sending an angel to help me, I sure do appreciate that." When I opened my eyes, I saw Lizzie's face glowing like a flame. Across the room, the guard blew a whistle, and Lizzie and I and all the other women began getting up from the tables and taking our trays to the big, stainless steel table where the kitchen prisoners would scrape the plates clean and get them ready for washing.

Lizzie said, "Just you be sure and remember that dream. You are blessed to have such a dream, and to have Jesus living in your heart! But I do so wonder where the River Jordan is, myself!"

"Could be just about anywhere I guess. But I know one thing for sure."

"What's that?" Lizzie was hanging on to my every word, just as if I had suddenly become someone famous to her.

"I know it ain't here in this prison!" I said.

"Maybe not," Lizzie agreed. "But that big laundry is here, and it's just waiting for us."

"Yes, Lord!" I said.

# CHAPTER ONE

ONLY A FEW DAYS after Pansy's nocturnal visit by the Lord Jesus, Peony—Pansy's baby sister—was doing what she had been doing six days a week for many years—working in the kitchen of the big white house on Lakeview Drive and taking care of the white family she worked for: Mr. Franklin, president of the only bank in town, and now Miss Alice, Mr. Franklin's new wife and Jordan, his new stepdaughter.

Peony was a large woman who wore a starched, white uniform that contrasted starkly with her black velvet skin, and she was slicing fresh tomatoes onto a platter. But her nose was running and her eyes were filled with tears, as if she were slicing pungent onions instead of mild tomatoes. On several occasions, she stopped, pulled a towel rag from the waist of her dress, and wiped her eyes.

Peony had sent Jordan to feed the fish in the pool out in front of the house, because she knew that Jordan would be sure to notice and ask about her tears.

*Nothing gets past that one!* Peony thought. *That strange, quiet little girl with the darting eyes that see everything, maybe even what folks are thinking! Something always going on behind those eyes!*

Likewise, Peony knew that neither Miss Alice nor Mr. Franklin would notice at all—because to them both, Peony was an invisible presence in the house—a nonperson who did the cooking and the serving and the cleaning up, but who was not supposed to cause any unfortunate ripples in the mirror-calm surface of the family home. So Peony went back to slicing the tomatoes and wiping her eyes, and all because of what she had in her apron pocket—a letter from her big sister, Pansy. From her sister *in prison*.

And Peony had been right about Jordan, because Jordan already knew that something was wrong—in that uncanny way some children have of knowing things like that. She thought that maybe it was because of Peony sending her to feed the fish in the pool. But maybe it was more—a thing she hadn't quite figured out yet, so that she simply felt a vague uneasiness that deepened the shadows near the front porch and put something lonely in the perfume of the fresh-turned earth in the kitchen garden out back.

Late spring—and the azalea bushes in the yard were showing slits of too-bright crimson and purple and fuchsia through the first cracks in the swollen green casings. Her mama said that the flowers were going to be absolutely beautiful, but Jordan knew better. Because to her, the dwarf azaleas were always far more beautiful than the big ones, and they were already in full bloom. Tiny, softest-pink flowers on little bushes planted all around the fish pool below the driveway. The flowers reflecting themselves in the dark, still water, and mirror clouds moving across a blue sky behind them, and deeper down, the fish sparkling their gold and red and pearl sequin-scales against the old black leaves at the very bottom of the pool.

Because the flowers were one thing and the satin surface of the water another thing and the clouds looking like they were below the surface, not on it, and finally, at the bottom, all the soggy brown ones that used to be red and yellow and orange. The ones Miss Amylee liked so much last fall.

That's what Jordan was thinking about that spring morning when once again, she knew that something was getting ready to happen. But there was nothing to do but wait for it to come out of the dark corners of the garden at twilight, ready to burst out like crimson and purple and fuchsia too-big flowers. Wait for the images of her father and taste the bittersweet memories of sitting in his lap, opening her mouth like a baby bird as he fed her choice bits of tender chicken from his own plate. Breathe the aroma memory of him, the sunshine smell of the warm earth he worked every day and the fresh wind and the warm perfume of his flesh.

It all seemed so long ago and far away, living with her mother and her father on the small farm set out from town, enjoying a free childhood that she hadn't even known how to appreciate, until it was gone. Until her father sickened and finally died, and her mother wringing her hands and crying. But her crying stopped the day she went to the bank, to settle up any debts and to change the existing accounts into her own name. For at the bank, the young and pretty widow was waited upon by none other than the president of the bank himself—Mr. Franklin. Alice stopped crying and started smiling more, and after only a few months, she agreed to marry him. So she traded the front porch of the old farmhouse for the wide, polished veranda of Mr. Franklin's house in town, towing a silent

Jordan behind her like a forgotten appendage. And as far as Jordan was concerned, only two good things had come from her mother's marriage to Mr. Franklin: Miss Amylee—Mr. Franklin's elderly mother—and Peony.

Outside of the reverie, the reflection of Peony's wide, black face appeared on the surface of the pool, her gold hoop earrings undulating like little halos in the ripples left by one of the fish.

"Miss Alice says for you to come on back inside now and have your lunch," Peony said. The voice came from above the reflection of her face in the water, and that fact alone added something else to the layers of things Jordan was thinking about. And Peony's black, white-stockinged legs like gauze-wrapped trees growing out of the dark rock wall on the far side of the pool, and the clean, white shoes that were there too, but that she couldn't see because of the low wall.

"You're not having a *spell*, are you?" Peony asked, putting her big fists on her hips in such a way that meant Jordan had better not be having one, and so Jordan said no, which wasn't exactly true. Because her thinking hard about things like she was doing was what they all called *having a spell*, and so, of course, that's exactly what was happening. But if she said yes, Peony would tell her mama, and Alice would get Peony to give her a big dose of castor oil. Because everybody knew that having spells happens to children whenever they aren't *regular*.

"Well, come on in and have some lunch then," Peony demanded, as if it were something Jordan had to do, just to prove she wasn't having a spell after all. But Jordan noticed how Peony had said "lunch" instead of dinner, which was the usual way to talk about the big meal in the middle of the day, so Jordan knew right away that her stepfather wasn't going to be home. And that's why she would have something light and cold and called lunch.

She stood up and came around the pool, looking to see if Peony was wearing her white shoes and wondering if the shoes were really there when she couldn't see them. But of course, she didn't say anything about that, because she didn't want a dose of castor oil. And she didn't say anything about thinking so hard about her own father. So she followed Peony silently up the driveway, listening to the silk-swishing sound of Peony's starched dress against her girdle. She had seen that formidable girdle one time, because on a very hot day last summer, Peony said, " 'Scuse me, honey, but I gotta loosen up my laces." So Peony closed the kitchen door and flipped up her snowy-white, starched dress and the not-so-white nylon slip to reveal the girdle, a huge swath of heavy, pink canvas and elastic, with bone-stiff staves and laces like the ones in shoes, except far bigger and stronger. She loosened the laces and took a deep, satisfied breath.

"Whooee! That's better!"

There was something about that pink girdle and the swollen green pods of the azaleas, but Jordan wasn't sure of what it was, and she knew not to try to talk about things like that anyway, so she followed Peony's broad bottom in the white dress and lower down, the white shoes, clean and well-polished, with her feet pushing over the outside edges and the black, white-stockinged ankles swelling over the edges of the shoes like biscuit dough.

In the kitchen, Jordan sat down at the table and Peony put a tomato sandwich in front of her. And a folded, snowy-white linen napkin and a glass of milk.

"When you're done, your mama says for you to wash your face and put on a Sunday dress," Peony said.

"Why?" Jordan asked, feeling her scalp prickle. *Something's wrong, and I don't know what it is.*

"Why, Peony? And are you done with your crying?" she asked.

"Don't know why," Peony said. "She didn't say why. Just said I was to tell you. And yes, I'm done with my crying for now."

As always, Jordan was careful to pronounce her name as *pay-oh-nay.* That's the way she wanted it said, because when Peony was little, all the other children called her *pee-on-me,* and that had hurt her feelings something awful.

"Lord have mercy!" she said one time. "What on earth was my sweet mama thinking about to name all us girls after flowers like she did? It isn't so bad for my sisters—Primrose and Petunia and poor old Pansy. Not one of those is too bad, I'd say. But *Peony? Why, I wouldn't wish that name on a dog!*" That was right about the same time when Jordan had noticed that Peony's last name was the very same as Jordan's own first name.

"How come we've got the same name?" Jordan had asked.

"Same name?"

"You know. Your last name and my first name."

"Oh."

"How come, you reckon?"

"Well." Peony pursed her lips. "I 'spect that's because somewhere way back yonder, somebody in your mama's family owned somebody in my family."

"*Owned?*" Jordan was perplexed.

"Back in slave times."

"Oh."

"Your mama said that Jordan was her maiden name, and so that's what she gave you, when you came along."

"Why?"

"Dunno. Just a tradition or something."

Jordan thought for a long moment and then said, "I like it—having the same name as you."

Peony laughed. "Well then, I guess I like it too."

In the here and now, Peony asked, "You listening to me?"

"I'm listening," Jordan said. And suddenly she knew exactly why she had to wash her face and put on a Sunday dress. Mama was going over to White Columns to see about Miss Amylee—her stepfather's mama—and she was having Jordan go along with her because she said that having company always made her feel better, even though all Jordan did was sit in the waiting room. It was against the rules for children to go into the part of the home where Miss Amylee lived. And Jordan didn't want to go in there anyway. Not even to see Miss Amylee. Not after what Jordan's mama and stepfather had done to Miss Amylee.

That afternoon Jordan sat once again in the antiseptic-smelling waiting room of White Columns, a linoleum-floored room where two old ladies sat in wheelchairs, watching soap operas on television. One of them was asleep, leaning over the arm of the chair, and with her chin all wet. The other old lady was eating dry Froot Loops, one at a time, out of a plastic bowl.

"You sit right here and watch TV, sugar," Mama had said. "And be sweet."

With that, her mama followed a lady in a navy-blue dress through the door marked *Private,* and after it closed behind them, a thin thread of cooler air wafted into the hot waiting room, because the private room was air-conditioned. Jordan sat on a chair that had a plastic cushion and already, she felt sweat gathering around her bare legs under the short dress.

The Froot Loop lady started talking to the television set, but Jordan couldn't tell what she was saying. Besides, the lady wasn't talking to Jordan, and it wasn't polite to stare at anyone. So Jordan looked away.

"Don't you believe a word he says!" the old lady yelled suddenly at the television set. On the screen, a beautiful young woman was hugging a handsome man to her and saying, "Oh, of course, I believe you, darling!"

Jordan watched the old lady's hand going from the bowl to her mouth, bowl to mouth, one Froot Loop at a time. A pink one, then a yellow, then a green. And the whole time, there was a green one stuck to the side of her little finger and she didn't know it.

"Don't believe him!" she yelled again, so loud that the other old lady snorted in her sleep and straightened up a little in her chair. Then the one who'd been yelling at the television looked right at Jordan.

"She believes him!" she yelped.

"She does?" Jordan asked back, because she don't know what else to say. And Mama had said for her to *be sweet*, which meant to be polite in every way, so she couldn't let the old lady say something to her and not say something back.

"She's a fool!" the old lady hissed, but she looked back at the television, so Jordan didn't have to think of anything else to say. She sat there wondering if Miss Amylee's hair had gotten all dry and yellow gray and her skin was parchment and with big, blue veins showing through it, like this lady's.

Because she hadn't seen Miss Amylee in three long months, not since the day her mama and stepdaddy got Miss Amylee all dressed up in her Sunday clothes and walked her out to the car between them, to take her to White Columns.

"We going to see Uncle Ned?" Miss Amylee had asked them.

"No, Mama," Franklin answered. "You know good and well Uncle Ned's been gone for years and years."

"Gone?"

"Passed away, Mama," Franklin said through clenched teeth.

"Why, I'm sure sorry to hear that," Miss Amylee said. "When did it happen? Why didn't somebody tell me?"

Franklin looked at Alice.

Jordan had watched them moving toward the car, her stepfather on one side, her mama on the other, and Miss Amylee ambling along between them and with her pocketbook hanging open.

Peony was standing on the porch that day, and Jordan was sitting on the steps.

"Pore old thing," Peony said real low as they watched them go across the yard.

"Why?" Jordan asked.

" 'Cause she's all confused."

"Where's she going?"

"Over to White Columns. Old folks' home," she added.

"Why?" Jordan asked again.

" 'Cause she needs more taking care of than we can do for her."

"But we took good care of her," Jordan argued, thinking of how she used to take Miss Amylee down to the fish pool and show her the red and golden fish shining like Christmas lights in the dark water. She liked that ever so much. It was the one and only time Jordan ever saw Miss Amylee smile. Because Miss Amylee was the saddest person on the face of the whole earth. Jordan was sure of it.

The stories Miss Amylee told her were full of beasts and monsters and the taste of blood. Stories that replayed themselves later, in Jordan's dreams, leaving her wide awake and shivering and with the stench of wet animal hair in the dark room in the dark night. Wonderful, terrible stories Jordan would be able to hear no more.

"We did the best we could," Peony said. "But it wasn't enough."

So Jordan and Peony had watched silently while Alice and Franklin got Miss Amylee into the car, and when it rolled down the driveway and turned into the tree-lined street,

"It wasn't?"

"That's right. 'Cause she was always looking for something. Always wanting something but not even knowing what it is."

"Oh." So maybe that's why she was always so sad, wanting something and maybe not even knowing what it was. Wanting it bad enough to go searching in darkness.

Peony moved toward the door. Then she turned and added, "Your mama and Mr. Franklin had to do something, before she wandered away and hurt herself . . . or got lost."

The door to the private office opened again and Alice and the lady came out and so did another thread of cool air into the hot room.

"Well, I just don't know what on earth we're going to do," Alice was saying to the lady. "Do you know if Aunt Rose is still taking care of old Miss Mary?"

"Seems to me she is," the lady said. Then she hesitated.

"But come to think of it, I heard somebody saying the other day that Aunt Rose said she was going to retire and stay home to take care of Crazy . . . of . . . Honey-Boy. But it sure wouldn't hurt for you to call her and see."

"Well, I just don't know what on earth we're going to do," Alice repeated, drawing on her white cotton gloves. "I'll call her soon as I get home."

Jordan was watching and listening and then suddenly, the image of the fish pool in the yard flashed before her eyes—superimposed itself right over her mama so that the pool was right there, this very minute, and she could see it as clear as day, even though she wasn't there. The same way she could see Peony's white shoes, even when she *couldn't* see them. And the pink girdle under the starched, white dress. Before she could stop herself, she became a bird with bright, black eyes, perching for a moment on the hot sun windowsill on the other side of the screen and then suddenly spreading her wings and flying upward, climbing the summer air until she was high above the towering pines on the too-green lawn of the White Columns and then tilting her wing feathers just the least little bit and soaring away high over the countryside around their little town, flying through the sweet aroma of biscuits coming from somebody's oven and over the green mounds of the small country club on the edge of town. On a hill in the town, her stepfather's house and the fish pool and then the down-tilting of the effortless flight until she glided in among the pines and lit on her little bird-feet on the cool, dark rocks of the fish pool and dipped her beak into the dark water.

"Sugar? Sugar?" Mama was shaking her shoulder, and Jordan looking up into her worried blue eyes.

"Is she all right?" asked the lady in the cool-private, navy blue dress. She was holding her hands palms-together under her chin, as if she were praying.

"She's okay now," Alice said, sighing. "She just needs a little dose of castor oil."

# CHAPTER TWO

A S SOON AS THEY CAME HOME from White Columns, Alice went straight to the phone, dialed Aunt Rose's number, and took off her earring as she waited for Aunt Rose to answer. Jordan lingered nearby, ready to listen and fill in the part of the conversation she couldn't hear.

"Aunt Rose?" Alice spoke loudly into the phone, as if she were speaking to someone hard of hearing. "This is Miss Alice calling."

*"Well, Miss Alice! How you all been doing?"*

"We're just fine, Aunt Rose. Listen, I just wanted to ask if you're still working for Mrs. Pritchett?"

*"Yessm. I'm still doing that."*

"Well, we're going to need you *here*, Aunt Rose. Need you awful bad."

*"Yessm. What for?"*

"For taking care of Miss Amylee. Franklin's mama," she added.

*"Yessm. I know who she is."*

Jordan pretended to unbuckle the strap on her black patent

leather Sunday shoes, but she was thinking, *Goodness! Miss Amylee's coming home?*

"Well then, you know how much we need you."

*"But I thought Miss Amylee was over to White Columns."*

"She was, Aunt Rose. But I just found out White Columns is going to close, and I've got to find someone to take care of her."

*"Well, I'm sorry to hear about that Miss Alice. I surely am."*

"We need you, Aunt Rose. To take care of Miss Amylee in her own house. I can't think of anyone else we could trust."

Jordan could imagine Miss Amylee's big white bungalow standing only one street over from her stepdaddy's house, see the windows looking out over the big front porch, all dark and blank in the twilight. Like something dead. And inside too, to where the furniture was covered with sheets.

*"Yessm. But I'm still looking after Miz Pritchett. Why, I can't leave her and come to you. That wouldn't be right."*

"But won't you even think about it, Aunt Rose? We need you something terrible."

*"Yessm. I know you do."* A very long pause, then, with no one saying a word. Then at last, Aunt Rose saying, *"Well, I'll think and see if there's someone else could do it."*

"But Aunt Rose," Alice almost wailed. "We can't have just anyone."

*"Yessm."*

"It has to be someone who will stay with her and watch out for her. She's awfully confused. And she's always liked you."

*"Yessm."*

"Just think about it. That's all I ask," Alice appealed.

*"Yessm."*

22

"Well, I'll talk with you again, Aunt Rose."

*"Yessm."*

"So bye-bye now." Alice's voice was false bright.

*"Yessm. Bye-bye."*

Alice put the receiver down slowly, as if she were reluctant to turn loose of her link with Aunt Rose.

"Is Miss Amylee coming home?" Jordan asked.

"She's coming home."

"Is she coming back here?"

Alice sighed and replaced her earring before she turned to Jordan.

"Well, I'm trying to fix things so she can stay in her own house instead of here with us. But we have to find somebody to take care of her."

"I can take care of her," Jordan offered. Alice smiled and shook her head. "I know you'd like to do that, but she's very confused and needs a grown-up person to stay with her day and night." Jordan remembered what Peony had said about Miss Amylee's wanting something and not even knowing what it was.

"You think Aunt Rose will do it?"

"I don't know. I just don't know." Then Alice looked at Jordan and patted her arm. "You go get your clothes changed, sugar. And be sure to hang up your dress like a good girl."

"Yes ma'm," Jordan said, and as she went down the hall, she heard Alice push open the swinging door to the kitchen and call out, "Peony? Did you fix that deep-dish chicken pie for tonight?"

After Jordan hung up her dress and put back on the shorts and T-shirt she had been wearing that morning, she went into the kitchen where Peony was just closing the oven door.

"Where's Mama?" Jordan asked.

"She went to lie down a little bit," Peony said, wiping her face with a towel rag she kept tucked into the waistband of her apron.

Jordan didn't say anything, but that was another way everything had changed since Mr. Franklin became her step-father—because when Alice had been a farmwife kind of person, she did all kinds of things, like putting up vegetables and putting corn shucks in a basket on the back porch, for feeding to the cow. She didn't seem to like doing those things, but she still did them, nonetheless. But now, in the new veranda-world of being a bank president's wife, she had taken to lying down in the early afternoon or sitting out on that shining veranda beneath the large umbrella that came out of the middle of the white enameled table, with her head leaning back and with her small white handkerchief blotting her neck and forehead, even though it was cool as could be in that shade.

Peony broke into Jordan's thoughts: "Whooee! It's way too hot to be running this oven on a day like this!"

"Why didn't you make chicken salad for supper?" Jordan asked. "That's nice and cool."

Pansy cut her eyes. " 'Cause your stepdaddy couldn't get home at noon for a proper dinner, so we're having it for supper. And cause he *wants* chicken pie, is why."

"How come he always gets what he wants?"

" 'Cause he's the man of the house." Peony spat the word *man* as if it were bitter on her tongue. "That's why I'm glad I don't have nobody like that at my house!"

"Where'd Willie go?" Jordan asked. Because for almost two years, Peony had been in love with him. But Jordan had heard her mama telling Peony that she didn't think it was a good idea for her to talk about Willie with Jordan anymore.

"Yessm," Peony had said.

"Gone," Peony said to Jordan, drawing her brows tight together to let Jordan know she wasn't going to say any more about it.

"But aren't you lonesome, living all alone?"

"No, I'm not lonesome, and I sure enough don't live alone—got my dog, got two yard cats. Them's enough."

Jordan thought for a moment and then said, "Well, why don't *you* take care of Miss Amylee then? You could live in her house with her and take care of her."

"Whatchu talking about?" Peony frowned deeply. "Miss Amylee's over to White Columns, isn't she? Isn't that where you and Miss Alice went today?"

"Yes, she is. But Mama says White Columns is going to close, so we got to find someone to take care of her."

"That so? Closing up, you say?"

"That's what Mama says."

"They going to bring Miss Amylee back *here*?"

"I don't think so. Mama's trying to get Aunt Rose to live with her in her own house."

"Well, that would be better, sure enough. I think your mama and stepdaddy bringing her here—taking her away from her own house—is what got her so confused in the first place."

Peony thought for a moment. "Miss Alice is trying to get Aunt Rose, you say?"

"That's right. But Aunt Rose says she can't leave Mrs. Pritchett."

"That's the truth," Peony agreed, adding, "Poor old thing."

"Mama says she doesn't know who else she can get. So how about *you?*"

"Lordy, child! I'm up to my earbobs now, taking care of you folks. If I was to go take care of Miss Amylee, who on earth would take care of you and Miss Alice and Mr. Franklin? You tell me *that!*"

"Oh." Jordan's voice was small and contrite, for she couldn't imagine what it would be like for them. Without Peony.

"But maybe I do know somebody would do it—come take care of Miss Amylee," Peony said, patting her apron pocket. "Got a letter right here might be the very answer."

"A letter from *who?*" Jordan asked.

"Well, just you wait a little bit, and I'll tell you," Peony said. "But don't you say a thing to your mama—not yet. Promise me, now, you hear?"

"I promise," Jordan said. "But why don't you go ahead and tell me who it is? That way, I can keep my promise lots better." Peony studied Jordan's wide-open and innocent face for a long moment before she finally said, "It's my very own sister. That's who."

Later, when Peony was once again alone in the hot kitchen, she took the letter out of her pocket, to read it for a second time, unfolding the eight or ten small, lined pages, with Pansy's running handwriting filling each and every page, front and back.

Dear Sister,
     I guess you're surprised to hear from me, specially since I haven't written to you in such a long time. That's

because I figured you all were pretty embarrassed about me having to go to jail, so I didn't like to remind you all about it. I even thought one time that maybe you would forget all about me, and it would be a good thing if you did. But now, something has happened to make me change my mind about thinking I'm not good enough for you all to love me.

You remember how Mama drug me to church every single Sunday and me just kicking and screaming and not wanting to go? And when I got a little older, I'd sneak out during services all the time so's I could smoke cigarettes?

Well, now I've found Jesus and gotten saved and am a new person.

And—my goodness!—if someone as important as Jesus loves me, then I guess I'm worth other folks loving me too! And that's why I'm writing to you.

It was a miracle is what it was. I was asleep one night, when I heard somebody say, "Wake up!" Sounded like they was right there in the room with me.

"Who is it?" I hollered back all gruff-like—because there's some women in here you don't want to sound nice to if they call out to you in the dark. I expect you know what I mean, but maybe not.

Anyway, it wasn't a woman's voice at all. It was a man's. You can imagine how that startled me, considering what all I went through with Earlie, specially after all the things he done to me until . . . well, anyways, I holler again, "Who is it?" And it comes right back and says, "It's Jesus. Your Lord and Savior!"

Well, you could have knocked me over with a feather!

"Whatchu doing in here with *me*?" I asked. " 'Cause after all, I'm sure not no angel or anything like that, and if it really was Jesus and he was planning on talking to somebody, it sure wouldn't be somebody like me. It would be someone who's very good and prays all the time and tries to convert people. So I thought maybe He had gotten into the wrong cell.

"I 'spect it's Lizzy you're looking for," I said. "She's right next door." Because Lizzie is a real God-fearing woman who's always telling us about how we got to accept the Lord Jesus as our personal savior and get ourselves saved and baptized so we can go to Heaven and all kinds of things like that. But I always got away from her by saying, "Lizzie, I'm not planning on going noplace for a while—not until I've served out my time, and specially not anywhere near Heaven for lots and lots of years yet!"

That's why I thought it was Lizzy Jesus would be looking for. And not me.

So after I said Lizzie was right next door, I just pulled the covers back over me and started trying to go back to sleep. I didn't want no dream I was having to make me all tired out, you see. Because I had a long, hard day ahead of me, working in the laundry.

"It's *you* I want, Pansy," He says, and in a voice so sweet and so pretty, it was like having tea-olive blossoms talking to you!

*"Me?"* I asked.

*"You,"* He says, and so I throw back the covers again and sit up and rub my eyes. If it was a dream I was having, that would sure enough get it to go away.

But when I looked, there was a light glowing in the corner where there isn't no light—usually.

"Come to me, Pansy," the voice said again. "And get yourself washed clean in the River Jordan."

And then the strangest thing of all happened—right there where the light had been was all of a sudden this angel, but not like no angel what I've ever seen in books or nothing like that. This angel—and I don't know how I knew what it was right then—was a great big black woman and she smiled right at me and showed me the biggest, solid gold front tooth you ever did see!

Why, any angel what I've ever seen in books was white and a baby, all fat and pink. But I know what I saw, and this wasn't no pink little baby at all. This was a woman even bigger than me. And right while she was standing there and smiling at me, she said, "I'm gonna hep you. I'm gonna hep you, sure enough!"

Then the light disappeared and so did she. Just like that. It was so dark in my cell, you could have put your finger in it and pulled it out and left a hole.

"My goodness! What a dream!" I says to myself. And I sit there wondering what on earth I could have eaten would make me have a dream like that!

Then another voice calls out to me—a woman's voice—and says, "Pansy?" And I know it's Lizzie's voice. "Pansy. The Lord Jesus loves you. He just came through here and asked me to make sure you understand that. And He's gonna send you a angel to show you the way! Goodness, Pansy—ain't that wonderful? Makes you so special!"

I didn't know what to say to that, and I still don't. So maybe this will sound crazy to you, and I don't blame you one little bit if you think I've just lost my mind, what with my being shut up in jail for three long years. But this is real, sister, and I wanted to share it with you.

I'm coming up for parole soon, and if they let me out, I'm going to do exactly what Jesus said for me to do and what he's sent me my own angel to help me out with—I'm gonna remember how much He loves me, and I'm going to do what He said—get myself baptized in the River Jordan, no matter how long it takes. I'm not even sure of where the real River Jordan is, but I'll figure it out. I'm going there, no matter how hard I have to work to earn the money for getting there and no matter how long it takes. And I guess that big angel is gonna help me.

So what I wanted to ask you is this: If I get out, could I maybe stay with you just for a little while, until I can get a place of my own? I've learned how to work hard, and I am a new woman. I will find a job and start putting money away for getting to the River Jordan one of these days. Just as soon as I find out where it is.

You don't have to be afraid of me, Sister. I didn't mean to do what I did to Earlie. Just that he had beat up on me all I could stand, and finally, I just pushed him away from me. And it was only that one time I ever put my hands on him, and I never meant for him to fall and hit his head so hard on the corner of that big old iron cookstove of mine. I never, ever meant for him to die. Just not to hit me no more.

So maybe the parole board will take pity on me because of all the beatings I took before I pushed him away just that one time and also because I'm gonna say how I've found Jesus and will be a good child of His from now on. But I'm not gonna say nothing 'bout that angel—I've got more sense than to tell a parole board full of white men about that!

One last thing now—I am changing my name from Pansy to River—as a promise of what Jesus said for me to do. Please let me know what you think about all this. And I sure do 'preciate it.

> Love,
> Your Sister, River (Pansy) Jordan

Peony's eyes lingered on Pansy's new name.
*River Jordan.*
She pulled the towel rag out of the waistband of her apron and wiped her eyes. *Poor old Pansy! Her in that jail all the time. And for what? For punching that old devil, Earlie, like she shoulda done a long time before. Then the jury not believing her*

*when she said over and over she didn't go to kill him. Probably
'cause she's such a big woman and outweighed old Earlie by a
hundred pounds. So they couldn't believe he'd been beating her
for so long and her just taking it. But they just didn't know how
much she needed somebody to love her, and as long as she had
Earlie, she could make-believe. In spite of all her black eyes and
broken teeth. Or maybe she should have thrown him out, like I
did Willie. Stinking man! Trying to steal my little bit of money!*

Getting mad again about Willie displaced some of her pain
about Pansy . . . River. She tucked the towel rag back into her
waistband, folded the letter, and put it in back in her pocket.
"Blamed *men!*" she muttered, opening the oven door to check
on the chicken pie. "Nothing but trouble! Every last one of
'em!"

At the fish pool, Jordan watched the pearl-white fish glim-
mering against the deep darkness of the bottom of the pool.

"Guess what?" she said to the fish. "Miss Amylee's going to
be able to come and see us again. Isn't that nice?" As soon as
Jordan said the words, she could remember Miss Amylee's face
reflected in the water over where the pearl fish was floating
lightly against the dark leaves at the bottom. Beneath Miss
Amylee's round, pink face, his silvery gills opened and closed
with mesmerizing regularity.

"Jordan?" someone called, and Miss Amylee's pink face
disappeared from the surface of the water. Below where it had
been, the silver-pearl fish opened and closed its mouth and the
gills moved in agreement.

"Jordan? You down there at the fish pool?"

Peony stood on the porch, shading her eyes against the blazing noontime sun and looking toward the fish pool. Beyond the

pool, on the other side of the carefully clipped hedges that separated the yard from the sidewalk, she saw her baby brother, Honey-Boy, shuffling along in his rhythmic, side-to-side gait, his lips frozen in a smile and muttering to himself happily.

*Wednesday,* Peony thought. Mama's *day off, so she's made Honey-Boy come home for his dinner 'stead of him staying in town all day and depending on someone buying him a hot dog from the Dairy Queen.*

She knew how Honey-Boy had been "marked" because his mama, Peony's mama, was frightened by a maddened sow while she was carrying him. That's what everyone in town said, anyway, and those who were old enough to remember said it was a terrible thing. Because Aunt Rose didn't know the sow had given birth to her babies during the long winter night and so she just went right into the pen. And the sow came at her like a wild beast, screaming like a banshee and with her mouth wide open and drool streaming out of it. She came out so fast, there were two little newborn pigs still hanging on to her. Aunt Rose was no spring chicken, even back that long ago and so heavy with child, and she'd scrambled over the hard-frozen ground, getting through the gate before that sow hit it just like a freight train.

That's why Honey-Boy was like he was.

Of course, at first nobody knew there was anything wrong with him. Not when he was just a little baby. Sure, he was scrawny, but all Aunt Rose's babies looked that way at first— even her daughters, Pansy, Peony, Petunia, and Primrose, who were already grown and gone from home when Honey-Boy was born—all looked like little burned-matchstick dolls when they were born, every one of them.

"Why, all I do is eat and eat," Aunt Rose said. "But don't

seem to make no nevermind. Gets *me* fat, but don't do a thing for my babies."

This time, she ate and ate, but she didn't put on a bit of weight.

"Maybe this time it's going to the baby," she said. But it wasn't.

Because when Honey-Boy was born, he was just as skinny as all the others. And more. Because his bony little legs were perfectly bowed out, just as if he'd been riding a mule for years and years. He had deep-set eyes and he came into the world looking around calmly, as if he had seen it all before. He didn't even cry. Never cried once, and Aunt Rose nursed him every few hours, for good measure, because it seemed he would have just looked around and starved without a sound. But other than those things, he seemed to be a good, quiet little baby. It wasn't until he started trying to toddle that it was pretty obvious his legs weren't going to straighten out. Miss Amylee heard about it and said to Aunt Rose, "Why don't you let me carry you and the little boy over to Atlanta. Maybe they got a doctor over there can do something for him."

Rose just shook her head. "Thank you, Miss Amylee. I sure do 'preciate your offering like that, but this is the way God handed Honey-Boy to me and that's how I'm supposed to love him. Just like he is."

Honey-Boy's legs never really did much growing, and they were so crooked, he had to waddle along in a side-to-side gait, as if his hip sockets were fused together. When he was close to reaching manhood, he started developing a chest on him that was so huge, it was almost twice the size it should have been. So that by the time he was a full-grown man, it seemed that the sheer weight of that huge chest was what was causing his little matchstick legs to bow out like that.

"Thank goodness we all know him," Alice said one time when he passed their house, walking down the street toward town. "Else it would scare a body to death, just to look at him."

But there was more wrong with him than the legs and that big barrel chest. Because he just never grew up. Not inside, anyway. That's when folks first started calling him Crazy Honey-Boy, though of course, they were very careful never to say that where Aunt Rose could hear. Honey-Boy remained a placid child who liked to walk into town from Aunt Rose's little house out on the Waynesboro Highway and stand around in the post office, telling people, "Santy Claus is coming tomorrow!" Because when he was three or four years old, something or other happened that got him stuck on a Christmas eve, so that the next morning, he wouldn't even open his present, but just went around saying "Santy Claus is coming tomorrow!" He'd been saying it ever since.

Miss Amylee said one time that she thought it must be a blessing God had given him to make up for those bad legs and that big misshapen chest—that he could spend his whole life in the perpetual glow of Christmas eve—and because Christmas day itself never came for him, he lived his whole life in sweet anticipation.

Everybody in town knew Honey-Boy, of course, because of Aunt Rose and because of him standing in the post office every single day, smiling in delight and spreading the news about what would happen the next day, on a day of ultimate joy. And besides, the people of the town cared for him and looked out for him because he belonged to Aunt Rose, and she was the most revered and highly respected black woman in the whole county. For four generations, she had been the ministering angel to families facing illness or death—or birth—and the joke went around that whenever Aunt Rose showed up at your back door, wearing her spotless apron, you knew you were either sick or dying or expecting a baby—maybe all three.

The strange thing was that no one ever had to send for her. She just seemed to know when people needed her, and she would show up silently. Come in the back door, roll up her sleeves, clean the kitchen, set a big pot of coffee on to boil, and start making her famous chicken and rice soup that was guaranteed to comfort, strengthen, and heal both man and beast.

Especially, she knew when babies were going to come into the world, and her thin hands had lifted almost every baby in the town into the world for many years. And more than all of that—because they all knew there was something purely healing or comforting in the sight of Aunt Rose, even when she was aged and shrunken—sitting in a chair in the corner of the kitchen like a bright little bird, waiting to use those gentle hands to soothe or clean or hold a newborn baby. And her cracked voice confirming what they already knew: that God would carry them in the palm of His hand through their illness or grief or a long, hard birth.

That's why people cared about Honey-Boy and looked out for him. Because after all the healing and the comforting Aunt Rose had done, and after all the plump, healthy, white babies she had brought into the world, it seemed especially sad somehow, that her own late-life son would never grow up, but would be a child forever. A child who wore the misshapen body of a big, black man like an ill-fitting garment.

"Jordan! You out there?"

Peony watched Crazy Honey-Boy moving on down the road.

Then she called again, "Jordan?"

"I'm here," Jordan finally called back, still caught up in wondering how the fish knew to do it all just so.

"Well, come on in here for a minute," Peony called. "Your mama said she wants you to have a little dose of castor oil."

# CHAPTER THREE

AT MISS SWEETIE-PIE'S CAFÉ next to the Gulf station, Gertie was slinging lunch dishes into the sink and wiping down the counter with vicious strokes. The lunch-hour rush always left her feeling more harried and petulant than ever, especially during the hot summers. Even the garbage can seemed to be especially putrid to her, with the half-eaten slices of tomato and the paper napkins with lipstick on them.

Because the only people who came into the café for lunch were travelers who didn't know there was a brand-new Dairy Queen just on down the highway—or men working on the new highway that was being built between Thompson and Wrens. All people who came in ate their hamburgers or grilled cheese sandwiches and then went away to their own lives—leaving Gertie to clean up their mess.

Maybe it wouldn't have been so bad if sometimes the better people in town came in, but most of those folks still clung to the old tradition of having a big, hot meal in the middle of the day. They were the lawyers and doctors and bankers, who lived on tree-shaded streets in big, quiet houses where fans blew cool air in rooms that had all the blinds and drapes drawn shut against the broiling summer air.

After the dinner flurry was over, some old-timers would come and sit beneath the swirling ceiling fan and swap stories over glasses of sweet tea. And every afternoon, Crazy Honey-Boy came to the back door, knocked on it gently, and called, "Miss Sweetie Pie? It's Honey-Boy here." And when he came like that, Gertie was supposed to cut a slice of whatever pie they'd had that day and hand it to him through the screen door out back. Gertie hated doing that. Hated the happy emptiness of his huge eyes and the animal smell of his big chest. Hated him telling her—every single day—that Santa Claus was coming and the wide, innocent smile that showed his strong, dazzling white teeth.

But later—after Honey-Boy had taken his pie and walked away—the sheriff would come in for his tea. Gertie liked him—liked his tanned face and blue eyes and his uniform. She had tried flirting with him once, but he seemed restless and uninterested in her. The fact was that no men liked her at all, even though she wasn't all that bad looking. Maybe it was her petulant attitude that turned them all off.

"Gertie, you keep slinging plates like that, you're gonna break something!" Miss Sweetie-Pie's voice came rumbling out of the tiny, hot kitchen at the back of the café.

"Yessm," Gertie mumbled. "Silly old bitch," she added under her breath.

At the sheriff's office, Amos was locking the door and getting ready to walk over to the café for his afternoon glass of tea. Silently, he was hoping that Gertie wouldn't be there. Wouldn't be ready to get off work and want somebody to talk to. Poor Gertie! he thought. Lonely and homely and only sixteen years old, but already as old as Methuselah. Griping and complaining all the time.

"Afternoon, Sheriff," she would say to him, before his eyes had adjusted from the glare of the sun.

"Afternoon, Gertie," he would say, sliding into a booth and hoping she would leave him alone. But it never happened that way. Because before Miss Sweetie-Pie would even have time to bring him a glass of tea, Gertie would move from her seat at the counter—uninvited, of course—and slide into the booth with him. And it would be the same conversation they always had—down to the last word.

"You wanta know what I was saying to Miss Sweetie-Pie just now? Just before you come in?" Gertie would blink at him darkly. And as always, he would gaze impassively at her, seeing the same sallow complexion and limp brown hair as always.

"What?" he would say.

"Well, I was saying I wisht I could go out there in the parking lot and find me a million dollars, so's I could go somewhere and do something. That's what I was just saying." The petulant and defeated tone of her voice said that such a thing would never happen to her. Poor Gertie! he would think, once again. Born so late to her mama and no daddy at all—Lord only knew who he had been!—and her mama spending all her time shampooing and setting hair. Still fixing all those old beehive hairdos and old, longtime customers of hers smiling and acting all pleased and tipping her and then getting outside and saying, "Lord have mercy!" and mashing their hair down so they could get into their cars!

Her spending all that time teasing hair and spraying it and then teasing it even more. And not having any time at all for her own unexpected daughter. And then running off like she did and leaving poor old Miss May, her mama, to try and raise Gertie.

"Where would you go, Gertie? And what would you do?" he always asked, but he didn't mean to. Her small eyes glittered.

"Somewheres exciting!" she breathed. "Somewhere *not* like this hot, boring old place!" That same old song from Gertie, day after day.

So, please, Lord, Amos was thinking. Please don't let her be there!

But before he could lock the door and finish thinking about it all, the phone started ringing. He hesitated, thinking of the cool café, the sweet amber tea, and the clinking of ice in the big glass. And maybe Gertie sitting there, just waiting for him. So he went back inside.

"Sheriff's office," he said into the receiver.

"Sheriff? Amos?" A woman. An elderly woman and upset.

"Yes, ma'm. Who's this?"

"Miss May, and I want you to come over here right away!"

He visualized the small, gray house on a side street not far away and the confused, elderly woman who used to be his Sunday school teacher long years ago, but who had forgotten almost everything that had ever happened and everybody it happened with. And Gertie's grandmother, as well.

"What's wrong, Miss May?" he asked lightly, because he thought that she was probably imagining something or other. And where was that girl of hers anyway?

"What's *wrong?* What's *wrong,* you say? Well, there's a big nigra man in my back yard, that's what's wrong! I just saw him through the window."

"Aunt Rose there with you?"

"Who?"

"Aunt Rose. Doesn't she take care of you?"

"Oh. Yes."

"Then is she there with you?"

"No. Not supposed to be here."

"She doesn't work for you anymore?"

"Sure she does. But she's not here today. Gertie was some-where around here earlier, but now I can't find her. . . ." Her voice shrilled suddenly. ". . . I tell you there's a big black nigra man in my yard!"

"I think Gertie's still at work. Maybe it's just Honey-Boy cutting through your yard?"

"Who?"

"Honey-Boy. You know—Aunt Rose's boy. He wouldn't hurt a fly."

No response from her—just a stiff, offended silence that almost shouted at him through the phone. Amos sighed. "I'll be right there."

He walked the short distance to the café, where Gertie was just finishing work and taking off her apron.

"Gertie, come on and let me give you a ride home. Your grandmama just called me and said there's a big nigra man in her yard."

Gertie came right away, and for one small moment, the bored, petulant face was lively and interested. "Miss Sweetie-Pie helped me find somebody to come rake up under the pecan trees. I told Grandmama about him, but she must have forgotten. Just that fast."

Amos thought for a minute and then said, "Well, I wanta make sure it's just the one that's supposed to be there."

They walked back to the office and got into the patrol car.

"Gertie, why don't you go back to school?" Amos asked, as he backed out of the parking space. And he asked that because of the fleeting expression of liveliness and curiosity that he had seen on Gertie's face.

"Don't wanna," came the brusque reply, and he glanced at her profile, with the chin jutted out stubbornly and the eye filled with a sullen gleam.

"But if you did go back to school—and graduate—then you really could 'go somewhere and do something.' " He came close to imitating Gertie's own thickly accented, sullen tone, but he stopped himself just in time. No answer from Gertie as they drove the few blocks to the small, gray house, but as Amos pulled into Miss May's driveway, Gertie mumbled, "Just don't wanna."

The curtains in the living room window moved and a few seconds later, Miss May came out on the porch to meet them, one hand fluttering in the air and the other pressed against her flat chest.

"Gracious me!" she twittered. "I'm glad somebody's come. I just didn't know what to do!" Gertie started up the steps, and the sheriff moved toward the side of the house.

"Be careful!" Miss May warned. "He's big!"

"Grandmama," Gertie said. "It's just the man I told you Miss Sweetie-Pie helped me find to rake up around back."

"Man? What man?"

Amos said, "I'll go on around back and you all go on through the house and meet me back there. We'll just make sure things are okay." He unsnapped the strap on his revolver and went around the side of the house. He could hear Miss May still talking as she and Gertie went through the dining room. "Nobody said a thing to me about getting somebody to rake up around back," Miss May protested.

"I did too tell you," Gertie argued. "I told you about him three different times, the last time just before I went to work."

"Well, you couldn't have! I wouldn't have forgotten something like that."

The sheriff ducked under the clothesline, smiling briefly at a pair of Miss May's neon-pink, ribbed cotton bloomers that brushed the top of his head, and met Gertie at the back porch steps. Miss May was standing at the screen door, still talking.

"You didn't say a thing to me. I'm sure of it!" Under the big pecan trees behind the garage, a man was raking methodically, humming under his breath.

"That him?" the sheriff asked.

"That's him," Gertie said, and Amos called to him. "Hey, Sam?" The man stopped raking and jerked halfway to attention when he saw the sheriff.

"Yessir?"

"You see anybody else around here?"

"Nawsir!" He shook his head vigorously. "Not nobody here 'cept me, and I been working hard the whole time, just like I'm supposed to be doing."

"There he is!" Miss May shouted from the back porch. She pointed at Sam, who was still standing stiffly. He looked at Gertie and the sheriff and then he grinned, relaxed a little, raised his hand, and waved at Miss May.

"Yessm," he called to her. "Nobody here but Sam, sure enough."

"Well, I better be going," Amos said. Gertie was staring at him in a most peculiar way. He almost expected her to go into her spiel about finding that million dollars and going some-where and doing something.

"I liked riding in your car," she said instead.

After the sheriff left, Sam returned to his raking, but he mut-tered under his breath, "Like to scared me to death! Somebody calling the sheriff and me just doing what I done been *told* to do!" He was still grumbling when Honey-Boy cut across the edge of the yard, holding a partially-eaten piece of pie in his hand and swaying along in that side-to-side gait, the child-sized legs bending under the weight of the huge upper body. As always, he was looking at the ground, grinning and talking to himself.

"Hey, Honey-Boy!" Sam called to him. "Where you headed?" Honey-Boy looked up briefly before he resumed grinning at the ground.

"Santy Claus is coming tomorrow," he said. "So you better be good!"


At exactly three minutes before six that evening, Peony placed the deep-dish chicken pie on the white tablecloth and stood looking at the table, silently checking to see that every-thing was done just so. Because Mr. Franklin was very particu-lar, especially about the table. While she stood there, Alice came into the dining room.

"I'll go tell Mr. Franklin dinner's ready," Peony said, satis-fied at last about the table. "Where's Miss Jordan?"

"I thought she was in the kitchen with you."

"Nome. She sure ain't there. She came in when I gave her a dose of castor oil, like you said to do, but then she went back outside."

"Was she real upset about getting a dose of oil?" Alice inquired.

"Nome. She took it right down. She sure don't like it none, but she took it right down. Didn't complain one little bit."

"Well, you go check out in the playhouse out back and I'll look down at the fish pool," Alice said. Then she added, "I hope this doesn't delay dinner."

In the playhouse, Jordan hugged her knees and rocked back and forth, thinking about Miss Amylee, who was the only good thing that had come out of her mama's marriage to Mr. Franklin—besides Peony, of course. Miss Amylee, with all her strange, dark stories that raised all the hairs on Jordan's arms and afterward, filled her dreams with great snuffling beasts and the sound of someone weeping far away. And now, once again Jordan would be able to be with her. Because once Mama got everything arranged and found someone—maybe even Peony's very own sister—to come and stay with Miss Amylee, Jordan could go to see her every single day, just the way it had all been before Mr. Franklin got a bee in his bonnet about his mama and brought her into his own house.

*Peony was right,* Jordan was thinking. *That's exactly when everything started to go wrong for Miss Amylee. When Mr. Franklin took her out of her own house.*

But just then, Jordan heard Peony's voice: "You back here, Jordan? Do, you better get yourself in to supper right this minute! Mr. Franklin's having to wait for his supper, and you know how much that upsets your mama!"

Supper was a very quiet occasion, as was always the case when they all sat at the table together—whether it was break-fast, or the usual hearty middle-of-the-day dinner, or the usual simple cold supper. Because children—Jordan—were not allowed to speak, except as necessary. "Please pass the butter" or "May I please be excused?"

Jordan's mother didn't say anything either, unless it was to gently inquire if Mr. Franklin needed anything. Does your tea need refreshing? or Is the chicken cooked to your liking? Mr. Franklin himself ate in a contemplative silence, looking off into the distance as he chewed each morsel, as if he were deciding whether the chicken or the green beans or the fluffy rice offended his sensibilities in any minute manner. It was his typical way of dining, and between her mother's solicitous murmurings and her stepfather's judgmental chewing, Jordan always felt as if she were tiptoeing through dry leaves and trying not to let them come forth with a loud crackle beneath her feet.

On that particular hot summer evening, Peony came into the dining room only twice—once to replenish the glasses of iced tea with fresh ice cubes and another time to bring in dessert—a creamy, well-chilled banana pudding. Both times, Jordan watched Peony's face, studied the unhappy scowl. Because usually, Peony went home at three o'clock, but whenever—on those thankfully rare occasions—Mr. Franklin had his "dinner" at suppertime, she had to stay late, and she hated it. Jordan hated it as well, because it meant that she had to try and manage to eat a hot meal at the hottest time of the day.

"Try to eat some more of your green beans before you have your dessert," Alice said, and her words caused Franklin's sharp eyes to land on Jordan, who, to his way of thinking, was a strange, thin, light-headed creature. Jordan managed two or three more green beans and about half of the pudding.

"May I be excused?" she asked, and when Alice nodded her head, Jordan placed her folded napkin back into its napkin ring and pushed in her chair, all under the gentle gaze of her mother and the sharper, somehow disquieting gaze of her stepfather. Jordan was only about halfway into the kitchen when she heard Alice mention White Columns in a low voice and Franklin responded with a louder *"what?"* She stopped the double swinging door from closing all the way and stood quietly.

"When?" Franklin's voice was full of irritation.

"We've got about a month to make other arrangements."

"Can we find another home?" Now, Franklin's voice sounded more weary than irritated.

"I don't think so," Alice said. "Not another one close enough, and heaven only knows how they treat folks who've got no family nearby to keep an eye on things."

"I don't want to bring her back here," Franklin admitted in a low voice.

"I've been thinking about that." Alice's voice sounded careful. "Seems to me she'd be better off back in her own house."

"Well, that can't be."

"It could, if we had someone staying there with her day and night," Alice suggested. "I was thinking about Aunt Rose."

Jordan let the door close.

Peony was sitting at the kitchen table, eating the same supper she'd served in the dining room. Jordan sat down with her, watching silently as Peony speared one, two, three pieces of green beans with her fork. On the kitchen counter, the oscillating fan hummed, blowing a fried-chicken aroma and squeaking sadly at either extreme of oscillation.

Peony studied the green beans critically before stuffing them into her mouth, while the breeze from the fan lifted first one side of her gauzy white collar and then the other.

Jordan could hear Alice and Franklin's voices continuing in discussion, but she couldn't tell what they were saying. Leaning forward toward Peony, she whispered, "When are you going to tell Mama about your sister?" Peony chewed and then swallowed, all the while looking right into Jordan's eyes.

"Don't you say nothing," she warned.

"I won't," Jordan assured her. "I just wondered."

"Well, you just get over wondering," Peony said, with an edge in her voice. "Gonna do this my way, Jordan, and don't you go saying something and spoiling what I got planned."

"What have you got planned?" Jordan asked before she could stop herself. But Peony scowled at her so hard that Jordan let her eyes drop back to Peony's plate. When she looked back up, Peony wagged her finger in warning.

"Just you hear what I say," she growled.

"Okay," Jordan whispered.

The muffled voices from the dining room gradually became softer until there was only silence beyond the swinging door. Jordan could picture her mama and Franklin walking toward the veranda, where they would sit and continue their conversation about Miss Amylee and their dilemma.

"Come on and help me clear this table, honey," Peony said. "I need to get finished up here so I can go see Mama."

"Why are you going to see Aunt Rose?" Jordan asked. "You going to try to get her to leave Miss Pritchett so she can take care of Miss Amylee? Or are you still thinking about your sister?"

"Now there you go again." Peony frowned. "I told you just to leave it alone!"

"I forgot," Jordan confessed in a small voice. And because

Peony was still scowling at her, she added, "I really did. I just forgot."

"Well." Peony softened a little. "You just work harder at remembering."

"I will."

# CHAPTER FOUR

"OH, GOODNESS! I don't know about that!" Alice placed an astonished hand over her heart as if to calm its wild fluttering. "Hire someone who's a murderer to take care of a helpless old lady?"

"Now Miss Alice, you know Pansy." Peony spoke in a soothing tone. "You know she's a good person. Just he beat up on her so bad and for so long, and she never meant to hurt him. It was an accident, that's what it was, and you know that. And I'll be careful about the mustard."

They were in the dining room, where Alice always sat at the great mahogany table to write out the week's menu. Peony stood, as she always did, waiting for Alice to hand her the menu so she could look at it and see if she had any questions about what Alice wanted served. Alice had just said, "Now don't put too much mustard in the potato salad on Wednesday. You know Mr. Franklin doesn't like it like that."

As always, the menu was in Alice's beautiful script, and written on a page of creamy linen paper. And that's when

Peony had brought up the idea about Pansy. She had already gone to see her mama about it.

"Why, that sure snuggles right up to near perfect!" Aunt Rose had said, pleased that Peony was trying to help her sister. Now if Peony—or any of them, for that matter—would only pay a little attention to Honey-Boy."

"I'm just so shocked!" Alice went on. "I just don't know."

"Well, I hope you'll think about it," Peony gently urged, reaching over and lifting the sheet of linen paper out of Alice's fingers. "She would do a good job for you, and it would help Miss Amylee to be in her own house, 'stead of here."

"Y-e-s-s-s." Alice drew out the word as she considered that. Yes, it would please Franklin. It would please him immensely not to have her come back here. But someone who's just coming out of jail?"

"And she's gotten saved," Peony added easily.

"Saved?" Alice wasn't sure whether she'd heard *saved* or *shaved*. A strange vision of the enormous Pansy with a shiny, black, bald head floated before her eyes.

"Saved," Peony repeated. "She's accepted Jesus as her Lord and Savior."

"Well . . ." Alice was thinking that Franklin would like that, as well. He was always one to try and help repentant sinners. "I'll think about it, Peony," and she didn't bother to pronounce the name the way Jordan always did. For Alice it was just plain old *pee-oh-nee*. "And I'll ask Mr. Franklin about it."

"Thank you, Miss Alice," Peony said sincerely, and then she disappeared back behind the swinging doors, carrying the carefully written menu with her.

Alice put the cap back onto her fountain pen and sat at the table for a few minutes, thinking about Peony's proposal. If she could only be sure that Pansy hadn't been mentally deranged by being in prison, it would all be perfect. She could envision Miss Amylee safely in her own home—close but not as close as having her right in the house. She also envisioned Pansy in a crisp, white uniform, taking care of Miss Amylee's every need. Suddenly, the solution came to her. She would ask Peony to get the Reverend Brown, pastor of the African Methodist Episcopal Church to go visit Pansy in the prison and report back to her. No need to say anything to Franklin until that had been accomplished. She smiled and nodded, pleased with herself and thinking about how happy Franklin would be that she had taken care of things without bothering him.

Then she got up, pushed open the swinging door to the kitchen, and said to Peony, "Would you ask your pastor if he'd be kind enough to go over to the jail and see what Pansy is like? I just feel that we have to find somebody who will let me know exactly what she's like now."

"Reverend Brown?"

"Yes, he's the one. I hope he'll see her himself and make sure she's not . . . changed . . . by this experience or anything like that."

"Yessm," Peony said. "I'll ask him. And I'll tell him about your concerns." She went back to wiping the sink, and Alice couldn't see her grinning into the spotless porcelain.

A few days later, Jordan was playing by the fish pool when a strange, dark car came up the driveway and went on to the rear parking area behind the house. Jordan followed it and watched as the biggest, blackest man she had ever seen in her life got out and started up the back steps. But when he saw Jordan, he stopped and smiled.

"How are you this afternoon, little miss?" he asked.

"Fine," Jordan said. "Who are you?"

"I . . ." He drew himself up to his full height. "I am Reverend Brown, of the AME Church, and I'm here to see Peony."

"Oh," Jordan murmured, wondering if maybe this Reverend Brown was a new man in Peony's life.

"Well, God bless you," he said easily, and knocked on the back screen door. In a few minutes, Peony came to the door, opened it, and made crooning sounds of welcome. Jordan followed him up the steps and into the kitchen. While Peony went to find Alice, Jordan stood in the kitchen, studying the man openly. He smiled at her again, and then he looked at his watch, then his fingernails, and at the last, he plucked imaginary bits of lint from both sleeves of his black jacket.

When Peony and Alice came into the kitchen, he stiffened to attention.

"Peony, would you please take Jordan and have a little walk so the reverend and I may speak in private?"

"Yessm," Peony said, grabbing Jordan's hand and casting a strong glance at the reverend before leading Jordan onto the back porch and down the steps.

Alice sat down at the kitchen table; the reverend remained standing at attention.

"Thank you for helping us," Alice said simply. He nodded his head gravely, looking at his shoes. There was a long moment of silence with Alice's unspoken *Well?* hanging in the air between them. He took a deep breath and let it out.

"I am convinced," he began importantly, "that Pansy is healthy, hearty, and completely contrite about the accident." He strongly emphasized the last word and glanced at Alice. "I saw her, I spoke with her at length, and I believe her to be ready to live in society again."

"You're sure?" Alice floated out the words.

"Yes ma'am, I am sure."

Alice worried her bottom lip with her teeth.

Then Alice's eyebrows went up almost to her hairline. "And what about her being saved?"

The Reverend Brown, of the AME Church studied her carefully. Presbyterian, he thought. Maybe even Episcopalian. Most surely, not charismatic! Then he said, "I am convinced that Pansy has experienced a religious conversion." Not another word, he thought. Not a single word about her visitation by the Lord Jesus Himself! Or a black angel!

Now, it was Alice's turn to take a deep breath and let it out slowly.

"Thank you," she breathed. "I appreciate your assurance."

"Yes ma'am," Reverend Brown said, bowing slightly.

"Now, we should pray for parole for her," Alice added, almost without thinking. Her words surprised him. Maybe not Presbyterian or Episcopalian. Maybe First Baptist. But no matter what denomination she was, if she wanted praying from him, it's praying she would get.

"*Lord!*" His booming voice filled the kitchen, and Alice almost fell out of her chair when the big man raised his arms, palms upward, and tilted his broad, dark face straight up toward the ceiling.

"*Lord!*" he called again, and Alice wanted to bow her head and close her eyes, but the dramatic stance he had taken held her surprised eyes like an irresistible force, so that for a brief moment, she felt like a helpless fish caught in the talons of an eagle. She glanced uneasily at the back door, as if the Lord Himself would appear, drawn by such a hearty exhortation.

The voice resumed, somewhat softer, but bursting from time to time into loud pleading.

"We come here before You today, asking for Your help in getting parole for Sister Pansy. She's needed here, Lord, to help a poor, elderly lady. To help this *family* take care of her. She's *needed,* Lord! Help her to *get here!* Soften the hearts of the parole board. *Help us, lord!* Help us bring Your brand-new child *here!*"

He held his stance, eyes still closed and lips moving silently for long minutes, while Alice felt that the echoes of his shouted words still bounced around from walls to table to stove to refrigerator.

"Amen!" he finally whispered as softly as if he were soothing a frightened child. The mighty arms slowly lowered, the head moved forward, and eyes slowly opened. Alice felt that she should say something. "Thank you," she breathed.

"You are most certainly welcome," he said, smiling. And then Alice sat silently as he let himself out of the door, leaving the kitchen strangely quiet.

"What's he here for?" Jordan asked Peony as they strolled toward the fish pool.

"Well, something important," Peony tried to hedge.

"I thought maybe he was your new boyfriend," Jordan said, smiling and looking up at Peony's startled face.

*"What?"* Peony shot the word out like a cannonball. "How come you to think such a thing as that?" Then she muffled a snicker.

Jordan didn't answer—just kept on holding Peony's hand

and smiling and starting to swing their hands back and forth, like Peony was a good friend and they were walking around the school yard at recess. When they reached the fish pool, Jordan asked, "Are they really gonna let Miss Amylee come back?"

"I hope so," Peony said.

"Oh! So do I!" The strong sincerity of Jordan's words surprised Peony.

"I didn't know you cared about her so much."

"Oh, yes!" Jordan's eyes were sparkling.

"How come?" Peony asked. "Her not even kin to you. Only Mr. Franklin's mama and him just your stepdaddy?"

Jordan thought for a long moment. "I like her stories," she said finally. Then she added, "And I guess she's the saddest person I ever knew."

"Amen to that," Peony added.

# CHAPTER FIVE

T HE NEXT DAY, Gertie was getting ready to go to work, and as she buttoned her dress, she looked at herself in the mirror. Even in repose, her face held a solid pout. She lifted the sides of her mouth with her fingers, but above the false smile, the eyes brooded darkly.

"Someday," she said to her reflection, "I'm gonna get out of this dead, stinking town and go somewheres and do something exciting. I gotta find a way. I just *gotta!*"

On the porch, Miss May was sitting in a rocking chair, a bowl of butter beans in her lap. Methodically, she prodded open each rich pod, releasing the swollen beans into the bowl, and dropped the empty pod into a paper bag on the floor. Gertie came out onto the porch, shading her eyes from the almost-noon glare of the sun. Miss May paused in her work and looked at Gertie.

"Oh, Grandmama," Gertie sighed. "Sometimes I get so sick of this place, I could just die. I wish I could go somewheres and do something."

Miss May sighed. "Well, honey, you're sure like your mama that way. She couldn't abide this little town. Always had to be heading off for someplace else."

"Wish she coulda taken me with her," Gertie said, pouting. And with that, she started down the front steps.

"Where you going off to, honey?" Miss May asked, with some alarm in her voice.

"Going to work, just like always," Gertie said. Then she added, "Grandmama, you ask me that question every single time I leave this house. Can't you remember that I work from eleven to two-thirty every single day for Miss Sweetie-Pie? Except for Sunday."

"You do?" Miss May seemed to treat the news as something she had never heard before.

"Yessm. When will Aunt Rose get here?" She didn't like going off and leaving her grandmother alone—too likely that she would put something on the stove to cook and then forget all about it and burn down the whole house.

"Aunt Rose," Miss May said.

"Yessm. Aunt Rose. When does she come?"

"Not sure," Miss May said, resuming the shelling of the butter beans.

"Well, I gotta go. Don't you try to cook those beans," Gertie warned. "You wait for Aunt Rose to get here. Okay?"

"I'll remember," Miss May said, and Gertie was halfway down the street before she realized that she didn't know whether her grandmother meant that she wouldn't forget the cooking beans or that she wouldn't forget *not* to cook them. At all. She started to turn around, but just then she saw Aunt Rose coming along the sidewalk, walking slowly and carefully.

"Talk about the blind leading the blind!" Gertie muttered

under her breath. She raised her hand to Aunt Rose as they passed, and then Gertie walked past the same houses, the same old one-story stores on Main Street—many of them deserted now—on past Miss Milly's Dressmaking Shop, past the Red and White Grocery and the sheriff's office. She walked slower as the peered in the window to try and see him, but the chair in front of the desk was empty and the patrol car was gone. She imagined him out in the countryside somewhere, talking to a farmer whose cow had mysteriously died. She could see the crisp, tan shirt, the impressive, shining badge, the sun-tanned arms and the sunglasses he always wore. For a brief moment, the sides of her mouth turned up all by themselves.

She felt strangely lighthearted as she helped Miss Sweetie-Pie get ready for the lunch crowd, and her employer noticed it right away.

"You sure seem happy about something or other today," she commented. "You got yourself a boyfriend?"

Gertie snorted. "No boyfriend. No friend. No nothing." Then she stopped and thought for a moment. "But I tell you one thing . . . something new is going to happen to me. I'm sure of it."

"Well, something new doesn't come around this old town very often," Miss Sweetie Pie noted. "But I hope you're right." She studied Gertie's face. "You know, you'd be a right pretty-looking girl if you'd just smile more. Maybe go to the dime store too and get yourself a bit of lipstick and some face powder."

Gertie touched her face. "You think so?" Maybe she would do just that. Get her face looking a whole new way. It was fun to think about that. Then the first of the lunchtime people started coming in, and for the next hour and a half, Gertie took people's orders, waited tables, and kept all the good food coming out of the kitchen moving in a steady line.

Finally, the crowd began to dwindle, and only moments before the serving line would have shut down, in walked three of the tallest, most handsome men Gertie had ever seen. They were wearing easy clothes and sunglasses and construction hard hats, and when Gertie went over to take their order, she couldn't help but notice the manly aroma of their clothes and the sun-tanned skin of their strong arms and thick necks. They had all piled their hard hats on a nearby chair, and two of them were busy studying the menu. But the third man glanced up at Gertie with sea-green eyes.

"Hi ya, pretty girl," he said, flashing even, white teeth at her. Gertie almost turned around to see what pretty girl was standing behind her, but she resisted that urge and struggled to keep her wits about her, all the while feeling red streaks coming up the side of her neck.

"Pretty . . ." he repeated. "And innocent too. Look at that blush!"

Gertie giggled nervously. The man reached up and gently pressed two of Gertie's fingers. She thought she would faint, right on the spot! "May I take your orders?" she stammered, instead of her usual, "What do you want?" Because somewhere deep down inside of her, she thought she probably already knew what this man *wanted*. The people who were building the new highway seldom stopped in at the little restaurant, but when they did, everything in the town seemed to change. Town folks looked at the strangers warily, and conversation humming in the café would go quieter.

The man turned loose of Gertie's fingers, and her flesh felt absolutely burned, where his touch had been. He turned his attention to the menu. In the end, they all ordered the same thing—cheeseburgers all-the-way, fries, and Cokes. When Gertie handed the order to a perspiring Miss Sweetie-Pie in the kitchen, she whispered, "Make 'em extra good!" Miss Sweetie-Pie looked up over the counter, and seeing the three handsome young men, smiled at Gertie and nodded.

Gertie continued cleaning tables, but she glanced at the men from time to time, feeling herself flush every time she did. They ate hungrily and genially, laughing often and sometimes leaning in toward the middle of the table to share something private. After one such consultation, they all looked up at her, and the one who had touched Gertie's fingers winked.

When Gertie presented their bill, she had put a folded paper napkin with her name and phone number on it under the bill. She handed it to *him*, but she didn't meet his eyes. He glanced at the napkin, smiled, and tucked it into his shirt pocket. When they left, he lingered in the doorway for a moment. "Bill," he said. "That's my name, Gertie."

The sound of her own name coming from his mouth made her dizzy, so that the glaring sunshine from the open door blinded her and she reached out and steadied herself by placing her hand on one of the tables. And then they were gone, just like that, leaving behind them a dull, boring, sleepy little town and a small café that had a faint lingering aroma of their maleness.

Peony received another letter from her sister the next day. In it, Pansy wrote about how hard she'd been praying about the parole hearing and how grateful she was to Peony for saying she could stay with her until she could find work and get a place of her own.

"Well, River Jordan—my dear sister—if that parole board lets you out, I've got a far better surprise for you—a job *and* a place to stay." Because Alice had wisely said that they shouldn't mention any of their plans to Pansy until they found out whether she would get paroled. No need in adding to her misery with dreams of what-might-have-been, if she had to stay in prison. Jordan silently pushed open the kitchen door, but when she saw Peony with head bowed, eyes closed, and lips moving, she backed out. Jordan knew only whatever little she had been able to overhear, but she sensed that, very soon, something important was going to happen.

# CHAPTER SIX

Pansy Jordan sat on a wooden bench in a long hallway, with a rigid, hooded-eyed prison matron sitting lightly dozing, beside her. Across the hall was the closed door with a frosted glass upper part, and from time to time, Pansy could see the silhouettes of people moving around inside the closed room. And she could hear the low voice tones of the white men who would determine her fate.

When she had gone into that room and faced that row of men, she knew for certain that she wasn't alone. Because she had picked out an empty chair on the other side of the room, and she pictured Jesus sitting in that chair. He was leaning forward in an engaging way, with his elbows resting on His knees and His deep, kind, love-overflowing eyes on her face. And beside Him, she pictured her very own angel. A big, black, gold-toothed, smiling angel.

So that when the parole board members began asking questions, she answered calmly, peacefully, and honestly. Finally, the questions stopped, and she was asked—almost courteously—to wait outside. Back outside in the hallway, she felt that the whole thing had been like a dream—and not a bad dream, either. Just a warm, peaceful dream that had Jesus and her own angel in it, and also strange faces and white hands and men writing things down on pieces of white paper.

The waiting wasn't at all bad, either. She sat quietly on the bench with the matron beside her, and she couldn't seem to worry about what would happen to her. If the men made her stay, that was all right. If they let her go, well, that would be better, of course. She would be able to go and stay with Peony and start looking for a job so she could take care of herself. The only thing that could possibly matter was having to wait to get herself baptized in the River Jordan, but that was going to take some time anyway, even if she got herself paroled and set free.

When the door opened, she didn't even feel anxious. She just went back inside of the room and stood quietly, waiting for whatever would come. Whatever was God's will for her.

Peony had just poured Franklin and Alice's coffee when the phone rang. She answered it in the kitchen. "This is the Lockhart residence."

When Peony went back into the dining room to take more hot biscuits, Alice glanced at her anxiously. Peony smiled and nodded her head once. Alice put a quick finger in front of her lips and nodded her head toward Mr. Franklin. Jordan watched this exchange silently, continuing to draw the tines of her fork disinterestedly through her grits.

Franklin, oblivious to the signaling going on around the table, continued reading the financial section of the morning newspaper, but when breakfast was done and he had left for his office, Alice went into the kitchen, where she and Peony chattered excitedly.

Jordan cracked open the swinging door and listened.

"When?" Alice asked.

"She's not sure. But *soon*. Just some paperwork needs to be done and filed with the court."

"We'll have to work fast to get the house cleaned and ready," Alice said. "Maybe we can get Petunia to come help us. We could get it all done tomorrow, with more help—and then it would be all ready for Miss Amylee and Pansy."

"H-m-m-m," Peony hesitated.

"What?" Alice asked.

"Well, I was just thinking—maybe we ought to work on getting them there at the same time. Just get everything taken care of all at once. I think that would be best."

"Maybe so," Alice agreed. "Once we find out when Pansy will be released, I can call over to White Columns and make arrangements to get Miss Amylee the same day."

"And I can ask Reverend Brown if he'll go over to the prison to bring Pansy to Miss Amylee's house," Peony added.

"That will be perfect!" Alice said, and at that moment, Jordan pushed open the kitchen door.

"I can help with cleaning the house. I can dust off all those little figurines Miss Amylee likes so much."

Because, Jordan was thinking, when Miss Amylee finds out that she's going to be living back in her very own house—and not here in this cold house with us—maybe she won't be the saddest person in the whole world anymore. Because maybe if she isn't so sad anymore, those big, swollen buds on the fuchsia azaleas wouldn't be so scary! Or the dead, dark leaves down at the bottom of the fish pool.

That night after supper, Alice asked Jordan to please go into her room so she and Mr. Franklin could talk. As always,

Jordan did as she was told, but also as usual, she left her door cracked open and tried to listen to the conversation in the living room. Alice and Franklin spoke in such low voices, she couldn't understand the words. Finally, she just settled down with a good book, because they were definitely talking about the arrangements Alice had made for Miss Amylee, and Jordan knew that her stepfather would not oppose any of it. Because doing that would put Miss Amylee back under his own roof, and he wasn't going to have that.

The words in the book blurred before Jordan's eyes, and suddenly the pages held only the image of Miss Amylee's house just down the street. The last evening light crept in around the shade-drawn windows, cast shadows on the dust-shrouded furniture, and highlighted the little figurines in the china cabinet. She could clearly see the one of a little boy in short pants, reared back and playing an accordion, and the tiny vase that was a miniature head of a beautiful lady with long dark eyelashes and tiny pearl dangle earrings, and the artificial violets stuck in the vase made the lady a big, purple hat. And the rotund little Benjamin Franklin in his tricornered hat—not a figurine, but a bell.

All the figurines swam in happy abandon before her eyes. And tomorrow, she would be able to dust them for Miss Amylee. It was the best story she ever read.

The next morning, Petunia—another one of Peony and Pansy's sisters—came with Peony, and they were certainly alike—except that Petunia carried a little more flesh on her big bones than did Peony. And they arrived ready to work on Miss Amylee's house, wearing old clothes and with their heads done up in bright blue scarves. Petunia brought her own bucket, scrub brush, bottle of pine oil, and a bundle of cleaning rags.

"You all go on over to the house and get started," Alice directed. "I'll fix Mr. Franklin's breakfast myself this morning." Peony cast a glance at Petunia—a glance that meant *he ain't gonna like her biscuits near as much as he likes mine.*

"Oh, let me go on over with them!" Jordan begged.

"But you haven't had your breakfast," Alice reminded her.

"Oh, I'm not hungry at all," Jordan argued. "Please?" Because she was thinking that she wanted to get over there just as soon as possible, and she wouldn't be able to bear having to sit at the big, polished table, listening to her stepfather chewing his food.

"Well, okay—but you do whatever Peony tells you."

For that whole day, they worked in Miss Amylee's house, taking all the dust covers off the furniture and scrubbing and mopping and cleaning until early afternoon, when the whole house was bright-looking and pine oil–smelling, and Joran had lovingly dusted every single one of the tiny figurines and put it back into its place. At the last, Jordan walked through the house once more, with her heart singing the glad tidings of *Miss Amylee's coming home!*

And indeed, only a few days later, two cars were making their way toward Miss Amylee's newly cleaned house. One car carried Pansy and was driven by Reverend Brown; the other, driven by Alice, carried a silent Miss Amylee in the passenger seat and an equally silent Jordan in the backseat, learning forward and with her arm draped lightly across Miss Amylee's bony shoulder. And what no one knew at the time was that the coming together of these two women was going to change the whole town forever.

\*　　\*　　\*

The Reverend Brown and Pansy were the first to pull into the driveway of Miss Amylee's house. Pansy studied the house for a while and then said, "Well, it's a right nice-looking house. Big front porch."

"Pansy, those are the first words you've spoken since you got into my car," the Reverend said in his honey-smooth, baritone voice.

"Name's River," she reminded him. "And you was humming hymns most of the way, so I figured I shouldn't interrupt. Maybe you was praying."

"Maybe we ought to hold off on using your new name for a little while," he suggested. "Give things a chance to settle down. And yes, I was praying—for a new start and a better life for you and for Miss Amylee."

At first, Pansy had glared at the Reverend's suggestion of putting off using her new name, but then she thought better of his judgment and settled herself back down. "I don't remember much about Miss Amylee," Pansy admitted. "Guess maybe she's something like Miss May, what my mama takes care of?"

"She gets a little confused, Miss Alice says." He tilted his head in a way that indicated perhaps it wasn't too bad. "And she's got a heavy heart," he added.

"What for?" Pansy snorted lightly. "She's got this here good house and her son's a rich man, so she's got no worries about money."

"Don't know," he admitted. "Just got a heavy heart, Peony says."

"Well, is us going in or not?" Pansy asked, reaching for the door handle.

He cleared his throat. "Uh, we're waiting for Miss Alice to get here. She's bringing Miss Amylee from White Columns."

"White Columns? What's that?" Pansy asked, drawing her eyebrows together.

He cleared his throat once again. "It's an old folks' home," he explained.

"That where she been?" Pansy was incredulous. "Well then, no wonder she's got a heavy heart! She'll be lots better off here in her own house." Pansy thought for a moment. "She needs her things around her. All the things she knows."

"I think you're right," he said.

"How come we gotta wait?" Pansy asked.

"Miss Alice thinks it's the best way—so you both come into the house at the same time. That way, Miss Amylee won't get confused and think she's at somebody else's house. *Your* house," he added.

"*My* house?" Pansy laughed. "Well, maybe Miss Alice is right. *My house?*" She chuckled. "And when did Mr. Franklin remarry?"

"About six months ago. Nice lady, Miss Alice is. Widow lady with a little girl."

"Well, I wish them happiness," Pansy said. "But I'm not sure they'll get it. It's a mighty cold house, that Mr. Franklin's house is. 'Specially for a little girl. Peony says so, anyway."

They heard car tires crunching on gravel behind them, and Alice's big black car came up beside their own. Alice's too-cheerful, let's-not-let-anything-impolite-happen face smiled into Pansy's thoughtful and completely sober-looking one.

"Hello! Hello!" Alice chirped. Then she turned to Miss Amylee, who was sitting passively in the passenger seat. Pansy noticed the little girl's arm draped across Miss Amylee's shoulder. "Miss Amylee?" Alice hollered, as if the elderly woman were deaf. "You see where you are? You see your very own house right there in front of you?"

Miss Amylee gave no indication that she heard Alice. "You see that?" Alice tried again, pointing her finger at the house and wiggling it up and down, to try to attract Miss Amylee's attention. But Miss Amylee didn't respond. So Alice got out and went around to open the passenger door. Reverend Brown and Pansy got out of their car, as well. Jordan remained in the backseat of Alice's car, but she pulled her arm off Miss Amylee's shoulder.

"Come on, Miss Amylee!" Alice almost shrieked as she guided the elderly woman out of the car. "Come meet Pansy!" Pansy glanced at the Reverend, who pursed his lips a bit and shook his head. He was right, of course. Plenty of time later to get everybody used to her new name. So she walked over close to where Miss Amylee was balancing carefully, with Alice holding on to her arm.

"Miss Amylee?" Alice started. "This is Pansy. She's going to be staying with you and helping you take care of yourself."

"How do?" Pansy said, nodding her head. Miss Amylee's head turned ever so slowly, and she finally looked up for the first time, casting milky-blue eyes on Pansy's broad, serious face. Miss Amylee's mouth opened a bit, but no sound came out of it.

"Well!" Alice said far too brightly. "Let's go inside!" As if all she could think about was dispelling the uncomfortable silence. She pulled gently on Miss Amylee's stick-thin arm, but Miss Amylee resisted. Alice waited in the unbearable silence, while Miss Amylee continued to stare, speechless, at Pansy. Finally, Miss Amylee's small, purple-veined hand came up, trembled briefly, and fluttered to a light landing on Pansy's arm. The wrinkled white hand on Pansy's strong, black arm. Two pats, and the hand retreated.

"Yessm," Pansy said. "I'm glad to meet you too."

At that moment, Jordan came out from behind the car door and stood, watching silently as her mother started guiding Miss Amylee toward the porch steps. Pansy got on the other side, to help Miss Amylee, but she was also watching Jordan carefully.

*Yes. Peony was right. This little child sure enough lives in a cold house.* But then she saw Jordan glance up at Miss Amylee, and the whole expression in that small face changed very much for the better. Why, she's almost pretty! Pansy thought.

"Thank you so much, Reverend Brown," Alice called over her shoulder, and that's how she let him know that he wasn't invited inside. "I'll let you know how things go."

"I'll have you all in my prayers," he said easily, and then he got into his car, backed out of the driveway, and briefly watched the small group moving ever so slowly toward the porch steps.

I will most certainly have you all in my prayers! he thought.

# CHAPTER SEVEN

WHEN THEY CAME into the house, they all stopped, with Alice and Pansy still on either side of Miss Amylee. Alice beamed at the spotless living room, while Pansy breathed in the wonderful aroma of pine oil. Alice looked at Miss Amylee expectantly, but Miss Amylee was merely staring at the wall.

Jordan bolted around the threesome, grabbing Miss Amylee's limp hand.

"Come see your figurines!" she said, pulling Miss Amylee away from Pansy and Alice. "Come see them!"

Miss Amylee toddled along with Jordan into the dining room.

"Careful, Jordan!" Alice called after her. "Don't pull her right off her feet!" But they made it into the dining room, where Jordan proudly pointed to the figurines in the china cabinet.

"Look! I dusted them for you, and I didn't break a single one."

Miss Amylee's eyes wandered around the room and finally rested on Jordan's pointing finger and then—oh so slowly—on the figurines. She stared silently, saying not a word. But she was thinking: Accordion boy. Old Ben Franklin. The lady with the violet hat. And where have I seen these before?

"Honey?" Alice said. "Let's get Miss Amylee settled in a chair, and you stay with her while I show Pansy around." So Alice guided Miss Amylee to a chintz-covered armchair in the living room, settled her into it and went off toward the kitchen, followed by Pansy. Jordan sat down on the floor at Miss Amylee's feet and studied her face.

"You see where you are, Miss Amylee?" Jordan asked, but with real hopefulness, instead of with her mother's false cheerfulness. Because Jordan, strangely, could spot things that were false easily. False was what they all were at the table together at her stepfather's house. And real was just on the other side of the kitchen door. Real was when she and Peony were together.

Miss Amylee's milky-blue eyes moved around the living room, looking at the furniture and the crisscrossed sheer curtains, and the mantle, and the big upright piano with all the framed photos on its top—including one of herself as a young woman, smiling into the camera and with her head tilted prettily. And where have I seen that young woman before? she wondered.

Then, at last, her eyes dropped down to her own lap and then to Jordan's expectant face, just beyond her knees. *And where have I seen this child before?*

Jordan smiled. "I think you know where you are," she said. "And I think you're going to kind of wake up and maybe not be so sad anymore. And I'll come see you every day Mama will

73

let me, and I'll beg her and beg her every single day!" Jordan thought she saw Miss Amylee's head nod just a little.

"You'll see," Jordan added.


Alice showed Pansy all through the house, with particular attention to the kitchen.

"You're pretty well stocked up with groceries," Alice said, opening the refrigerator and also the door to the pantry. Pansy muttered her satisfaction. "Flour, sugar, lard, milk, eggs."

"And Pansy," Alice said, suddenly serious. "Only bland foods for Miss Amylee. She's got trouble with her digestion."

"Yessm."

"And," Alice went on, "normally I'd say for you to stay in that little room off the back porch, but you need to be able to hear her if she needs anything in the night, so you can use that regular bedroom so the bathroom is between Miss Amylee's room and yours."

"Yessm."

"At night, keep both the bathroom doors open," Alice went on. "Oh yes, Mr. Franklin had latches put on all the outside doors and they are too high for Miss Amylee to reach them, but you won't have any trouble, since you're pretty tall. Now I want you to always use those latches at night."

"Yessm."

"Remember I'm only half a block away, and I put my phone number by the telephone.

"Yessm. We'll be fine," Pansy assured her.

"Well, Jordan and I will go along now and let you all get settled in."

As they came back into the living room, Jordan jumped to her feet. "Oh, please let me stay!" she begged.

"No, Jordan—not today," Miss Alice said. "You just wait until Miss Amylee and Pansy here get settled."

To Pansy, Alice added, "Now, Jordan will want to be over here all the time, but don't you let her wear out her welcome, you hear?"

"Yessm."

Pansy looked down at Jordan's stricken face. But I sure hate to send her away to Mr. Franklin's cold, cold house, she thought. But to Alice she said, "Yessm."

When Franklin came home for the noonday dinner, he questioned Alice right away about Miss Amylee. "They seem to be getting along all right?" he asked, just before he bit into a piece of fried chicken.

"Seems they are okay," Alice said. "Of course, they will have to take a little time to get all adjusted to each other."

"Mama know she's at her own home?" he added, wiping his mouth with the napkin.

"Hard to tell," Alice said. "But she didn't seem upset about anything, so again, maybe it will just take a little time."

Jordan listened, but she didn't make any eye contact. She focused herself on moving her rice around on her plate so that all of the kernels lined up with each other, like tiny, white soldiers all in a row.

"Jordan, try to eat your dinner," Alice admonished her, and as usual, Alice's words drew Mr. Franklin's immediate attention. His chilling blue eyes bored into her as he continued chewing, with his small moustache moving slowly up and down simultaneously with his working jaw. Jordan wondered for a brief moment if Miss Amylee's eyes had been that exact shade of icy blue when she was younger. Then "Yessm," Jordan replied.

After dinner, Jordan sat in the kitchen with Peony. "I think I like Pansy," Jordan said. "And I know Miss Amylee likes her too."

"Well, that will certainly help things along, if that's true."

"Why won't Mama let me stay over there today?" Jordan asked.

"I expect she wants Pansy and Miss Amylee to have a chance to get to know each other and get settled in," Peony answered. "I imagine she will let you go over there a little bit tomorrow."

"You think so?" Jordan's tone was one of desperate hope.

"I think so," Peony answered. "Now you go on and play outside a little bit, before it gets too hot."

So Jordan went out to the fish pool, and from there, could just barely see the corner of Miss Amylee's front porch down the street. She wondered what Miss Amylee and Pansy were doing right at that very moment, so she sat down on the edge of the pool, closed her eyes, and tilted her head back as far as she could. In only a few moments, she could clearly see herself sitting at the kitchen table with Miss Amylee and Pansy standing at the stove, stirring a good-smelling pot of field peas. The aroma of cornbread came from the oven of the heavy stove, and she had already put the salt, pepper, hot sauce, and a dish of pickle relish on the kitchen table. It was all so real that Jordan felt tiny droplets of saliva popping up under her tongue, just from imagining the smell of that good food.

But right in the middle of her lovely reverie, she could suddenly see the rice grains on her plate at dinnertime—cold, uniform, tasteless.

Tomorrow! she thought. Mama will let me go tomorrow!

\*     \*     \*

The next morning, Jordan was especially quiet at breakfast, and she made sure to eat everything on her plate.

"Well, I'm glad to see your appetite improving," Alice commented, drawing that same sharp look from Franklin that he gave to Jordan when her mother reminded her to eat more.

"May I be excused?" Jordan asked, feeling that she would suffocate if she didn't get away from the table.

"You may," Alice said. And as always, Jordan folded her napkin carefully and replaced it in the napkin ring. After she got out of the chair, she pushed it in quietly, went through the living room, and right out the front door. She ran lightly around the house, tiptoed up the back steps, and went into the kitchen. Peony was wiping down the counter, and when she turned and saw Jordan, she put her finger to her lips. Jordan tiptoed across the kitchen, put her hand on Peony's shoulder, and started whispering.

"What are we to be quiet about?" she asked.

"Just don't want to see you start right in pestering your mama about letting you go see Miss Amylee first thing this morning," Peony whispered back.

"Why?"

" 'Cause you'll stand a better chance of going if you don't pester her," Peony said. "Just leave things alone and let me see can I get it done for you," she added. So Jordan sat down at the kitchen table and waited. In a little while, Alice came to the kitchen door. "You can clear the table now, Peony," she said.

"Yessm," Peony answered. "And Miss Alice? I've got extra biscuits left over this morning, and I was wondering if we could let Jordan run them over to Miss Amylee's before they get cold."

"Well, I don't know," Alice hesitated, while Jordan's heart pounded crazily in her ears. "Seems to me we should let them get settled in first."

"But on the other hand . . . " Peony went on, carefully . . . "Jordan could be a big help to Pansy—being as Pansy doesn't know where things are kept, and I expect Miss Amylee doesn't remember either."

"I could help," Jordan chirped with what she hoped was complete sincerity.

"Okay," Alice said, simply. "But don't stay too long," she added to Jordan. When the door closed, Jordan went up behind Peony, who was placing the fragrant biscuits into a warmed pie tin, and wrapped her arms around Peony's ample waist.

"Thank you!" she whispered, and Peony just smiled.

Carrying the tin of biscuits wrapped in a towel to keep them warm, Jordan fairly skipped the short distance to Miss Amylee's house, believing with all her heart that Miss Amylee, after a night in her own house, would be feeling ever so much better. Would maybe even tell Jordan some of her wonderful, terrible stories.

While Jordan was happily skipping along on her way to Miss Amylee's, Gertie was sitting at the dresser in her room, looking delightedly at all the new cosmetics she had bought the day before. They had cost almost a whole week's salary, but she didn't care. Lipsticks, rouge, a glittery green eye shadow, an eyebrow pencil, and best of all, a bottle of shampoo that had lilac perfume in it. Or at least, that's what the label said: *Enjoy the luxurious shampoo that leaves your hair smelling like lilac blossoms in the spring.* She had already taken off the top and smelled of it several times. And she had opened and looked at and smelled all the other things, as well. But she hadn't used them. Indeed, she kept them hidden away in her sock drawer, each item hidden in a rolled-up sock—the shampoo was so large that it took two socks to hide it. Because Miss May would never have allowed Gertie to use such things.

"You look prettiest when you're natural," she said when Gertie had turned thirteen and wanted to use cosmetics the way the other girls did. "Girls who paint themselves up will find nothing but trouble. Makes a man think you're easy."

Gertie looked past the cosmetics now and at her reflection in the mirror. The same pouty-looking mouth, but when it would be glossed by candy-apple-red lipstick, it could become one of her best features. And she wanted to look absolutely ravishing when Bill came to get her on Saturday afternoon.

Because he had called her only a few days after they met, saying, "It's Bill—you remember me?" And he didn't give her a chance to answer before he went on: "You wanta go out Saturday night? Go somewhere? Do something?" At first, Gertie had been unable to speak, especially hearing Bill speak the very words she had used for so long to describe her desperate situation of being stuck in a hot, dead little town. Finally she heard her own voice: "I'd love to."

"Okay—why don't we meet in front of that little café at seven o'clock?"

"Oh, yes," Gertie was trying hard to keep her voice melodious and even.

"See you then!" Bill blurted and then hung up. Gertie's head was swimming. Where would they go? They would have to go someplace, because there was absolutely nothing to do in the small town. No movie, no café open late, and on Saturday, even the drug store closed early, so they couldn't go for sodas there. Yes, they would have to go someplace else. Maybe even all the way over to Augusta! And what would they do? Gertie's mind was filled with visions of amusement parks and bright lights and Bill—how he would pay attention to her, think that she was charming and beautiful!

That's when she'd made the decision to buy the cosmetics—and the shampoo. Come Saturday evening, she meant to be as beautiful, as sweet-smelling, as glamorous as anyone could possibly be.

"Gertie?" Miss May's voice from downstairs. "Gertie? Gertrude?"

Gertie swept all of the cosmetics into the top drawer. She would remember later to hide them among her socks.

"Yessm?" Gertie called back.

"Breakfast is ready," came the answering call.

"Coming!" Gertie hollered, and then she started planning her means of escape for the date with Bill on Saturday night. She didn't know quite how she was going to arrange it so Miss May wouldn't find out, but she meant to find a way. There had to be a way!

# CHAPTER EIGHT

WHEN JORDAN CAME across the grass in Miss Amylee's front yard—carefully carrying Peony's good biscuits—the very first thing she thought was that even the grass looked different, now that Miss Anylee's house wasn't all empty and lonely anymore. The steps had been carefully swept and all the dead leaves from last fall were gone from the corners of the porch. And the very windows looked as if they had sunshine glowing in them.

Jordan reached to open the screen door, but it was latched, so she balanced the tin of biscuits in one hand and knocked loudly on the door with the other. Through the porch floor, she could feel the vibrations of someone coming toward the front of the house. Pansy's face appeared behind the screen, and she unlatched the door.

"Good morning, Pansy!" Jordan chirped. "Peony made too many biscuits this morning, and she's sent these over for you and Miss Amylee. Can I come in?"

"Sure, sure, come on in," Pansy invited, but when she looked at the biscuits, some little bitter-looking look flicked behind her eyes. But she didn't say anything, so Jordan followed her into the big kitchen at the back of the house. Miss Amylee was sitting at the kitchen table, with her hands lying quietly on either side of an empty plate. Jordan kissed her cheek and took a moment to breathe in Miss Amylee's own particular fragrance—a mixture, perhaps of violet toilet water and liniment and the warm, slightly musty aroma of her hair.

"Good morning, Miss Amylee," Jordan said, and Miss Amylee produced a vacant half-smile and patted Jordan's arm. "See?" Jordan went on. "I told you you'd feel better, now that you're back in your very own house."

"She slept right good too," Pansy added. "Both of us slept good. You want some breakfast?"

"Yes, thank you. If you have enough," Jordan answered, and she slipped into the chair beside Miss Amylee. Pansy put a big platter of scrambled eggs and country ham slices on the table, but when she picked up the basket of biscuits, a low harrumph started in her throat. But then she stopped herself, turned around to lean with both hands against the sink and with her head bowed.

Jordan glanced back and forth between Pansy and Miss Amylee, who was still sitting quietly, with her fingers resting on the edge of her plate. Pansy let out a low moan and raised her head.

"Forgive me!" she whispered fervently, and when she turned around, she said, "Now old Pansy Jordan almost came out there for a little minute—all offended and thinking Peony sent biscuits 'cause she thinks my own aren't good enough." Then a broad smile filled Pansy's face. "But this woman, this River Jordan has asked the Lord's forgiveness—and she even feels grateful for her sister's kindness!"

"River Jordan?" Jordan parroted. "Who's this new woman?"

"Me!" Pansy's voice thundered joyously across the cool, quiet kitchen. "Me!" she repeated. "I'm River!"

Miss Amylee jumped a little at Pansy's booming voice, but then she actually focused her eyes directly onto Pansy, who stared right back at Miss Amylee and with her smile growing even broader.

"Well, hello to you, Miss Amylee," she said in the softest voice Jordan had ever heard. Miss Amylee's eyes stayed on Pansy and her slightly bobbing head nodded a bit and then slowly swiveled around to look at Jordan. Eyes not such a milky-looking blue, but a soft, gentle blue and with life in them.

"Hi, Miss Amylee," Jordan said in a small voice. And she was thinking *I knew everything would be fine, once you were back in your own house!*

Pansy's voice broke in, still soft. "Well, I guess we're all gonna be okay, so thank you, Father! Now let's get some breakfast into us, and while we're eating, I'll tell you both the story about River Jordan!"

Jordan felt a pleasant flutter in her stomach, because maybe this Pansy-person would turn out to be as good a storyteller as Miss Amylee herself. And indeed, as Pansy told them the story about her actual visitation from the Lord Jesus Himself and the big angel He was sending to help her, Miss Amylee and Jordan ate silently. When Pansy finished, Jordan could smell the dank cell, see the glowing light that was the Lord, and hear His very own voice in her ears. And she could see the big angel woman and the gold tooth that glistened when she smiled.

"So now, you're not Pansy anymore?" Jordan asked, when she could speak.

"That's right," Pansy said. "My name is River Jordan, 'cause that's where I'm gonna get me baptized!"

"Where is it?" Jordan bit into one of Peony's soft, high biscuits.

"Dunno," Pansy admitted. "But I'm gonna find it. You can bet on that."

Miss Amylee's faint, creaky voice surprised them both: "Jordan."

"Ma'am?" Jordan responded.

"No," Miss Amylee searched for the words she wanted. "Jordan Creek," she whispered. Pansy and Jordan both leaned toward her.

"Come again?" Pansy urged.

Miss Amylee's eyes slowly went from one to the other. Then she took a deep breath. "Jordan . . . Creek," she repeated.

"Well, ma'am, I sure enough don't know anything about a place like that. Do you?" She turned to Jordan.

"I don't know either," Jordan said. "Maybe Mama or Mr. Franklin knows," she added, only to be cut off by the ringing telephone. Pansy went to answer it, leaving Jordan and Miss Amylee sitting at the table.

"Jordan Creek," Miss Amylee repeated, and Jordan could tell that Miss Amylee was pleased to be able to say the words.

"Yessm," Jordan answered.

"That was your mama saying for you to come on back home now," Pansy said.

Jordan sighed deeply, but she reasoned that if she didn't put up too much of a fuss about wanting to be with Miss Amylee, then maybe her mama would get busy with something or other and forget about making her come home too soon all the time.

"Tell Peony we sure do thank her for those good biscuits," Pansy added, with a sidelong glance that warned Jordan not to say anything about Pansy's initial reaction and her correction of it.

When Jordan went back through the living room where the shades were already drawn down against the hot sunshine, she thought for a minute that the room reminded her of the Sweetwater Baptist Church, where Mr. Franklin and her mother took her every Sunday morning and evening too, and sometimes Wednesday evenings, as well. The cool, peaceful aroma of it. And what was the word . . . sanctuary. That was it. So this was another sanctuary for Jordan. A place she could come to. A place away from Franklin's icy-blue, slightly startled gaze. Away from Alice's sugary-sweet voice. Away from doses of castor oil.

# CHAPTER NINE

IN THE END, Gertie found the perfect solution for getting away to be with Bill, but she had to plan most carefully. First, she asked Miss Sweetie-Pie if she would please come and stay with Miss May on Saturday evening, so Gertie could go "out with some friends," and when Gertie asked that favor, she used a pleading look that she had rehearsed in her dresser mirror for several days. "Just until she gets into bed," Gertie added. "Once she's asleep, you can go on home, because I won't be too late getting back myself."

Miss Sweetie-Pie somewhat reluctantly had agreed, and Gertie explained to her grandmother that she was going out with friends. For that conversation, Gertie used her very best "you can trust me" look, again well-rehearsed before her mirror.

"Well," Miss May finally admitted. "Maybe you should get to go out once in a while. Must be awful hard for someone young to be cooped up with an old lady all the time." At that, Gertie planted a kiss on Miss May's cheek and smiled her best Sunday school smile.

And that is how it came to be that Gertie sneaked her makeup out of the house early in the week and hid it behind the counter at Miss Sweetie-Pie's. Then, on Saturday, she used her own key that evening, let herself into the diner, and put on the makeup and a pair of dangle earrings she'd bought at the dime store. So she felt quite beautiful when she met Bill in front of the diner, and they drove off together into the darkness. And once she was with Bill, Gertie never again thought about Miss Sweetie-Pie or Miss May for a single minute.

Gertie had been right about where they would go on their date. Bill drove all the way over to Augusta, and during the drive, Gertie felt herself coming more and more alive and vibrant. At the beginning of the drive, when they simply went through long stretches of empty highways with fields and trees on either side, Gertie felt that she was traveling down a long, dark birth canal, away from everything dead and dull and always the same, and toward . . . what, she didn't know, but she was with Bill and she felt pretty and young. She almost held her breath as they eventually reached the outskirts of the city. Bill drove carefully and deliberately, and they spoke very little, but about halfway there, he reached over and silently covered Gertie's hand with his own. She resisted the impulse to grab his hand, but she turned her own hand over beneath his and slowly and gently entwined their fingers. Gertie was thinking: it's really happening! At last, I am getting to go somewhere and do something exciting!

"Where are we going?" she finally ventured.

"Real nice place I know about," Bill answered. "I think you'll like it."

"I *know* I will," Gertie said, sighing, and with that, she slid a little closer to Bill, tucked her arm through his, and rested her head lightly on his shoulder.

When Bill and Gertie finally reached the Starlight Roadhouse, Gertie could hear the pounding bass beat from the jukebox, even before they got in the door. And as they went across the parking lot, Gertie noticed a small motel at the back of the main building. She glanced up at Bill, but he didn't seem to notice. When Bill opened the roadhouse door for Gertie, she was completely unprepared for the rush of loud music and raucous laughter. There was almost more to see and hear than she could comprehend. Suddenly, the mental image of the dead little town she lived in crept into her mind, and she felt a rush of sheer joy. She had always believed that far away, beyond some hill, *life* was going on, without her. And now, here it was, in its full glory!

Inside, so many people—mostly young—sat around at tables covered with red-checkered tablecloths, while a vast mob of dancing men and women occupied the center of the room. Around and around they went, stomping and laughing and whistling, while an array of brightly colored lights swept back and forth over the dancers.

Bill guided the stunned Gertie to a small table in the corner and pulled out the chair for her.

"Beer?" he yelled the question, and she nodded dumbly.

But Gertie adjusted to the atmosphere quickly, especially after she'd had two glasses of icy cold beer. Her stomach warmed and her ears and eyes grew accustomed to the noise and activity. When Bill held out his hand and nodded his head toward the dance floor, she took his hand joyfully, and they joined in with the throbbing, milling throng. Gertie danced and danced and laughed and thought that, surely, here was what she would call *pure heaven*.

Hours later, Bill guided her to the door and they stepped out into a moist, cool night. Instead of guiding her to the car, however, he turned her toward the small motel she had noticed earlier.

"You want to go in here for a little while?" he asked, and she could tell by the expression on his face that he would understand if she refused. But Gertie, flushed with beer and sheer excitement, nodded her head vigorously.

It was very close to dawn when Bill stopped his car in front of the diner and drew Gertie into his arms, once again.

"Why don't you let me take you on to your house?" he asked. "I don't like you having to walk from here, what with it being so late and all." But Gertie had already determined that she didn't want him to see that she lived in such an ugly old house, one that needed painting so badly and had those big, crooked rocking chairs on the front porch. And all those begonia plants in coffee cans.

So when Gertie finally got out of the car, she started walking down the street, looking back to wave her fingers at Bill one last time. She waited, to be sure he had driven on, and then she turned into the familiar street, now so strange and quiet in what was the very earliest of the morning light. But when she came up on the porch, she was completely surprised to find Miss Sweetie-Pie sound asleep in one of the rocking chairs.

"Miss Sweetie-Pie!" Gertie whispered, shaking Miss Sweetie-Pie's shoulder. "What on earth are you doing here?"

Miss Sweetie-Pie stirred slowly, and when she saw Gertie, she sat bolt-upright and grabbed the chair arms with both hands.

*"Gertie!"* she fairly bellowed. *"What are you doing coming home so late?"* She glanced around at the pearl-gray dawn light. *"Coming home so early?"* she amended.

*"S-h-h-h!"* Gertie urged, and she sat down in the other rocking chair and scooted it close.

"I said for you to go on home, once Grandmama got to sleep!" she whispered.

Miss Sweetie-Pie swept a strand of hair out of her eyes. "Miss May was awful restless. Why, she didn't get good asleep until around two in the morning, and by then, I was worrying myself sick about you! Miss May asked me what time it was, and I even lied for you!" Her loud whispering almost broke into full, spoken speech, and Gertie put her finger to her lips.

"Well, where were you?" Miss Sweetie-Pie whispered viciously.

"I was in heaven!" Gertie whispered back. "I was in heaven with Bill!" Miss Sweetie-Pie sat back with her hand over her heart. "Lord help us all!" she breathed.

"Oh, Miss Sweetie-Pie," Gertie went on, and the glitter in Gertie's eyes was not lost on Miss Sweetie-Pie. "I'm so in love!" Gertie said the last word in such fullness of tone that Miss Sweetie-Pie almost expected it to bloom from Gertie's mouth and float across the dim front porch like a great, iridescent bubble.

For a long moment, neither of them spoke, and then Miss Sweetie-Pie said in the lowest possible whisper, "Oh my Lord, Gertie! Did you let him *know* you?"

Gertie's mouth dropped open. "Why of course, he knows me. We met right there in your very own restaurant." But Miss

Sweetie-Pie shook her head in frustration. "No, Gertie! I mean did you let him *know* you, in the biblical sense?"

Gertie frowned in confusion. Miss Sweetie-Pie took a deep breath and leaned forward to take Gertie's hands in her own. "Gertie," she went on. "Did you go to bed with him?" The look of confusion on Gertie's face dissipated, and she blushed and looked down at the floor.

"Oh, Heaven help us!" Miss Sweetie-Pie repeated.

"I'm so in *l-l-o-o-o-v-v-e-e!*" Gertie whispered melodically, sighing deeply, smiling, and closing her eyes. But what had suddenly dawned upon Miss Sweetie-Pie was that she had been used by Gertie. Used to enable Gertie to spend a night in *sin*!

"Gertie, you did me wrong," she whispered. "And don't you ever do something like that to me again!" Miss Sweetie-Pie's jowls shook with the whispered fury of her words. "If it wasn't for my deep respect for Miss May, I'd tell you right here and now not to come back to my café!" She expected those harsh words to elicit some sort of remorse from Gertie, but there was that same self-centered, bland face she'd always seen—with some heightened color in the cheeks. "I love your grandmother too much to take your job away from you," Miss Sweetie-Pie said again. "And Lord knows, somebody's got to give you some guidance, whether you want it or not, and I guess that job has fallen on me. Lord, give me strength!"

"I know it was wrong," Gertie whined. "But I just couldn't help myself. Seems to me I've been lonely and blue for my whole life, and he gave me such a wonderful feeling, like I was very, very special!"

"Well, let's hope that's all he gave you," Miss Sweetie-Pie

said, but Gertie looked at her in a completely confused way. "And don't you be late for work!" Miss Sweetie-Pie added. With that, she went down the steps and out into the quiet street.

About the same time that Gertie was watching Miss Sweetie-Pie walking down the street in a rapid, stiff, you-have-offended-me gait, Aunt Rose, in her small house out on the Waynesboro Highway, was taking a pan of biscuits out of the oven. She had already fed her few chickens and ironed a fresh shirt for Honey-Boy to wear that day. In her mind's eye, she could see him walking along the highway toward town well ahead of her own departure for Miss May's house. As everyone else in town, she had long ago memorized his peculiar gait so that the instant she thought of him, she could see his swaying, side-to-side "dance," as she called it. "Honey-Boy's dancing," she always thought, and even though she knew that some people privately called him "Crazy Honey-Boy," she was grateful that, for the most part, the people of the town knew that he was as harmless as a child. "Thank you, Father!" she whispered. "And thank you for this new day and a new life for Pansy. Amen!" She moved around the small kitchen, thinking about maybe stopping by to see Pansy and Miss Amylee, once she was done for the day at Miss May's. Yes. That's exactly what she would do. Then, without a moment of hesitation, she entered back into prayer: "Oh yes—and bless Miss Alice for hiring my sweet Pansy! And Reverend Brown and Peony for helping Miss Alice make up her mind. And this time, sweet Lord, I'm done. Amen!"

"Honey-Boy?" she called out. "Come on now, get you

some good, hot biscuits!" She put a plateful of the fragrant biscuits on the kitchen table, along with two cups of coffee and the big jar of the sorghum syrup that he always liked. Then she went across the dim living room and plugged in the Christmas tree. Twelve months of the year, the tree stayed in the corner of that small room, and every single morning, Rose plugged in the lights before Honey-Boy came out of his room. Once, many years ago, she had forgotten, and Honey-Boy had broken down in tears. After that, she never forgot again. There had been a time long ago when she kept a live tree, but Miss Amylee had told her that was too dangerous—that it would get dried out and maybe start a fire. So Miss Amylee sent off to some company that made artificial trees—not at all easy to find! And she ordered one for Aunt Rose and Honey-Boy. Ever since, that was the tree they used all year long. And now, with the colorful lights casting a rainbow of colors around the room, Aunt Rose knew that her day was well begun.

Honey-Boy came into the kitchen, smiling and silent, as almost always, and Aunt Rose helped him into the freshly ironed shirt before he sat down at the table. She split open three biscuits, put them on his plate, and poured his beloved sorghum onto them. All the while, he gazed at his plate with bright, happy eyes.

"Yes, I know," she said to him. "I know all about it. You sure do love your biscuits and syrup, and . . ." She hesitated, and Honey-Boy looked at her with a breathless stare. She laughed. "And Santy Claus is coming tomorrow!" Honey-Boy grinned and wriggled and then settled down to the serious business of the fragrant biscuits and the palate-tingling sorghum and the steaming cup of coffee. When he was done, he reached out and put one clumsy hand on her head as he got up from the table.

"You're welcome," she said.

A few minutes later, Aunt Rose stood at the kitchen sink with her hands in hot, soapy water, washing the dishes. From the small window over the sink, she watched Honey-Boy go dancing down the grassy strip beside the road.

"And thank you for taking good care of Honey-Boy," she murmured.

Miss May said, "Gertie tells me your Pansy has moved into Miss Amylee's house with her, and they're going to be staying there together?"

"Yessm," Aunt Rose answered, as she wiped down the kitchen counters.

"Well, that's good," Miss May said. "Good that poor old Miss Amylee doesn't have to live in an old folks' home. I always thought Franklin and Alice were wrong about putting her there."

"Yessm."

"And it's good that she's right in her own house and with Pansy to take care of her."

"Yessm."

"And how is Pansy?" Miss May added, with the curiosity oozing out of each word.

"Right fine, I reckon," Aunt Rose said, busying herself by starting to clean out the refrigerator. "You want to save this little bit of dried-up store-bought jelly?"

"Let's throw it out but keep the jar," Miss May directed. And then she repeated her question: "How is Pansy?"

"I haven't seen her yet," Aunt Rose said. "Mean to stop by

there after I'm done here," she added. Then she turned and looked full into Miss May's face. "But I 'spect she's just fine," she whispered. "I'm at peace about her."

Miss May nodded her head. "That's good," she pronounced. She studied the coffee in the bottom of her cup and then added, "I sure do wish I could feel at peace about Gertie." Aunt Rose didn't say anything, but she studied Miss May's face, waiting for her to elaborate. "I worry about that girl," Miss May finally admitted. "So much like her mama, and I couldn't do a thing with her either."

"She was a hard one," Aunt Rose finally admitted. "And I think you've done real good to raise Gertie like you done."

"Thank you," Miss May said. "I've done the best I could."

"That's all any of us can do," Aunt Rose agreed.

Miss May heaved a great sigh and said, "Maybe I'll make a little casserole and get Gertie to take it over to Miss Amylee's when she gets home from work. Be a good idea to send something over there for them. Let them know we're thinking about them."

Aunt Rose hesitated. "You want me to fix up a casserole for you?"

"No," Miss May said absently. "I kind of feel like cooking, myself."

Aunt Rose didn't say another thing, but if the big jug of tea in the bottom of the refrigerator had eyes, they would have seen Aunt Rose's eyebrows going almost up to her hairline. "Well," Aunt Rose finally offered. "You've been having a bit of trouble with cooking lately." She lifted out the words softly and gently, as if trying to reduce the consternation they might bring to the elderly lady.

"Aunt Rose!" the wounded words following right away. "I

am too a good cook, and there's nothing wrong with my cooking now! Just because I'm a bit older, doesn't mean I can't still make a mighty good casserole!"

"Yessm," Aunt Rose answered.

Miss May glanced at her sharply, because she knew all too well that Aunt Rose was capable of masterful manipulation, when she needed to be. "I am *too* a good cook!" Miss May repeated, and to punctuate her resolve, she opened the freezer compartment and plunked a rock-hard package of frozen pork chops on the counter. "Gonna take some time for those to thaw," Aunt Rose said, lifting her chin.

"That's okay," Miss May replied. "I'll wait."

And wait, she certainly did. The whole time Aunt Rose dusted and cleaned and did the hand laundry, Miss May sat at the kitchen table, staring at the frozen pork chops, as if her ardent stare, by itself, could hasten the thawing. By the time Aunt Rose was ready to leave, Miss May was breaking apart the pork chops and heating up an iron skillet. Aunt Rose stood in the doorway, studying the thin, rigid back.

"I sure wish you'd wait until Gertie gets home before you try cooking those pork chops," Aunt Rose said in gentle tones.

Miss May didn't answer.

"Did you hear?" Aunt Rose inquired in a louder voice.

"I heard you!" Miss May almost snarled. "And if you're done, then you can go on now," she added.

"If you'll just wait until tomorrow, I'll help you with your pork chops," Aunt Rose tried once again. "And I'll even take them over to Miss Amylee's myself."

"Gertie can take them," Miss May said. And Aunt Rose was thinking, Oh, Lord! Not Gertie, Miss May! Gertie can sure enough be a big bother! "We ought to let them get settled be-fore we go bothering them," Aunt Rose offered.

"Bothering them?" Miss May said. "What could be a bother about my good, pan-roasted pork chops?"

Just then, Aunt Rose heard Gertie's footsteps on the front porch and the squeaking of the screen door. As Aunt Rose passed Gertie in the front hallway, she whispered, "You help her keep an eye on those pork chops. She's bound and deter-mined she's going to cook them!"

"Oh, Lord!" Gertie sighed. But by the time Gertie could get to the kitchen, dark smoke was roiling out of the old cast-iron skillet, and Miss May was gasping, coughing, and fanning helplessly at the smoke with her apron. Gertie stepped forward, reached through the smoke, and turned off the unit. Then she grabbed a kitchen towel and pulled the burning mess of pork chops to the side. Miss May opened the back door and was swinging it to and fro, drawing out some of the acrid smoke with every swing. Gertie leaned wearily against the counter, watching her grandmother with unkind eyes.

"Don't you say a single word to me!" Miss May snarled. "Just you wait until you get as old as me, and the same things are gonna happen to you.

The words hit Gertie like a curse. I won't get old! Gertie silently promised herself. I won't get old! And somehow, I'm gonna find me a way to get outta here. Outta this hot, dead, old town and old women who've forgotten what it's like to be young!

Suddenly, Gertie turned away from the kitchen and ran to her own room. She slammed the door behind her, went to the drawer where she had hidden her cosmetics, and rested her fingers on the smooth, plastic cover of the powdered blush and the cool cylinder of lipstick.

"Okay, Billy," she whispered. "I'm already head-over-heels in love with you, and now, you're gonna be my ticket outta here!"

# CHAPTER TEN

A LL THE NEXT DAY, Gertie looked up every single time anyone came into Miss Sweetie-Pie's, but Bill and the others in the construction crew didn't come. So Gertie's time at work seemed as if it would never end, with the afternoon sunshine glaring against the front window, and some powdery old lady sitting endlessly in the chair where he had sat. And Gertie didn't even hope the sheriff would come in for his usual glass of iced tea, because after all, he too was stuck in this dead old town, and even if she could manage to get him interested in her, he wouldn't give her what she really wanted: to escape from that stupid, hot town forever and ever.

But Bill was an entirely different matter. She daydreamed about the two of them driving along a highway in a red convertible, on their way to some exotic place where they would live, and she would cook and clean their pretty house and buy lots of nail polish and lipsticks and bubble bath beads. Where he would come home every night and tell her how beautiful she was, and she would never, ever have to put up with her grandmother again. Where she could be young and exciting, and they would go dancing every single night.

Call me, Bill! she screamed silently.

When Gertie went home from work, she found that Aunt Rose was putting the finishing touches on a high, white coconut cake, and Miss May was sitting at the kitchen table, watching her.

"You take this cake over to Miss Amylee's for me," Miss May said. "Sin and a shame for me being so late in sending something to them over there." Aunt Rose rolled her eyes, but in such a way that Miss May didn't see her do it. Gertie did, however, and she bristled. "I won't stay and *bother* anybody," she said to Aunt Rose, but as soon as she had left the house, she thought, Actually, I'll do any damned thing I like! That's what I'll do!

Only a few minutes later, Gertie knocked on Miss Amylee's front door, and Jordan came to answer it.

"Hi," Gertie said, trying to remember who Jordan was and how she was related to old Miss Amylee. Jordan said nothing but studied Gertie carefully before letting her eyes drop to the cake in Gertie's hands.

"Who is it, Jordan?" Pansy called from the kitchen.

"Who are you?" Jordan asked, bluntly.

"Gertie. Miss May's granddaughter. My grandmama said for me to bring this cake over to you all."

By then, Pansy had come into the living room and stood behind Jordan like a great, dark mountain. She reached around Jordan and pushed open the screen door.

"Come right in," Pansy said, smiling, drawing a glance

from Jordan that was filled with sharp rebuke. Gertie stepped into the living room, and Pansy lifted the cake out of her hands.

"That's sure nice of Miss May," Pansy said politely. "Won't you come in and sit down?" Her invitation to Gertie drew yet another unsmiling glance from Jordan. And frankly, Pansy knew that she was getting herself into trouble right then and there—both because of Jordan's anger and also because she knew from her mama exactly what kind of petulant, rude child Gertie really was. But she gritted her teeth and forced a smile onto her face.

"Gertie, this here is Jordan, Miss Amylee's step-grand-daughter." Jordan continued staring at Gertie but said nothing, and Gertie was thinking to herself: *Yes, I already know her. Or I know about her. Spoiled little snot who's always gotten everything she ever wanted. Without even once scraping plates or pouring coffee or working her fingers to the bone for a quarter tip!*

"How do you do," Gertie said, in a hoity-toity tone and with a bitter smile on her face. But then, Gertie suddenly noticed something else: "What's that I smell?" she asked as her mouth suddenly watered.

Pansy beamed at her and nodded slowly. "That's my specialty," she announced. "My good fried chicken." Then she added, with a modest casting down of her eyes: "Some folks say it's the best in the world. We're just awful late getting our dinner today."

"Sure does smell good," Gertie said, with a hopeful, almost pleading look in her eyes. "Does it taste as good as it smells?"

Uh-oh! Pansy was thinking. Miss Amylee had come into the living room, and Pansy glanced at her hopefully, then without hope, because the face was blank as a baby's. *Not up to her to be mannerly with folks, even folks who're being rude themselves!* Then Pansy glanced at Jordan. *Just a child,* Pansy thought. *Just a child who don't like this Gertie-person one little bit! Not really up to either of them to do the polite thing. All up to me to keep honor in this house!*

"I said, does it taste as good as it smells?" Gertie persisted.

"Well, we'll be happy for you to stay for some dinner, and then you can decide for yourself," Pansy said—drawing another sharp, offended glance from Jordan.

"Thanks!" Gertie yelped, plopping herself down on the couch. She looked happily from one of them to another, popping her gum loudly.

"Be ready in just a few minutes," Pansy said, getting Miss Amylee seated in an armchair and then turning and heading back to the kitchen, with Jordan right on her heels.

"What'd you do *that* for?" Jordan whispered in an angry growl.

" 'Cause it was the only thing I could do! Unless good manners don't mean nothing anymore!" Pansy defended herself. "Now you go back in there and be good company for our guest. *That's* good manners too."

"I don't like her," Jordan protested, thinking at once that she didn't know why. She just truthfully didn't like Gertie, not one little bit.

"Don't matter," Pansy fumed softly at her. "Don't matter whether you like her or not. She's your *company* and you got to make her happy." Then she added, "Leastwise while she's under this roof." Pansy didn't say another word, but she was thinking, Oh, good Lord, please don't let her stay long!

Jordan made her way back into the living room, where Miss

Amylee was sitting passively in the chair and Gertie was still firmly planted on the couch, openly gazing around the room.

"You all sure got nice stuff," Gertie finally offered.

"Thank you." Jordan's voice was as stiff and cold as she could make it. But somewhere in the back of her mind, her mother's voice came through in gentle, clear tones: *Be sweet, sugar! Always be sweet! That's a good girl.* "Miss Amylee does have nice things," Jordan offered, as a conditioned response to her mother's deeply entrenched admonitions.

"Nice furniture," Gertie offered, passing her hand over the arm of the couch. *Not a crocheted doily in sight,* she was thinking. *I sure wish I had me a nice house like this to live in, instead of Grandmama's house. All those old yellowed crocheted doilies on every single piece of furniture, and the linoleum in the kitchen all worn right down to the floorboards.*

"Dinner's ready," Pansy announced. Gertie shot up off the couch and raced into the dining room, so that she was the first one to sit down at the table. Pansy narrowed her eyes at Jordan and tilted her head to the side, which meant: *don't you say a word!* Then she helped Miss Amylee to the table. When they were all seated, Gertie grinned openly, taking in the gleaming silver tableware and the delicate china plates and only at the last letting her gaze fall upon the platter of fried chicken.

"You all always use silver and china?" she asked, thinking of Miss May's old plastic plates and the mismatched tableware—some of it stainless steel and some of it old and stained, with yellowed plastic handle coverings. Pansy didn't answer her; she just bowed her head and closed her eyes, as did Jordan and finally, Miss Amylee.

"Lord, we thank You for this food and for Your love. And we especially thank You for the beautiful cake Miss May sent over to us." Pansy hesitated and drew a brief glance from Jordan. "And thank you for Gertie breaking bread with us today. Amen."

Pansy passed the platter of fried chicken to Gertie, who scraped three big pieces from the platter, including both breast pieces. Jordan looked sharply at Pansy, whose face was as calm as a summer pond at noontime.

"Hey!" Jordan suddenly yelled. "That's not fair! She took all the white meat!"

Pansy's sharp intake of breath went suddenly inaudible as she and Jordan studied Gertie's face. It was a grinning, comic mask with *Gotcha!* written all over it.

"Well, I *like* the white meat," Gertie said, with petulance dripping from her voice.

*"S-h-h!"* Pansy whispered to Jordan, then she added in a louder voice, "After Gertie brought us that beautiful coconut cake, I think she deserves the best pieces." And that was how Pansy tried to smooth things over, because having anything unpleasant happen at the dinner table was something she simply could not allow to happen. Jordan, though she said not another word, sat rigidly and with a thundercloud face. But the more she thought, she also could imagine the dining table in her stepfather's house—the stiffness in the air and the faint curled edge of his lip, and she decided that even Gertie's terrible manners were better to put up with than the cold glance of Franklin's electric blue eyes.

Gertie shrugged her shoulders flippantly, and then she bit into a well-crusted, tender chicken breast and kept her eyes on Jordan the whole time. After that, she poured almost all the gravy over her mountain of mashed potatoes and gazed at Jordan once again. *Spoiled little rich kid,* Gertie was thinking.

*This is one time when I'll have my way and you won't have yours!*

When Pansy brought out the coconut cake, she cut Gertie a slice almost twice as large as the other slices. As Pansy handed the plate to Gertie, she bored her eyes into Jordan's eyes. Another *don't you say a single word* command.

After Gertie had wolfed down the monstrous slice of cake and had repeatedly and noisily licked her fork, she belched loudly, drawing a somewhat startled glance even from Miss Amylee herself. "Well, I gotta go now," Gertie said. "But I'll come back again."

"Thank Miss May again for sending over such a fine cake," Pansy said, and once the screen door had shut behind Gertie, Jordan let out a deep and terrible sigh.

"She's rude!" Jordan said. "She's the rudest person I've ever known!"

"Well . . ." Once again, Pansy tried to smooth things over. "I guess she just hasn't had many advantages. Mama says it's purely a shame that such a young girl had her mama run off and leave her, and now her being saddled down taking care of old Miss May. Maybe that's why Gertie is like she is." Then Pansy added, "But you're absolutely right—she's gotta be the rudest person I've ever known either."

"Jordan?" Miss Amylee's cracked voice startled both Jordan and Pansy.

"Yessm?" Jordan asked.

"Jordan!" Miss Amylee fairly shouted. "That's it! Jordan Creek!" While Pansy and Jordan sat in complete shock, Miss Amylee's voice kept right on. "Right down behind my grand-daddy's farm, it was. Why, we used to go fishing there almost all the time. Swimming too." For the briefest possible moment, the faded eyes warmed to a more vibrant blue, and the thin lips curved into the memory of a smile.

"What's that you saying?" Pansy asked her. But just that fast, the smile and the vibrant blue of the eyes both faded. And Miss Amylee became exactly the same as she had been before.

"You know what?" Jordan asked Pansy. "I'll bet you anything that Miss Amylee got better for a little bit because of the shock of her watching Gertie lick her fork and then burp! Right at the table!"

On her way back to her grandmother's house, Gertie belched once again. And her thoughts re-created everything she had seen at Miss Amylee's house, but with a tight and bitter aftertaste, as she remembered Jordan's thinly disguised anger. *Stinking little bitch!* She was thinking. *And I sure do wish I could live in such a nice place and have a servant like Pansy take care of me,* she thought. *Then I could invite Bill to dinner and introduce him to my family: my little sister—that stinking Jordan! And my grandmama—Miss Amylee. And our servant woman! I'll bet that would impress him! Maybe he would even think I was a rich girl, and that would make him want me all the more!* The sensation that coursed through Gertie at that thought was the same she'd felt when she held all the new cosmetics in her hands. But right away, another thought crowded into her head. *What was it Miss Sweetie-Pie said, that night when I was first with him and when I told her that he gave me such a wonderful, wonderful feeling. She said, "I hope that's all he gave you."* Gertie was so taken by this new, brazen idea that she stopped walking. Stood right there on the sidewalk and hatched yet another plan for getting him to take her away.

A baby! A baby! That would certainly do it! But in the

meantime, until Gertie could make Bill give her a baby, she would certainly use the cosmetics—and maybe, just maybe she had found a way to make him think she was rich, as well.

At supper that night, Franklin, Alice, and Jordan sat together around the dining table in the typical silence that was broken only by Alice's offering more ice for Franklin's tea or another serving of the cold chicken and biscuits, or fruit salad that usually composed the cold supper at the end of the day.

When Franklin suddenly spoke, Alice and Jordan both jumped a little. "So!" he started out. "Mama seem to be doing okay with that Pansy person?" Jordan watched carefully, but she said not a thing about Pansy's having changed her own name. Alice glanced toward the kitchen, but then she remembered that Peony had left hours ago, not long after she'd served the hot dinner at noontime.

"Everything seems to be fine," Alice said—too brightly, as always.

Jordan considered telling them about Gertie's visit, how she brought the cake but then ate up all the best pieces of chicken and used up almost all the gravy, and especially how she licked and licked her fork right at the table! And burped! Right in front of God and everybody else! But then she thought better of it and remained silent.

"Jordan spending too much time over there?" Franklin asked Alice, as if Jordan herself were not sitting at the very table with him. Jordan felt her scalp prickle.

"Oh, no," Alice said quickly, glancing at Jordan. "At least, I don't think so. Pansy said your mama seems to like having Jordan around. Said she's a big help."

"Good!" Franklin pronounced, surprising both Alice and

Jordan. He looked up, his electric blue eyes sweeping first to Jordan and then to Alice, touched his napkin to his lips, and pushed his chair back a few inches.

"You like some more tea?" Alice asked, poised on the edge of her chair,

"No."

As always, his speech was clipped in a strange way. Early on, Jordan had mentioned this to Peony and wondered why her stepfather always sounded so curt and rushed.

"Sugar," Peony had explained. "Mr. Franklin's daddy sent him off to school way up in Mass-a-toosets . . ." Peony's voice took on a dark tone, as if she were trying to describe a place so completely foreign, she was reluctant to have it on her tongue. "And—from what I hear—folks up there just come right out and say exactly what they mean."

"Say what they mean?" Jordan had questioned. Such a thing was unthinkable.

"Yes, honey. They just say whatever they think needs saying, and they don't add a lot of stuff for making it sound polite. He don't mean nothing by talking like he does," Peony added. Jordan thought for a moment. "Makes him sound like he's mad at somebody," she had offered. And now, Jordan heard his curt *no* hanging in the air and making the whole dining room feel uncomfortable to her. But then, in what was an extremely rare gesture, Franklin smiled, reached over, and covered Alice's hand with his own.

"Listen," he started, as if Alice and Jordan would do anything else. "I have to make a trip to Savannah in July, and I thought maybe you'd like to come with me. It'll only be for a few days, but I thought you could do some sight-seeing and a bit of shopping during the days, and we could go out to dinner every evening. Just the two of us," he added, casting one of his electric glances at Jordan. "Like a second honeymoon," he added in a whisper.

Alice reddened and smiled, but then she glanced at Jordan—and Franklin already knew what she was going to say. So he said, "Jordan can stay with Mama and this Pansy person. That way, we could give Peony some time off too. And we have plenty of time for getting everything planned." He rubbed a slender finger along his chin. "We haven't been off together since our honeymoon," he reminded Alice.

"I don't know," Alice said. Because after all, Alice herself knew about Pansy having been in prison—a fact she had definitely not shared with Franklin. But then she envisioned the Reverend Brown, heard his deep, honeyed voice reassuring her. And besides, she had plenty of time to keep an eye on Pansy and Miss Amylee, to make sure everything was fine before leaving Jordan with them.

"I think that would be just wonderful," Alice said. "I'd love to see Savannah again."

Jordan forced herself not to smile. *A few days!* That much time without Franklin's electric glances at her, without being reminded to eat more of her green beans. That much time without any castor oil! And that much time to be with Miss Amylee and Pansy!

But then—somehow—the word *Savannah* began floating around in her mind, and she should have known what was about to happen, but she didn't. Or, if she did, she simply let it come, fueled by images of the postcards her mother had sent to her from Savannah when she and Franklin were on their real honeymoon. Jordan had been staying with Miss Amylee, who hadn't been at all confused or distant back then. It had been a heavenly week of listening to all the stories Miss Amylee loved to tell her and making tea cakes and having them with iced tea on the porch. And she and Miss Amylee had marveled together over the postcards that came every single day, and now the pictures from those cards floated into Jordan's mind like leaves falling from a tree in autumn: *Savannah, with the enormous, damp trees and curled moss hanging from them and livid-green grass in the shaded places and marble statues and benches with a different kind of moss growing on them. The dank aroma of that city so completely familiar to Jordan, somehow, that she had pressed the cards to her nose and tried to inhale the images. Clopping of horses' hooves on the warm pavement and the steady squeaking of carriage wheels.*

But into that reverie came Jordan's mother suddenly leaping up from her chair and rushing over to put a trembling hand on Jordan's forehead and then the unbelievably loud *smack!* of Franklin's open palms on the flat, mahogany surface of the table, the table itself resounding with the shock and anger, and the images in Jordan's mind suddenly cracking and tilting and her return to the terrible here and now. She looked right into Franklin's blue eyes, eyes that were filled with an electric rage.

"W*hy* do you do that?" Franklin yelled, his voice exceedingly sharp and brilliant with anger. "*Why?*" Once again, the strong flat palms smacked the tabletop. The sound exploded in Jordan's ears.

Alice was looking at Franklin as if she had never seen him before. "*Why?*" Franklin demanded again.

"Franklin, please! She's just a child! It's happened before—you know that! She can't help it!" Even then, even with those words, there was a softness in her voice that bordered on pleading.

"You scare your mother half to death when you do that!" Franklin yelled. "And you know that! So *why* do you keep on doing it?"

Jordan's mouth fell open, and what was waiting to fall out of it was her own honest question: *Why do I do what?* But then she thought better of saying anything, her head clearing a little as the last of the clopping hooves and squeaking carriages and Spanish moss and the dank aroma all finally fell away. She remained silent, because it had occurred to her that even if *she* didn't know what happened to her at times like this, maybe *he* did, and she couldn't bear for him to name it. The naming of it, whenever that would happen, could not—would not!—come from him! Not from him!

Suddenly and instinctively, Jordan knew that her mother was completely wrong about her "spells"—had been wrong all along. That they had absolutely nothing to do with not being *regular*. Still, Jordan clung to that familiar explanation, even anticipating with a strange, new joy the appalling thickness of castor oil on her tongue—the viscous elixir of absolution.

For several days following Jordan's latest *spell*, Alice wouldn't let her go to Miss Amylee's at all, and Jordan knew that the less fuss she made, the sooner she would be able to go back. Peony had, upon Alice's instructions, administered the dose of castor oil, and Jordan had almost welcomed it. Peony frowned at Jordan's strange willingness, and she peered closely into Jordan's eyes. But she could see nothing in them that would explain it. Alice and Peony watched her carefully, even coming to check on her in her room, where she was reading. Best of all, Jordan was excused from having to eat in the dining room, receiving instead trays in her own quiet room. For the first day or so after her stepfather's frustrated outburst, the loud explosion of his angry palms on the table resounded over and over in her ears. But after that, she gradually forgot the sound. In her own quiet room, she determined to eat every bite of food that was brought to her, and in only a few days, her cheeks were a healthy pink. Whenever Franklin wasn't at home, she skipped happily up and down the front porch.

While Jordan was "recovering,"—Alice's term for the enforced rest and relative isolation—Gertie finally received another phone call from Bill. She was quite careful in her conversation with him, knowing as she did that Miss Sweetie-Pie was hovering close by, openly eavesdropping. Gertie tried to shield the receiver so that her words would be as inaudible as possible. "Would you like to come to my house for lunch this Saturday?" she whispered. "Around one o'clock? I'll meet you in front of the diner and show you how to get there."

Then, when Gertie got home, she asked Aunt Rose to make one of her best pecan pies on Friday and to hide it in the highest cabinet, where her grandmother wouldn't see it. That pie was going to be the ticket for getting herself—and Bill—included for dinner at Miss Amylee's house, and he would think that Gertie came from a very wealthy family that ate every meal off of fine china. As for Pansy and Miss Amylee and that stinking Jordan, well . . . what they didn't know wouldn't hurt them!

# CHAPTER ELEVEN

O N THE NEXT SATURDAY MORNING, Alice finally allowed
Jordan to go to Miss Amylee's house again, and from
the look in Alice's eyes when she gave her permission, Jordan knew that perhaps her stepfather's angry outburst had
provided her with a hidden blessing—because Alice seemed
relieved to let Jordan go. If Jordan wasn't in the house, it
would be less likely that Franklin would get upset about anything.

The screen door at Miss Amylee's was latched, of course,
and after Jordan knocked and called to Pansy to let her in,
Pansy appeared at the door, wiping her hands on her apron
and smiling.

"Well, come on in here, Little Miss Jordan!" she boomed.
"Miss Alice said you'd been feeling poorly, and we've missed
you. Got a surprise for you too."

"What kind of surprise?" Jordan asked, walking into the
cool, gentle living room and instantly loving the way the blinds
were pulled against the hot sunshine. She inhaled the perfume
of peace.

"Something your mama alredy knows about, but I asked her not to tell you, so we could surprise you ourselves," Pansy said.

*Surprise? A surprise like Mr. Franklin's hands coming down hard onto the tabletop and his voice shattering the images in my mind?*

"A good surprise?" she queried.

"Oh, yes!"

"Well, I already know about Mama and him going off to Savannah in July," Jordan said. She didn't add: *Now that really was a good surprise!*

"That's not it," Pansy said, and then she actually added some of the words that Jordan didn't say: "That's a good surprise, sure enough. Means you'll be able to stay with me and Miss Amylee. But this is something else. Come on."

With that, Pansy turned and headed for the kitchen with Jordan close on her heels.

Miss Amylee was sitting at the kitchen table with a bowl of buttered grits in front of her. Jordan glanced around the kitchen, then shrugged her shoulders. "I don't see any surprise," she complained.

"Then you aren't looking hard enough," Peony said, and she tilted her head toward where Miss Amylee was sitting. Jordan sat down at the table, directly across from Miss Amylee, put her elbows on the table, and rested her chin in her hands.

*New hairdo for Miss Amylee? New dress? What?*

Then a truly surprised Jordan saw that Miss Amylee was looking at her steadily and clearly and with a big smile on her face.

"Oh, Miss Amylee!" Jordan laughed. "You're lots better aren't you?"

Because the face Jordan was looking into was the face she had loved. The face she had seen before White Columns. The comical lift of the left eyebrow. The lively eyes and the twitching half-smile of a consummate storyteller.

Miss Amylee smiled and nodded her head once, emphatically.

"Good grits!" she announced, spooning up more of the buttery, creamy-white confection.

"You already had your breakfast?" Pansy asked Jordan.

"I had biscuits in the kitchen with Peony," Jordan answered, still engaged in watching Miss Amylee. Clear-eyed, smiling, and enjoying her breakfast. "How come she got better all of a sudden?" Jordan asked Peony. "Being back in her own house?"

"I expect so," Peony said, and then she added, "How come you to be having your breakfast in the kitchen with Peony, 'stead of in the dining room with your mama and stepdaddy?" Jordan's brows pulled together, but she said nothing.

"You got trouble at your house?" Peony asked. "I thought your mama sounded way too cheerful when I called to tell her about Miss Amylee here being so much better, and she said you was sick." Pansy thought for a moment and then chose her words carefully. "But I guess I think she always sounds like that."

"Mr. Franklin got mad at me," Jordan whispered.

"What for?" Pansy asked in a soft voice.

"Yes, what for?" Miss Amylee added and both Pansy and Jordan jumped a little at the clear, lucid question.

Jordan glanced into Miss Amylee's eyes, the eyes so like Franklin's, but lacking the hair-trigger sparkle of bitterness always waiting in his. Soft, tender blue eyes, tilted down a little, as if already exuding sympathy. Then Jordan looked at Pansy and into the deep brown-black eyes, tender and warm, the color of the good earth.

*If I lived in a place like that* . . . Jordan started thinking. And suddenly, she was two tiny, tiny Jordans in the fertile, brown, loving eyes, those tiny twins walking around slowly and dreamily, carefully avoiding the black, pupil-pits and then gracefully reclining on the brown-earth parts, joining in with a love-root that went all the way to the soul.

"Jordan? Jordan?" From far away, Pansy's voice. And then Miss Amylee's, echoing. The tiny Jordans in Pansy's eyes shrugged their shoulders, slid into the tears on Pansy's face, and then disappeared.

"Jordan!"

"What?"

"You okay?"

"I'm okay," Jordan mumbled sleepily.

"That what Peony's told me about? Spells? And how much they scare your mama?" Jordan was silent for a long moment, and then she nodded.

"Not a *spell*!" Miss Amylee pronounced, reaching across the table and covering Jordan's small, pink hand with her pale, blue-veined one.

"Not a spell," she said again. "Just a child *dreaming*, is all."

Pansy's large hand slowly descended upon the others, like a great, dark bird of warmth and kindness.

"I'm gonna make you some breakfast," Pansy announced. "Growing girl like you needs more'n a biscuit or two." The warm brown hand lifted off, exposing the two pale hands beneath it—one paper-skinned and old and one small and richly pink.

"You've got a rich imagination, Jordan," Miss Amylee said, as Pansy began frying fragrant sausage patties and breaking eggs into a bowl. "I knew that about you the first time I met you. Right now, it's a burden to you, but as you get older, you'll see what a gift it really is."

"Imagination's a *good* thing to have," Pansy called from the stove. "Helped me imagine I was free, even when I was shut up in a prison cell."

Miss Amylee's eyes grew wide, and she twisted around in her chair to stare at Pansy's back. "You were in prison?" Miss Amylee's voice held on the slightest twinge of alarm. Pansy turned around to face her, holding a spatula that dripped sausage grease onto the floor.

"Yes, ma'am. I sure was," Pansy said. "I was in prison when the Lord Jesus came right into my cell and told me he loved me. And that I should get myself baptized in the River Jordan. So that's what I am bound to do. I already told you about all that, but I guess you weren't . . . awake enough to really hear it."

Pansy turned back to the stove, and Miss Amylee said, "Jordan, please go get my Bible for me. It's got maps in the back so I can show Pansy here where the River Jordan really is."

Jordan knew exactly where Miss Amylee's Bible was kept, because she had dusted it off the same day she'd cleaned all the little figurines. When she came back into the kitchen, Pansy was putting a big platter of sausage and scrambled eggs onto the table.

"You go ahead and serve your plate," Miss Amylee said to Jordan. "Eat while the food is still hot." Miss Amylee opened the very back pages of her Bible and thumbed through the maps until she came to one labeled *Palestine in the time of*

117

*Christ.* Jordan paused in eating her breakfast to look over at the map. The only things she recognized were Galilee and the Sea of Galilee. Miss Amylee planted a finger on the Sea of Galilee and then followed a crooked, blue line all the way down to another sea, called the Salt Sea.

"Here it is," she pronounced, and Pansy leaned over Miss Amylee's shoulder to study the map with her brows drawn together.

"The River Jordan," Miss Amylee said, with a soft reverence in her voice.

"The River Jordan," Pansy repeated after her. "And what's this?" Pansy asked, pointing to the Great Sea.

"Let me think a minute," Miss Amylee said, looking at the Great Sea as if its modern name would leap from the ancient one.

"Dead Sea," Jordan said, drawing surprised glances from Pansy and Miss Amylee. "I know, because there's a map on the wall at Sunday school."

"And what's that?" Pansy said, poking her finger onto the smaller of the two seas.

"The Sea of Galilee," Miss Amylee said. Then she put her finger onto a thin, blue line that ran between the two seas. "River Jordan," she repeated.

"How far away is it?" Pansy asked. A long silence followed her question, and Jordan went back to her sausage and eggs.

"Well?" Pansy pressed.

"It's a long way," Miss Amylee admitted. "Across the whole Atlantic Ocean from here. And then on across part of Europe too."

"Across the ocean?" Pansy frowned. "How'm I supposed to get all the way across the ocean?" And then she added, "I guess there's no sense in trying to get folks to call me River 'stead of Pansy after all. Ain't no way in this world I can get across a whole ocean." The defeated sound of her voice drew troubled glances from Jordan and Miss Amylee.

"Are you sure that's what Jesus said?" Jordan asked. Because she was thinking that maybe Pansy hadn't heard Him right.

"I'm right sure," said," Pansy murmured, but with a drawing together of her eyebrows and a squinting of her eyes as if she would be able to *see* His very words if she just tried hard enough.

Miss Amylee sat for a few minutes, staring at the map. "Maybe He'd let you settle for Jordan *Creek,* instead of the River Jordan? You'd stand a lots better chance of getting there, sure enough."

"Jordan Creek?" Pansy asked. "Jesus sure didn't say nothing to me about no *creek*. Where's it at?" The eyebrows lifted hopefully.

"A few miles outside Valdosta, down in south Georgia. Almost to Florida," Miss Amylee added.

"How far away is that from us?" Pansy asked.

"Oh, five or six hours, by car." Miss Amylee got a dreamy look in her eyes, but it wasn't the same kind of dreamy, "gone" look she'd had when she first came home from White Columns. This look was a somewhat bittersweet dreaminess. "Jordan Creek used to run through a wide crevice way down at the back of a pecan orchard on my granddaddy's old farm." She smiled and then snorted softly. "I used to love going to that creek . . . until . . ." Her voice tapered off.

"Until what?" Jordan asked, but Miss Amylee just waved her hand as if brushing away some pesky south Georgia gnats. "Nothing," she said.

"Jordan Creek?" Pansy was clearly pondering whether Jesus might just settle for that. "Get myself washed clean in Jordan Creek? Well, I'll have to think about that a little bit, I reckon. Pray about it too."

Just before noon on that same Saturday, Honey-Boy stopped by the back door of Miss Sweetie-Pie's restaurant to receive his customary piece of free pie. Gertie, reluctant as always, shoved the slice of pie at him and then—purely because Miss Sweetie-Pie wasn't in the kitchen at that moment, she slammed the door shut right in his face, so she wouldn't have to see that grin or listen to that ridiculous voice telling her the same old thing about Santa Claus coming.

"What you don't know, you crazy fool," she whispered to Honey-Boy, "is that *my* Santa Claus is coming *today*!" About fifteen minutes later, Gertie cleared a table, glanced at the clock, and then went into the kitchen where Miss Sweetie-Pie was flipping hamburgers.

"Miss Sweetie-Pie, I'm awful sick," Gertie said, holding on to her stomach and frowning. "I gotta go home."

"Gertie! It's right in the middle of rush hour!" Miss Sweetie-Pie's face mirrored the alarm she felt at the mere thought of trying to do the cooking and the serving and the clearing off of tables all by herself.

"I'm awful sick, I tell you." Gertie raised her voice and punctuated her statement with a groan. She clamped a hand over her mouth and ran into the bathroom.

120

"Oh, good Lord!" Miss Sweetie-Pie whispered. She went straight to the phone and called Miss May's house. She knew Aunt Rose herself couldn't leave Miss May to come help out, but Miss Sweetie-Pie seemed to recall that she knew there was another flower-named daughter in the family, besides the one helping old Miss Amylee.

Aunt Rose answered the phone. "Aunt Rose, this is Miss Sweetie-Pie, down at the restaurant."

"Yessm?"

"Don't you have another daughter, besides the one helping Miss Amylee?"

"Yessm, I have another daughter. Petunia."

"You think she would come help me with the last of the dinnertime serving today? Gertie's taken sick, and I expect she'll be heading home any minute. I just gotta have me some help. Please?"

"Yessm. She's between jobs right now. I'll call her and tell her to get herself down there right away. I don't know as she cares much for waiting tables, but I'll get her to come anyway. And she'll be glad to make a little piece of change—got bills to pay, you know."

"Oh, thank you, Aunt Rose. Tell her to drop whatever she's doing and come on down here as fast as she's able!" As she hung up, Miss Sweetie-Pie breathed a sigh of relief, but that sigh died right there when the bathroom door opened and Gertie—complete with full makeup and wearing a fresh dress—came out of the bathroom.

"I thought you said you were sick," Miss Sweetie-Pie accused.

"I am!" Gertie announced with a jutting chin and a lift of her shoulders that added unspoken words: *I don't care!* While the astonished Miss Sweetie-Pie watched, Gertie went to the cabinet and took out a whole pie wrapped in waxed paper. Pie in hand, she walked almost insolently through the kitchen doorway and through the restaurant.

"Miss?" one of the customers called out. "Could I please have some more tea?"

Gertie stopped and gazed at him coldly. "Get it yourself," she whispered, and then she was gone.

For the fifteen minutes before Petunia showed up to help out, Miss Sweetie-Pie did everything herself. She cooked, plated, served, cleaned tables, so that when, at last, Petunia came, Miss Sweetie-Pie's hair was hanging in her face, her eyes were bitter-looking, and her mouth was set in a dreadful line. Because every time she cleared tables or took lunch orders into the serving area, she could see Gertie standing right in front of the restaurant, one hip thrust out and brightly colored lips pursed. What Miss Sweetie-Pie really wanted to do was go right out there on the sidewalk and smack Gertie right in the face! That ferocious thought startled Miss Sweetie-Pie, because she had always thought of herself as a good, Christian lady.

"Well," she consoled herself, "even Jesus got mad at the money changers in the Temple!" And Gertie was pulling something so positively a complete and bold-faced lie, she could hardly comprehend it. But then Miss Sweetie-Pie knew she would never, ever do such a thing as slap Gertie. Perhaps there was no such thing as a perfect Christian, but there was such a thing as being a lady, and no lady would ever strike anyone. Not in public, anyway. And later, when Miss Sweetie-Pie came out of the kitchen to help Petunia deliver an especially large order, Gertie was gone.

"Lordy, Miss May—I just don't know how much longer I can take this, even for you!" she whispered. Then louder, she said, "Now Petunia, clear that table over there and get some more tea for the folks in the corner booth."

# CHAPTER TWELVE

Pansy and Jordan were in the kitchen, putting the finishing touches on their dinner, and Miss Amylee was lightly dozing in a living room chair that faced a television soap opera in progress when Gertie and Bill opened the door and entered without knocking. Only at the last moment had Gertie realized that it was going to look quite strange for her to be knocking on the door of "her own house," and she made a note to be more thorough the next time she had to create a setting for attracting Bill. If there was a next time.

When she saw Miss Amylee asleep in the chair, she put her finger on her lips, indicating to Bill that they shouldn't awaken her.

"That's my grandmama," she whispered. Bill smiled and nodded his head at Miss Amylee, as if she were wide awake. Then he became completely absorbed in looking around the large living room, at what, to him, were lavish furnishings—the glass cabinet full of expensive-looking china figurines, the elegant mahogany tables and delicate lamps. Watching him with suppressed glee, Gertie led him on into the dining room where, as she had expected, the table was set with gleaming silverware and gold-edged china plates and with the small chandelier reflecting light from the window.

She could hear that stinking Jordan talking in the kitchen— *but what sisters didn't dislike each other once in a while?* she reasoned, *so even if he noticed her cool contempt, he would chalk it up to sibling rivalry, wouldn't he?* But she also noticed the enticing, spicy aroma of baking ham and the golden-sweet perfume of fresh cornbread wafting out of the kitchen.

*Yes!* She thought triumphantly. *It was a risk, showing up like this with Bill, but I've won! I know I've won! The servant woman won't dare say a word. Now if I can just get past that stinking Jordan.* Gertie paused at the kitchen doorway, held the big pecan pie out in front of her, and walked right in, with Bill at her heels.

"I see we're just in time!" Gertie chirped brightly, drawing completely startled stares from Pansy and Jordan. "Here's a pecan pie my aunt Rose made and wanted me to bring."

Dimly, Pansy noticed the "my" Aunt Rose reference. That was completely inappropriate! Pansy's mama had the honorary title of aunt because of her advanced age and years of faithful work for white people, but her mama was certainly *not* Gertie's aunt! Still, all the years of never saying anything offensive—at least to any white person—clamped her jaw shut.

"This is Bill," Gertie hurried on.

"Howdy, folks!" Bill said, bobbing his head at them.

"This is Jordan," Gertie said and added nothing else. Jordan's face was a perfect design of incredulity. "Close your mouth," Gertie ordered sharply. "Or you'll attract flies!"

"And this is Pansy," Gertie said, studying Pansy's shocked face. "She's been with us forever."

"How do, Pansy?" Bill said, smiling. "And hi, Jordan."

"But . . ." Jordan could manage only the one word.

"We're gonna go sit with Grandmama," Gertie said, and she turned, pushing Bill ahead of her and left the kitchen hurriedly. "You tell us when dinner's ready, Pansy," she called back over her shoulder.

In the now silent kitchen, Pansy and Jordan stared at each other for long moments. Finally, Pansy broke the silence. "What on earth? What's going on here?"

"I don't know," Jordan managed. "But I didn't like her when she came before, and I don't like her even more now!"

"Imagine her just showing up here like this, with no invitation!" Pansy sputtered.

"Let's throw her out!" Jordan suggested happily. Pansy studied Jordan's face carefully, as if that idea truly had some merit.

"That's exactly what I'd like to do!" Pansy said. "But let me think for a little minute here." Long, silent moments passed, with Pansy pressing her lips together and rubbing her fingers across her forehead. Jordan watched her in joyful anticipation that she would, indeed, get to witness strong-armed Pansy throwing that puny little Gertie right out of the house.

"Well, here," Pansy finally said. "That boy seems to be right nice, and Gertie—that rude, silly little b—" Pansy hesitated, studied Jordan, and then added "girl . . . is trying to fool him. But I dunno why. So only thing to do is the best we can in this . . . situation today," she announced. "But I'm gonna have a long talk with Mama and get her to tell Miss May to make Gertie not to do this ever again! Coming over here without so much as an invitation! And make her tell that boy the truth, that we ain't family at all!" As she spoke, her jowls began to shake with suppressed fury. "Imagine! Her making out to him that we're *family*! You get on in there, Jordan, and set two more places," she added roughly.

"Wait a minute," Jordan whined. *"I* didn't do anything wrong. It's that silly Gertie you're mad with, not me!"

Pansy was grabbing another can of English peas out of the cupboard and another can of sweet potatoes. She dug through the drawer, furiously looking for the can opener, and then she came to a grinding stop, resting her hands on the counter and leaning her body forward onto locked elbows.

"You're right," she breathed. "I'm sorry."

"It's okay," Jordan finally said.

"So let me try this again. Jordan, would you please set two more places at the table for me?"

"I will," Jordan answered. "But I sure don't want to."

"Thank you, Jordan," Pansy said in a sweet voice. Then she added in a rough whisper, "While you're in the dining room, peek and see what's going on in the living room."

While Pansy sliced more ham and cut each golden square of cornbread in half, hoping it would serve two more people, she heard the faint clatter of plates and tinkling of silverware in the dining room. Then silence. When Jordan came back into the kitchen, Pansy looked at her sharply.

"Well?"

"They're sitting on the couch—kissing!" Jordan said, with her nose wrinkled in disgust.

"What about Miss Amylee?" Pansy whispered.

"She's still asleep in front of her soap opera."

"Well, thank you, Jesus, for that!"

In the living room, Gertie had one part of her mind on Bill's hot, provocative kisses and another part on Miss Amylee.

*She seemed so out of it the other day. Will she be that way again today?*

It was Gertie's lucky day. When all the food was on the table, Pansy coughed loudly—to announce herself to Gertie and Bill, who were absolutely lip-locked on the couch. Bill had the manners to blush mightily, but Gertie just gazed at Pansy with cold, narrow eyes. Pansy touched Miss Amylee's shoulder, and Gertie could tell as soon as Miss Amylee opened her eyes that both her mind and her eyes were deeply clouded over. .

What luck! Gertie thought to herself.

They all sat down at the table, with Miss Amylee glancing only briefly at Gertie and Bill. *Oh! That nice young couple from the soap opera!* she thought. *I should tell them something, but I can't remember what it is.*

Gertie ate rapidly, not making any eye contact with anyone other than Bill. He made a few futile attempts at conversation and then gave up, pouring his full concentration onto the food. When Pansy served the pecan pie, Bill said to Gertie, "So . . . have you always lived here?"

"Oh, yes," Gertie gushed. "I was lucky to be born into such a wealthy family."

Pansy and Jordan stared at each other in surprise. *Ah-hah!* Pansy thought. *So that's what this is all about!* Miss Amylee stared at the beautiful couple from her soap opera and smiled. Gertie gobbled her pie and then stood up, grabbing Bill's hand. Hurriedly, he shoved the last bite of pie into his mouth.

"We'll be late if we don't hurry," Gertie said. "We're driving over to Augusta to see a movie," she added. "So, 'bye now!"

"Nice to have met you all," Bill tried to say around the mouthful of pie. And just like that, they were gone.

"Such nice young people," Miss Amylee announced.

"I'm gonna go call Mama right now!" Pansy declared. "Put an end to Gertie's antics, once and for all! She's not going to impose on us and embarrass us like that again!"

So Pansy went to the telephone, leaving Jordan and Miss Amylee sitting at the table together.

"Did you ever hear of such a thing as Gertie's done, Miss Amylee?" Jordan posed the question and then waited patiently for the eyes to shift around to her.

"They're on my soap opera," Miss Amylee announced.

"They what?" Jordan asked, frowning.

The blue eyes blinked, and Miss Amylee's mind suddenly cleared. "Who were those young people anyway?" she asked.

Aunt Rose answered Miss May's phone on the third ring.

"Mama?" Pansy said, "have you got a little minute? I want to tell you something you just won't believe! But be careful what you say on your end until we can figure out how to let Miss May know about it."

"What on earth?" Aunt Rose murmured. "And Miss May's taking a nap right now, so it's a good time for us to talk."

When Pansy was done telling Aunt Rose everything that had happened to them during what was supposed to have been a normal dinnertime, Aunt Rose let out her breath in a whoosh. "I figured Gertie would do almost anything to get away out of this old town, but I never thought she'd go *this* far! Making out like you all was her family?" Then Aunt Rose's voice settled down a bit. "And yes, we've gotta find a way to get Miss May in on this, sure enough. But we have to be careful. I expect it would truly hurt her feelings if she knew about Gertie pretending to the young man that you all were her family."

"Yes, that would break her heart," Pansy agreed.

"So she and the boy have gone off to Augusta to see a movie?" Aunt Rose asked.

"That's what she said."

"Well, if that's true, likely she won't be back in time for me to leave, and I can't leave Miss May all alone. Lord only knows what time Gertie will come in—if she comes in at all," Aunt Rose added. "Tell you what . . . Miss Sweetie-Pie called me early this afternoon and asked me to get Petunia to come over and help her out. Seems Gertie was already up to no good, simply walking off the job, and right in the middle of the busy time. I declare, I just don't know what's going to happen to that girl! But I can get Petunia to come stay with Miss May, until we find out what's going on."

"That's a good idea," Pansy agreed. "And I think what's going on is that Gertie is out to catch that nice boy. Sure do hate to see that. He just doesn't know what he's getting into, with that girl."

"She's a wild one," Aunt Rose said. "So much like her mama."

"Well, let's think on things a little bit. I don't want Gertie just showing up over here whenever she takes a notion. No invitation, no nothing. *Huumph!* But I also don't want to hurt Miss May's feelings."

"We'll get it all figured out," Aunt Rose assured her. "So now, let me call Petunia—likely, she's home from the restaurant by now."

Later that afternoon, Jordan sat on the stool in the kitchen of her stepfather's house, telling Peony all about the day's unusual happenings. Jordan related every detail with relish, enjoying the way Peony rolled her eyes and acted shocked at every word.

"I guess Pansy handled everything all right," Peony said. "If there's a *right* way to handle something so embarrassing."

"I'm glad I was there and got to see it," Jordan confessed. "Why, I've never seen anything like that in all my life!"

Peony gave a short, sharp laugh. "Sure woulda been different if Gertie had showed up over here like that." Jordan had an immediate vision of Mr. Franklin throwing Gertie off the front veranda. But the thought of Mr. Franklin brought Jordan's glee to a crashing halt.

"Mama doesn't like it when Mr. Franklin gets mad," she said simply.

"Well, honey, your mama was raised to keep anything unpleasant from happening in the first place, like most of the white ladies around here. But I never really understood that. Unpleasant things is what goes along with living life, and some times you can't get around them no way at all."

"I'm glad Mama lets me go over to Miss Amylee's so often, but I've been wondering if you mind it."

"Mind?" Peony questioned. "No, honey, I don't mind it. I miss you sometimes, but I know you like being over there. Pansy likes it too," she added.

"Did she tell you that?" Jordan asked, delighted to think of Pansy saying something so nice about her to Peony.

"She sure did."

"Tell me about it," Jordan begged. "Tell me exactly what words she said."

Peony smiled and rolled her eyes. "No, I can't tell you exactly what she said, and besides, it's time for me to go home now. My old feet are killing me today."

"Oh." Jordan's word was deflated.

"Listen, Jordan." Peony cupped her hand under Jordan's chin. "I expect that when your mama and Mr. Franklin get back from having a second honeymoon in Savannah, things will start being a little better around here. They both need a little break in the routine."

"And you get a break too, don't you?" Jordan asked.

"Sure do, sure do." Peony almost sang the words. "And you get to spend all that time with Pansy and Miss Amylee, and that's good."

"Yes," Jordan agreed. "That's very good!"

The next day, Aunt Rose called Pansy at Miss Amylee's house and said that Gertie hadn't come home at all.

"Thank goodness Petunia could stay with Miss May, but what's gonna happen if Petunia gets another job? She doesn't mind taking care of Miss May, but she never has liked to wait tables. And suppose Gertie never comes back?"

"I just hope that boy didn't act a fool and *marry* her, for heaven's sake," Pansy lamented.

There was a long silence on the other end of the line, and then Aunt Rose said, "I'm worried that she's *with* him and he's *not* a fool and he *didn't* marry her."

"Oh, Lord!" Pansy breathed. "How is Miss May taking all this?"

"Well, of course, she doesn't know the whole story, but she's worried all right. Why, she's raised that child on her own and all by herself since Gertie's mama ran off, so she's acting more like a mama than a grandmama right now."

"Just do the best you can," Pansy replied. "And let me know if there's anything we can do."

"I've got a feeling in my bones Gertie's finally gotten her wish—to get away from this town. Maybe she'll never come back."

"That would be bad for old Miss May, but it might be the best thing for Gertie. Girl gets that desperate and unhappy, she's gonna explode all over everybody someday."

"That's the truth," Aunt Rose agreed. "That's surely the truth!"

Gertie did not come home the next night, or the one after that. And so they all waited to see what would happen about her. They waited and then waited some more.

Every morning, Aunt Rose begged Miss May to let her call Sheriff Amos about Gertie, but Miss May resisted, saying, "Let's wait just a little longer. Maybe she'll come home this very afternoon."

Of course, in a small town, nothing can be kept quiet, and the sheriff soon heard about Gertie's disappearance. He stopped by Miss May's house, and they sat in the living room, drinking iced tea and speaking in low voices. Aunt Rose couldn't hear what they were saying, but nearly every time she glanced into the living room, she saw Amos leaning forward in his chair and Miss May sitting on the couch, shaking her head no.

When he finally stood up and thanked Miss May for the tea, Aunt Rose heard him say, "At least let me make sure she's okay. That should ease your mind a little bit."

Miss May hesitated before she finally whispered, "Yes, please."

Meanwhile, Petunia became more and more sullen about waiting tables, and her glum attitude reduced her tips and Miss Sweetie-Pie's revenues. But Petunia was perfectly fine

133

when she was with Miss May, even when Miss May waked up in the middle of the night and wandered around the house, calling for Gertie. At those times, Petunia was at her best, soothing Miss May, guiding her back to bed, and staying with her until she had fallen asleep again.

Finally, almost a month after Gertie's disappearance, the sheriff came back to Miss May's house, and once again, they sat together in the living room, speaking in low voices. But this time, Aunt Rose crept into the dining room specifically to listen in on the conversation. After all, she reasoned with herself, Miss May's my responsibility, at least sometimes, and I can't help her if I don't know what's going on!

"Gertie's okay, Miss May," Amos said, and Miss May put a hand over her heart.

"Thank the good Lord!" she breathed. "Is she coming home?" she added, and the hopefulness in her voice made Amos take a quick breath. He stared at Miss May for a brief, silent moment before he said, "No, ma'am. I don't think so."

"Oh!" The soft utterance almost broke Aunt Rose's heart.

"Gertie's living in Augusta. She's well and says she's happy."

Miss May waited patiently for him to go on. He pulled a small notebook out of his pocket and flipped through a few pages, but still he said nothing.

"Is there more?" Miss May inquired.

"Yes, ma'am," he said. "You might not like to hear it."

"No, you may as well go on and tell me all of it," she whispered.

"She's living with a man," he said. "Leastwise, the apartment lease is in his name."

"Are they married?" Miss May posed the question he was dreading.

"No, ma'am. I don't think so." Then he quickly added, "I had him checked out, and he seems to be all right. No police record or anything like that. Works in road construction."

Miss May heaved a deep sigh. "I'm surely glad to know she's okay. Thank you."

After seeing Amos out, Miss May turned toward her room. "Without benefit of clergy!" Aunt Rose heard her exclaim.

It didn't take long before the rest of the story of Gertie's disappearance got around town, but most folks had figured out themselves that Gertie had simply run off with that nice young man, and they certainly clucked their tongues about it. But then they got back to their own routines, only occasionally thinking to say, "Poor old Miss May!"

Miss Sweetie-Pie hired a replacement helper, a young, buxom girl from a nearby town that was even smaller than the one they all lived in, and she had a winning smile and a cheerful giggle and she always said "yes, ma'am" and "yes, sir" to the customers, and she brought in many new customers, folks who drove all the way over from her own little town, just to see "little Mary Lou in her first paying job." Best of all, she thought that Crazy Honey-Boy was delightful, and when she handed him his pie every noontime, and he told her about Santa Claus coming, she giggled in delight, sending his quizzical eyebrows far up onto his forehead and making him smile even more than usual.

Petunia was left with the job she seemed to love the most, and she and Aunt Rose exchanged staying with Miss May, just as Aunt Rose and Gertie had done. As for Jordan, she was finally invited back into the dining room table in her stepfather's house, after Alice gave her a long, long talk about how important it was that she not upset Mr. Franklin. At the table, Jordan worked hard to keep herself from having any of her *spells*. If she felt herself drifting toward any reverie, even a small one, she silently pinched her upper leg—unseen, of course, by her mother or Franklin—until the sheer force of self-inflicted pain drove away her dreaminess.

Hurry! Hurry, time! Hurry for Savannah! she chanted to herself every time Franklin's startling, terribly frightening blue eyes flicked toward her, and in the course of her efforts, she pinched her legs black and blue to keep from going into another Savannah reverie.

So that on the last night before Alice and Franklin's trip was to begin, Jordan tossed restlessly in her bed, trying to find a way to keep her bruised legs from hurting and feeling frustrated at her inability to fall asleep. Because if only she could go deeply into the timelessness of sleep, her stay with Miss Amylee and Pansy would come faster, would be right there in her hands with the rising of the sun.

Only a few miles away, Aunt Rose was also counting off the hours, but she was searching not for sleep, but for the sound of a door opening and familiar footsteps across the living room. Yes, there had been a few other nights when Honey-Boy hadn't come home, and she reminded herself of that. Reminded herself that those times had worked out all right. But she still feared for him. The people in town and those who lived along the road to town knew Honey-Boy, knew he was harmless, and that in his mind, he was only a sweet child. But a stranger might not know that. A stranger might see only the big chest of a fully-grown man—and a *black* man, at that. He would be no match for anyone who decided to hurt him. Or worse.

\*     \*     \*

On the morning of Alice and Franklin's departure, Jordan watched as the big, black car went slowly down the long driveway, with Alice's white-gloved hand still fluttering from the passenger-side window. The brake lights flickered briefly at the end of the drive, and then the car made a slow turn onto the highway. When it disappeared completely, Jordan stood, almost transfixed for a long moment, and then she laughed, threw out her arms, and began twirling and twirling—an overly wound top spinning endlessly.

"Come on in, now," Peony called from the porch. "Make yourself sick, do you keep on twirling like that! Besides, we gotta get your things packed so you can go stay with Miss Amylee and Pansy. And I gotta water the plants and shut up the house good and proper."

Jordan dashed past Peony and went into her room. Her suitcase had been packed for weeks but hidden quietly under her bed.

"I'm ready!" she called, but Peony was going from room to room, closing the blinds, so that when Jordan came into the living room, it was in a sort of twilight and very peaceful looking. For some reason she could not fathom, she put her suitcase by the front door, went into the dim dining room, and sat down in her customary chair. Around her, the silence spoke softly and with beautiful words she couldn't quite make out. She sat in her chair, remembering all the times of pinching herself, so as not to go into a reverie. She could clearly see a mountain of green beans on her plate and suddenly, Alice's voice was there: *Please try to eat a little more,* she pleaded, and Franklin's icy blue eyes turning on her were like neon warning lights in the dim light. Jordan gasped at the realness of the vision.

"Whatchu doing, honey?" Peony's concerned voice, and

Jordan figured right away that even Peony was happy to get away from her and from her reveries. Little did she know that it was the administering of the castor oil that bothered Peony the most about Jordan. Pore little thing! she lamented to Aunt Rose from time to time. Pore little thing! Miserable in her own home! What is it with these white folks makes them be so mean to they own children?

Peony's voice again, "I said whatchu doing sitting in here all by yourself?"

"Don't worry," Jordan chirped. "I'm not having a spell at all."

"Well, that's good. Now we got to get you over to Miss Amylee's and me down to the station, else I'll miss my bus."

"You're going away? I forgot all about that."

"Sure am. First time in years. Going to visit my big sister and her family in Nashville."

"Does she have a flower name too?"

"Name's Primrose."

"That's pretty." Jordan was thinking that Aunt Rose did a good job of naming her daughters—except for Peony—but she didn't say anything. Jordan's next question surprised Peony: "Did you pack the castor oil for me to take with me?" Peony drew a sharp breath.

"Honey, you ain't gonna need no castor oil over at Miss Amylee's. You ain't gonna need it at all."

Jordan helped Peony to make sure all of the windows were closed and locked and the blinds all drawn shut, and then they both took their suitcases out onto the front porch. Jordan watched while Peony locked the big front door and tried the knob, making sure the house was locked up all tight and safe.

When they started down the road toward Miss Amylee's house, Jordan had a strange feeling . . . as if she were walking away from the old Jordan, but she couldn't explain that feeling to herself, and she really didn't want to try. For the next few days, she was going to be free!

About halfway to Miss Amylee's, Peony grunted, "This old suitcase kinda' heavy."

"Mine too," Jordan confessed.

"What you got in yours, could make it heavy?" Peony asked, shifting her own suitcase to the other hand.

"Books, mostly," Jordan answered.

"Well, you are the reading-est child I ever did see," Peony grunted. "Just the reading-est child there ever was."

"That's okay," Jordan said, in her own defense.

"Oh, I didn't mean it's a bad thing," Peony insisted. "Fact is, I think it's probably good!"

"Oh!" Jordan sounded relieved, discovering that someone could say anything about her, and it wasn't something neces- sarily bad.

"What you got in *your* suitcase, makes it so heavy?" Jor- dan asked, realizing as soon as she spoke that she was lapsing automatically into Peony's speech patterns. That was some- thing that often happened when the two of them were alone—when Alice or Franklin weren't around to cast star- tled, then admonishing, glances at Jordan. But the first few times Jordan started picking up Peony's way of speaking, Peony had glanced suspiciously at Jordan and demanded, "You making *fun* of me?"

"Oh no," Jordan had protested. "I like the way you talk." But when Peony just kept on frowning, Jordan added, "It's so *real!*" When the frown was still there, Jordan went on yet again. "It has a rhythm to it—like music."

"Well . . ." Peony wasn't sure Jordan was telling her the absolute truth, but she decided to give that poor little white child the benefit of the doubt. "Just so you don't be making fun of me!"

So that now, Jordan's question rang in Peony's ears almost pleasantly.

"Got me a five-pound fruitcake in there," Peony said. "Present for my sister."

"Pansy?" Jordan asked.

"No . . . it's for Primrose and her family," Peony said.

By then, they were approaching Miss Amylee's front porch. Peony stopped just before the steps.

"You didn't put no bottle of castor oil in your suitcase yourself, did you?" she asked, and Jordan laughed—a sound that gladdened Peony's heart. "I sure didn't," Jordan said. "You said I wouldn't need it, and I believe you!"

"Good!" Peony nodded her head, and then she put down her own suitcase and helped Jordan take hers up on the porch. The screen door was latched, of course, as Alice had asked Pansy to do every single day, even though Miss Amylee was much more clearheaded than she had been at first. Pansy came to the door, wiping her hands on her apron, and lifted the latch.

"Here's Jordan," Peony said, unnecessarily. "Now sometimes, Jordan here gets little . . . uh . . ." She paused, frowned, and then brightened . . . "little flights of fancy!" Peony said with a flourish in her voice. "And she won't seem to hear anything you say to her. But that's okay, you understand?"

Pansy nodded her head. "This child's got a good, rich imagination, is all," she pronounced. "And sometimes, I think she just doesn't quite know what to do with it. But she'll be just fine." Jordan had heard only the word *good*, something she had never heard used when anyone was talking about her *spells*.

"And Mama says for you to stop in at Miss May's," Pansy added. "She's got something to send along to Primrose, and besides, Miss May's is right on your way to the bus station."

"Sure hope it's not something heavy," Peony growled and went back down the steps to get her suitcase. But then she turned back to Jordan and said, "Have fun, sugar!" before she headed off to Miss May's.

As soon as Peony came into Miss May's kitchen, she knew that something was wrong with Aunt Rose. Because Peony knew all the stories her mama's shoulders could tell, just by how they were raised up a little bit when she was mad about something, or squared solidly if she was determined, or . . . as in this case . . . slumped in worry. Whatever Aunt Rose couldn't bring herself to say with words was expressed perfectly by her shoulders.

"Mama?" Peony asked, and Aunt Rose jumped a little, turning from the sink. "Mama? What's wrong?" Aunt Rose glanced toward the living room, where Miss May was supposed to be watching her favorite early morning cooking show on television, but she usually enjoyed a post-breakfast nap instead. Aunt Rose motioned Peony back out onto the back porch.

"Honey-Boy didn't come home last night," Aunt Rose said simply. Peony frowned. "I'm worried about him," Aunt Rose confessed, prompting Peony to step forward and wrap her tiny mother in her arms.

141

"But don't you remember, Mama, that time he saw a cartoon about Huckleberry Finn, and he went off and stayed down at the creek for the longest kind of time?"

"I remember," Aunt Rose said against Peony's warm chest. "But I'm still worried."

"Of course you are." Peony released her and studied her face closely. "You're just being a mama, is all. You want me to stay home? I don't have to go see Primrose."

"No, of course not." Aunt Rose shook her head, as if she were trying to shake all of her worries right out of it. "I made some tea towels I want you to take to her."

Aunt Rose started back into the kitchen, but Peony caught her hand. "He'll be all right, Mama," she said. "He'll be just fine."

# CHAPTER THIRTEEN

RIGHT AFTER AUNT ROSE FINISHED clearing up the dinner dishes, she called Miss Sweetie-Pie's restaurant. "Did my Honey-Boy come by for his pie today?" she asked timorously.

"Why, I'm sure I don't know," Miss Sweetie-Pie answered. "Let me ask Mary Lou." Then Aunt Rose heard the muffled words. "Mary Lou? Did you see Aunt Rose's Honey-Boy today?"

"No ma'am, he didn't come by today," Mary Lou called back. "I was wondering where he was."

"I'm afraid we haven't seen him, Aunt Rose. Is everything all right?"

"I hope so, Miss Sweetie-Pie," Aunt Rose answered. "I certainly do hope so."

"Your mama said for me to stay in the room closest to Miss Amylee," Pansy explained to Jordan. "So we fixed up that little room off the back porch for you." Jordan followed Pansy through the kitchen, where Jordan noticed that a deep-dish chicken pie was cooling on the sideboard. Small beads of saliva popped up under her tongue, but she forgot about the chicken pie when she entered the small room behind Pansy. Helium-filled balloons of every size and color bounced lazily against the low ceiling, and the bed was newly made up, with crisp sheets that smelled of sunshine and were topped with a light quilt that reflected all of the colors in the balloons.

"You like what we done in here?" Pansy asked.

"For me?" Jordan breathed. "Just for me?"

"Sure enough, just for you. We wanted you to know how glad we are you're here—even if it's just for a little while. Now you get unpacked and come on into the kitchen. I expect that chicken pie is about cool enough for us to eat."

After Pansy left the room, Jordan flopped down upon the brightly colored quilt and stared up at the rainbow of balloons. Within an instant, the balloons became people to her. The large, red ones were stout, red-faced women who all laughed openly and without putting their hands over their mouths; the small green ones became apples that sang and danced at the feet of the laughing women; the medium-sized blue ones were grumpy-gusses who were ignored by everyone else; and the small, yellow ones were baby chicks who peeped and scratched the ground for seeds. Beneath her, the quilt seemed to roll gently, as if she were in the bottom of a boat that floated on a lazy creek in the summer sunshine. Jordan closed her eyes and breathed in the precious scent of . . . freedom!

"Come on, honey." Pansy's voice actually cut through the reverie, and Jordan was spared, for the moment, from that terrible feeling of being sucked away from something wonderful.

After Petunia had taken over with Miss May, Aunt Rose went home and sat on her own porch, reading her Bible, waiting for Honey-Boy, and frequently looking far down the road. And—miraculously!—she finally saw him coming, saw again his blessed, gangling gait. She put her Bible in the chair and muttered, "Thank you, Lord!" as she ran to meet him. But as soon as she got close enough, she could see that instead of his usual open smile, his face was contorted and his eyes held a strange sadness she had never seen before.

"Are you all right?" she asked anxiously, worried more for the strange light in his eyes than in the scratches on his arms and the bruise at the corner of his mouth. "What happened? Where have you been? Tell me now!"

"Fall down," he answered simply, and no matter how hard she pressed him, that was all he could tell her. But something cold touched Aunt Rose's heart at that very moment. She looked at him, drinking him in with her eyes, the way of all mothers, and she feared for him. Oh, something is coming! she thought. Something as surprising and as terrifying as that mad sow mother who marked my boy before he was even born. Suddenly, she knew exactly what that sow had felt like, because good, gentle Aunt Rose suddenly felt like attacking the whole world and everybody in it. "This is my son!" she wanted to scream. "This is a good man!" And then her mind spoke some other words that she had lived with ever since he was born: *A big black man in body; a child in spirit. And he lives in a world where he will always be treated with suspicion because of the body he lives in!* A white-hot pain seared upward from her heart and settled into a throbbing throat-ache known by mothers the world over when they realize how cruel life is going to be to their children and that there isn't a thing in this world a mother can do to prevent it.

"My baby!" she whispered, wrapping her arms around him and pressing her cheek into his massive chest. "You're safe now. You're with your mama and nothing can hurt you." But even as she whispered the words, she knew that they weren't true. Not one bit true at all. Just said in a whispered plea to Heaven.

"Santy Claus coming tomorrow?" he asked.

"Yes, baby. Yes!" she answered and felt a shiver of anticipation go through her son.


"Can we have fried chicken tomorrow?" Jordan asked. Miss Amylee was lying down, as was her custom after a big middle-of-the-day dinner, and Jordan was helping Pansy wash the dishes.

"Sure, we can," Pansy answered, obviously pleased that Jordan remembered how much she had enjoyed the chicken that infamous day when Gertie had imposed herself and Bill into their quiet meal. "But didn't you like my deep-dish chicken pie?" she added.

"Oh yes," Jordan said hastily. "But I like your fried chicken even better."

"Well, that's easy to do," Pansy said. "So tomorrow it's fried chicken sure enough."

Pansy untied her apron. "Now why don't you go on out on the porch and read for a little while. I think I'm gonna get off my feet a little bit while Miss Amylee is resting." Later, while Jordan was rocking in a porch chair and reading, she suddenly thought about how little babies and old people always have to have naps. And she decided right on the spot that she would never, ever get old.

\*     \*     \*

True to her word, Pansy made her good fried chicken for dinner the next day, while Jordan snapped green beans.

"Do I have to eat all the green beans you put on my plate?" Jordan asked.

"Well, why don't you just serve yourself, and then you can decide how much you want." Jordan smiled into the bowl of beans, because being with Miss Amylee and Pansy was just as wonderful as Jordan had believed it would be. Little did any of them know that things were about to take a completely unexpected turn.

When they sat down to their fried chicken dinner that day, Jordan was indeed thinking about how wonderful it was that Gertie wasn't going to come barging in on them. Of course, Jordan knew from listening to Peony's phone conversations with Petunia just how heartbroken old Miss May was over Gertie's sudden, unannounced leaving, but Jordan's sympathy for Miss May wasn't nearly as strong as her dislike for Gertie.

In the middle of dinner, the phone rang, and Pansy went to answer it. Jordan and Miss Amylee waited to see what Pansy was going to say into the receiver, but Pansy just stood there for the longest kind of time, listening and frowning. Jordan and Miss Amylee looked at each other and shrugged their shoulders. Finally, Pansy said, "Give me your number, and I'll see what I can do. No, don't cry no more."

Pansy wrote down a phone number on the pad of paper beside the phone and hung up, without even saying good-bye. When she came back to the table, there was a deep scowl on her face.

"Who was it?" Jordan asked. "And why are they crying?"

Pansy shook her head. "Just you let me think for a little

minute," she said. Again, Miss Amylee and Jordan glanced at each other, but resumed eating their dinner, while Pansy sat stony-faced and silent. When Jordan had finished her chicken but not her green beans, Pansy said, "Honey, take your book and go out on the porch a little minute, please. I need to talk with Miss Amylee here in private."

For an instant, Jordan's heart leaped in her chest. Had something happened to her mother and stepfather? "Are Mama and Mr. Franklin okay?" she finally managed to ask.

"Oh yes—this don't have nothing to do with them," Pansy assured her. "So please just do as I'm asking and let me talk with Miss Amylee here." Jordan obeyed, glancing back at the uneaten green beans on her plate—a strangely beautiful sight. She went into her room to get her book and then started down the long hallway toward the front porch. But as she passed the dining room, she heard Pansy's low voice, and despite her best intentions, she stopped and held her breath.

"That was Gertie," she heard Pansy tell Miss Amylee, and Jordan felt hot little sparks of anger popping inside her head. "Said she didn't have nobody else she could call. Seems that Bill's gone off and left her, and she's . . . *expecting*." The way Pansy pronounced *expecting* told Jordan right away that this was something far more serious than any kind of regular expecting—but expecting what?

Miss Amylee breathed out a soft "oh Lord!" followed immediately by a "poor Miss May!"

"He's left her where they were living, in Augusta," Pansy continued. "The rent's due and she's got no money, and she wants us to come get her."

"Why'd he go off and leave her without anything?" Miss Amylee said. And Pansy clucked her tongue. "He probably thinks she's from wealthy people, just like she wanted him to think, and that we'll take care of her." A bitter tone crept into Pansy's voice. "Gertie says he went off to work on a road crew somewhere in south Georgia, and he was going to send for her as soon as he had enough money for her bus ticket. But that was a month ago, and she hasn't heard anything from him."

Jordan couldn't stand it any longer, so she took a deep breath and stepped into the dining room. Pansy and Miss Amylee looked up.

"I'm sorry," Jordan confessed. "I didn't mean to listen in, but I got started with it and just couldn't stop."

"So what did you hear?" Pansy asked, her eyebrows drawn down and her eyes narrowing.

"I heard that stinking Gertie wants us to do something for her. But what does *expecting* mean? What is she expecting?" Pansy glanced at Miss Amylee, who nodded once.

"She's expecting a baby," Pansy whispered.

"Gertie and Bill got married?" Jordan asked, drawing yet another scowl from Pansy and a slightly surprised expression from Miss Amylee.

"Don't know," Pansy finally admitted.

"You have to be married to get a baby," Jordan announced in a serious voice.

"Well, I guess they're married then," Pansy admitted. "But Bill went off to work in another place and he didn't leave her any money. Rent's due, and she's all upset. Wants us to come get her."

"I don't understand," Jordan said. "If they're married, he's supposed to take care of her himself." Pansy and Miss Amylee stared at each other and sighed.

"It doesn't always work like that, Jordan," Pansy finally

said. "Well, let me think. Just let me think." After a long pause, Pansy sighed and said, "Well, she's right about one thing—she doesn't have anybody else she can call. Can't call old Miss May—she can't do anything. But what're we gonna do?"

"I hate Gertie!" Jordan's angry whisper startled Pansy. "That mean Gertie has gone and done it again!"

"Done what again?" Pansy asked.

"Messed things up!" A vein in Jordan's neck was bulging and throbbing, just like her stepfather's. If she could have seen herself, the sight would have sickened her. "I waited a long time for this." Jordan's voice almost broke. "And now look what Gertie's done again!" Pansy said not another word, but she got up from the table and went into her room, and while she was praying, she thought she heard Jesus talking to her again: *Do it for me, Pansy—and by the way, Jordan Creek is just fine.* Miss Amylee and Jordan still sat at the table, waiting to see what would happen.

"A real lady never raises her voice," Miss Amylee pronounced, and Jordan felt hot streaks of embarrassment coming up the sides of her neck. But then Miss Amylee reached over and covered one of Jordan's hands with her own. "You try and remember that." Stupidly, Jordan thought about Mr. Franklin. Too bad that's just for ladies, she was thinking. Maybe if she'd told Mr. Franklin not to raise *his* voice, things would be a lot better. But of course, Jordan would never say such a thing aloud. When Pansy came out of her room, she was wearing a Sunday dress, a small hat with a nose veil, and pushing her hands into white gloves. "Miss Amylee, you go ahead, please ma'm, and take your rest. Jordan, you read in the living room so you can hear Miss Amylee calling if she needs anything. Leave the dishes alone. I'll take care of them later."

"Where you going?" Jordan asked, careful to keep her voice modulated.

"Going to see Reverend Brown," Pansy explained. "Won't be gone long."

As Pansy had asked, Miss Amylee went into her room for her after-dinner rest, and Jordan sat in the living room, reading. Always before, Walter Farley's *Black Stallion* books had transported her into another, wonderful world, but that day, the story failed to draw her in. Instead, she imagined Gertie's mean face and wondered why on earth Pansy thought she had to do *anything* for that stupid Gertie! Finally, Jordan checked on Miss Amylee, who was snoring softly in her bed, and then she started clearing the table, careful not to chip any of Miss Amylee's plates. She just had to do something . . . anything . . . to feel better, and helping to clear the table was something so familiar that she actually enjoyed it.

After the table was cleared and the dishes scraped and stacked in the sink, Jordan checked on Miss Amylee yet again and then sat back down in the chair. But as soon as she sat down, she heard a car driving in under the portico. She ran to the window and saw that it was a big, dark green car with shiny chrome. And Pansy was driving it.

"Where'd you get the car?" Jordan asked as Pansy came into the room.

"That's Mrs. Reverend Brown's car," Pansy answered. "She's visiting her sister in Atlanta, and the Reverend, he won't ever let her drive in Atlanta traffic anyway, so he sent her on the bus. He said I could use her car so we can go and get Gertie. Take her down to that little town in south Georgia to see if we can find Bill. Said he'd do it himself, or at least go along with us, but he's got a doctor's appointment all set up. Said it's *somebody's* Christian duty, and so I guess that somebody's us!"

"All of us?" Jordan asked.

"Yep—think about it, Jordan. I can't go off and leave you and Miss Amylee here alone. Peony's gone, Mama and Petunia are taking care of Miss May. Your mama and stepdaddy are in Savannah. It's all of us or none of us."

"Then let it be none of us!" Jordan said in a vicious whisper, glancing at the door to Miss Amylee's room. *A real lady never raises her voice.*

Pansy rubbed her chin, thinking fast about what to do to make Jordan feel better. "I hear there's a real alligator farm down in south Georgia. Maybe we can go there after we get Gertie and start looking for Bill."

Jordan couldn't answer, because she was all caught up in imagining what on earth an alligator "farm" would be like. And suddenly, she could see shiny white teeth rising out in even rows in an open field, and small, green scales growing on trees whose smooth, black bark was spotted with blood. A hoe leaned against the sun-bleached door of a barn, and inside the barn, an old man in blue coveralls worked in the center aisle, assembling alligators from the various bins full of alligator parts—teeth and scales and claws and flat, black eyes.

"Honey?" Pansy called. Jordan didn't answer, and Pansy sighed lightly, and waited. Only after Jordan had watched while one perfect alligator was assembled, did she begin to notice Pansy's expectant expression and look at her.

"Okay," Jordan said in a dreamy voice.

"Well, let me call Gertie back and then we need to get ready for our trip. I need to tell Mama where we're going too. And we got to help Miss Amylee get ready. *Whoo-ee!* Lots to get done!"

# CHAPTER FOURTEEN

Aᶠᵀᴱᴿ Jᴏʀᴅᴀɴ ᴀɴᴅ Pᴀɴsʏ ɢᴏᴛ all the dinner dishes washed, dried, and put away, Pansy wrapped up the leftover chicken and put it into the refrigerator. "We can take this with us. We'll finish off the chicken pie tonight for supper."

"Take it with us *where*?" Miss Amylee stood in the kitchen doorway, her eyes only a little clouded from her long nap.

"Miss Amylee, you sit down here and let me tell you," Pansy said, taking Miss Amylee's arm and guiding her to a chair at the kitchen table. "Reverend Brown has loaned me Mrs. Reverend Brown's car so we can go get Gertie and take her to Bill, down in south Georgia."

"We're going to south Georgia?" Miss Amylee suddenly seemed more coherent and interested. "Good! While we're down there, we'll go find my grandpapa's old farm and get you baptized in Jordan Creek!" Pansy seemed taken aback at that, and she sat there for long minutes, looking right into Miss Amylee's eyes.

"That too," Pansy finally conceded. "Yes, that too. Soon

as we take Gertie to find Bill and make an honest woman out of her."

"An honest woman?" Jordan asked. "What does that mean? Gertie's *not* honest, and I bet she never will be!"

Miss Amylee and Pansy exchanged glances. "Well, at least we'll try," Pansy said at last.

Without saying another word, Jordan suddenly realized that it meant something about Gertie getting herself a baby.

The rest of the day was spent in a flurry of preparation, with Pansy calling Gertie back and getting the directions to where she was living. They talked for a long time, with Gertie bursting into tears at regular intervals. When Pansy told her that they were going to try to find Bill, Gertie cried even harder.

"Oh yes!" Gertie yelped. "I can't go back to Grandmama's! I can't go back to that boring old town!"

"Best not to say what you *can't* do," Pansy warned.

"But I can't!" Gertie insisted. "I gotta find Bill. I just gotta! Bill will help me to go somewhere and do something!"

Pansy hesitated before she said, "Well, Gertie, tell me this: does he have a legal responsibility to take care of you?"

"Legal?"

"Did y'all get married—legal-like?"

A long silence then, before Gertie's muffled "no."

"Well, we'll be there to get you tomorrow, and then we'll just have to see what happens. You got the name of a town or something we can start with?"

"Albany?" Gertie turned the answer into a question because she wasn't completely sure. "I think that's it. Only Bill calls it all-*benny*."

"All-benny," Pansy repeated. "We'll find it."

\*　　\*　　\*

After she hung up the phone, Pansy called her mama at Miss May's house, warning Aunt Rose not to say anything on her end, in case Miss May could overhear her. Last, she called Peony at Primrose's house in Nashville.

"You all want me to come on back?" Peony asked. "I can do that, if it'll help."

"No, I think we can handle things," Pansy answered. "Only thing I worry about is maybe Miss Alice or Mr. Franklin calling to check on things, and not getting an answer."

"Well, there's not much we can do about that," Peony said. "Just have to take a chance about that. But I still say that I can come on back home and see after Miss Amylee and Jordan."

"No," Pansy said. "We'll manage, and you just enjoy your visit with Primrose. Tell her I said hello."

"Well, y'all just have a safe trip," Peony said. "I'll say prayers for all of you, Gertie included."

"She's gonna need prayers more'n all the rest of us put together, I reckon," Pansy answered.

By very early the next morning, they completed all of the preparations for their trip. Suitcases were loaded into the trunk of Mrs. Reverend Brown's big car, and also a basket holding peanut butter, jelly, bread, apples, cold baked sweet potatoes, and the leftover fried chicken. Pansy put Miss Amylee in the passenger seat, and Jordan sat in the back. After they backed out of the driveway, the first thing Pansy did was to go to the Gulf station to buy a map of Georgia. But she parked down the street and walked to the station, because of Miss Sweetie-Pie's restaurant being in the same building. One thing Pansy didn't want was to have to answer any questions about where they were going.

Back in the car, Pansy and Miss Amylee struggled with un-folding and refolding the map and finally finding a listing for Albany.

"Albany is R-Six," Pansy pronounced, and Miss Amylee found the letter on the right-hand side of the map, while Pansy found the number at the bottom. Both their hands started moving across the map, and when their fingers met, they found Albany.

"Gonna be a long drive, sure enough," Pansy muttered.

"Do you see a Spring, Georgia near there?" Miss Amylee asked.

Pansy studied the map carefully. "No, Miss Amylee, I sure don't. What's Spring, Georgia?"

"Where my granddaddy's farm was when I was a child," Miss Amylee said. "But it's such a little town, I expect it's not on any map. I could find it, though. Find the old farm and Jordan Creek too. Get you baptized," she added, suddenly heav-ing a deep sigh and chewing worriedly on her bottom lip. "You okay?" Pansy inquired.

"It's a lot of memory," Miss Amylee said. And then cleared her throat and busied herself refolding the map.

"On to Augusta," Pansy said, swinging Mrs. Reverend Brown's car onto the highway. "Don't need a map to tell me how to get there, either, 'cause that's where I was in prison," she said easily.

It was almost noon when they arrived in Augusta and found the tree-lined street where Gertie had been living in an effi-ciency apartment in the back of a large, old house with a wrap-around porch. Miss Amylee and Jordan watched from the car as Pansy went across a small backyard and met Gertie coming out of the back door with a big brown grocery bag in her arms. And the Gertie they all saw bore little resemblance to the smirking, lying Gertie they had last seen sitting with Bill, uninvited, at their own table. This Gertie would have been incapable of a smirk at all, because her face was swollen, with blotchy patches on her cheeks and reddened, swollen eyes.

"How come you to cause your sweet grandmama so much worry?" Pansy spat out the rough-sounding words, surprising herself, because she'd had no idea she was going to say such a thing.

"I'm sorry," Gertie mumbled.

"You should have let her know you were okay," Pansy said in a softer voice.

"But I'm *not* okay!" Gertie protested, shifting the bag in her arms.

"Those your things?" Pansy asked.

"Yes," came the choked-sounding answer.

"Then get in the car," Pansy ordered.

Gertie got into the backseat, next to Jordan, but she didn't meet Jordan's eyes at all. If she had, she would have seen a glaring blue gaze that would have withered her. Miss Amylee noticed Jordan's glare, however, and she said softly, "Wonder where you learned to look at folks like that?" Jordan was taken aback by the question, and it took her a little moment to realize that Miss Amylee was making a hopeless little joke. Of all the people in this world, Miss Amylee certainly knew the answer to that. So Jordan turned her eyes back to the window and watched the camelia bushes beside the driveway slide past the car as they backed away from the big house.

In what was left of that day, they got all the way to Macon, where they pulled off onto a roadside park and had a picnic supper while the sun went down. Gertie's eyes sparkled as she looked at the good, leftover chicken Pansy had brought, but to her credit, she took not a single piece, contenting herself with a peanut butter and jelly sandwich and an apple. The sparkle in Gertie's eyes didn't go entirely unnoticed by Jordan, however. Jordan helped herself to a cold drumstick and glanced quickly at Gertie as she bit into it. *What goes around, comes around,* she was thinking. That was one of Peony's favorite sayings, and anytime anybody was mean to her, she just said that, smiled, and went on with her life, secure in her belief that the offending person would one day be treated exactly the same way. Most of the time, people never were around to see it happen, though, so Jordan counted herself as quite fortunate.

"I don't like to drive in the dark," Pansy said. "So maybe we can just get in the car, make sure all the doors are locked, and go to sleep right here."

"Why don't we rent us a motel room?" Gertie asked.

" 'Cause we don't have money for any foolishness such as that," Pansy shot back at her.

Gertie offered, "Well, I can drive."

"You got a license?" Pansy asked.

"No, but Bill taught me how."

"Can't let you drive Mrs. Reverend Brown's car without a license," Pansy declared. "Reverend Brown trusted me to take good care of his car, and maybe you'd wreck us." Gertie said nothing else about it. They cleaned up their picnic supper things and settled into the car, to sleep as well as they possibly could.

In the early hours of the morning, Gertie sneaked out of the car and awakened the others with the sounds of her morning sickness. When she came back, pale and smelly, Pansy got out, opened the trunk, and came back with a package of saltine crackers, which she tossed to the miserable Gertie huddled in the backseat. Jordan had moved just as far away from Gertie as possible, jamming herself against the other door.

"Eat some of these crackers," Pansy ordered. "They'll settle your stomach."

Miss Amylee stretched slowly and yawned, tucking some stray hairs back into her hairpins. "We're here?"

"Well, no, Miss Amylee. We're still where we stopped last night. Now us better find some bushes—for privacy," she added. "And take care of business. Then we'll get back on the road. Shouldn't be more than another couple of hours to Albany."

Gertie spoke around the crackers she had jammed into her mouth: "I was bad to you all that time I brought Bill to your house and pretended you all was my family. I'm sorry I did that." Fat tears welled up in her eyes. "But I'd have done anything in this whole world to get away from that town, no matter what it was."

"Well, you sure did get away, didn't you?" Gertie couldn't tell whether Pansy was being sarcastic or not.

"Yes, I got away—and it was lots of fun living in Augusta." She hesitated and then added, "At first."

"And then what happened?" Pansy asked.

Gertie swallowed the crackers. "Well, at first, Bill give me a little bit of money every morning, and I got to take a bus downtown and see all the exciting things there are to see in a real city. Had me enough to get a grilled cheese and a Coke at the drugstore and just walk around, looking at everything. And then I'd take the bus back to the apartment and be there when he got back from work."

Gertie stopped and looked at the three faces riveted on her expectantly. "But then, he stopped giving me my walk-around money. Just give me enough to get something at the grocery store for our supper, and he expected me to cook for him!"

"N-o-o-o!" Pansy drew out the word in mock surprise, but it was lost on Gertie.

"Since I didn't have any money to go anywhere, all I could do was watch television all day and then heat up some canned hash for dinner—or make us tuna sandwiches." Her face took on an even more downward expression. " 'Cause I didn't do the cooking at Miss Sweetie-Pie's, and so I don't know how to cook. Just how to bring the food what's already cooked and put it on the table without spilling it all over folks."

"What else did you do to make Bill run away from you?" Pansy asked, suspiciously. "He struck me as being a right good boy, and you must've done something else."

"Well . . ." Gertie's reluctant tone was obvious to all. "When he said I should find me some work at a place I could walk to, I got to thinking that I really hadn't gone anywhere or done anything. It was all going to be just like it was for me at Miss Sweetie-Pie's, only in another place. When I told him I didn't want another waitress job, he said I should send off to my rich family for some walking-around money!"

"So *that* came back to bite you in the ass!" Pansy whispered. "So why didn't you do like he asked and get you another waitress job?" Pansy asked, and Gertie just nodded miserably.

"I just told you," Gertie argued. "I wanted something different."

"Yes," Pansy agreed. "You wanted him to work all day just so's you could have money for walking around and eating at drugstore counters. So . . . if we can find him, what makes you think he'll want you back?" The question was delivered at point-blank range.

Gertie frowned. " 'Cause I'm gonna change," she announced. She glanced around and saw the unbelieving stares. "Well, I *am*!" she protested. Pansy shook her head the slightest little bit.

"Let's get business taken care of and make us some sandwiches and get on down the road to Albany. We'll just take it one step at a time."

At the outskirts of Albany, they stopped in a filling station and while the attendant was pumping gas, Gertie used the restroom to wash her face and hands and make herself look a little better by running a comb through her hair. After that, she came back to the car, rummaged through her paper sack, found a dress that was in a little better shape than the one she was wearing, and disappeared back in the rest room. When she came out and went to give back the restroom key, she did look better, and it was more than just being clean and having on a clean dress. Because there was almost a little air of sweetness about her. Pansy watched Gertie approaching the car, and she muttered to Miss Amylee, "Uh oh, I think she's gearing up to charm the pants right off that boy. Poor thing," she added. "I sure hope she can do it, though, else we got problems sure enough!"

When the service station attendant finished filling the gas tank of Mrs. Reverend Brown's big car, Pansy paid him and then she added, "Sir, do you know of any highway work being done around these parts?"

The man scratched his head while he thought. "Seems to me there's some resurfacing going on around Highway Ninety-one. Y'all going that way?"

"Wasn't planning on it, but I guess it's as good a place as any to start," Pansy said. "Thank you very much, sir."

Miss Amylee and Pansy pored over the map once again, locating Highway 91. But just as they drove away from the station, Jordan suddenly yelled, "Look! There it is!"

Pansy automatically slammed on the brakes, and she turned to see what Jordan was talking about. Jordan was bouncing up and down on the seat and pointing across the highway. Another filling station? Except, on that one, the pumps were missing. Above the open door was a sign that read *Bobby's Bait and Bible Shop.*

"Bait and Bible?" Pansy muttered. "What on earth is that?"

"I wanta go in there," Jordan insisted.

"You wanta go in a bait shop?"

"No. Look at the other sign!" Sure enough, under the sign announcing *Bobby's Bait and Bible Shop* was a smaller one that read *Brother Eddie's Alligator Farm.*

"It's an alligator farm!" Jordan announced fervently. "And I wanta go in."

"Honey," Pansy tried to argue. "Let's us get on down the road and find Bill before we go see any alligators."

Gertie interrupted, "She's gonna make me be sick, does she keep jumping up and down like that!"

"Stop jumping, Jordan," Pansy ordered, and Jordan obeyed, but she still argued. "I wanta go in! I wanta go in!"

Once again, Pansy tried to argue. "Listen, Jordan, we've got more important things to do than see an alligator farm!"

"You promised!" Jordan yelled. "It's not fair! You promised!"

Miss Amylee had been watching the fracas with a frown, but now she joined in. "You certainly did promise, Pansy," she said, and then she clamped her jaw.

"Okay! Okay!" Pansy admitted. "Look, there's a big shade tree right here, so Miss Amylee, you and Gertie stay in the car, and I'll walk Jordan over there so she can see the alligator farm." By the time the words were out of her mouth, Jordan had opened the back door, leaped out of the car, and bounced up and down beside Pansy's door. "Come on!" she urged.

"Now, we can't be gone long," Pansy mumbled, as she got out. "Gonna get too hot in this car for Miss Amylee and Gertie."

Joyously, Jordan took Pansy's hand, and they crossed the highway.

"Don't like the sound of something being a bait and Bible shop!" Pansy grumbled.

"It'll be okay!" Jordan assured her, but as they entered into the gloomy interior of the shop, leaving the bright sunshine behind them, Pansy looked around worriedly. The inside of the shop was filled with the sound of chirping crickets, and as their eyes became accustomed to the gloom, they were able to make out a large wire cage filled with crickets, rusted coolers holding earthworms, and farther along on the shelves, row upon row of Bibles. Beyond them, cane-fishing poles were sticking out of a barrel. Hanging high on the wall above them was a picture of two children crossing a bridge, with a large guardian angel looming over them, protecting them from the icy-looking, rushing water under the bridge.

"Can I help you folks?" A man's voice came out of the darkest gloom, far at the rear.

"Sir?" Pansy called. "This here little girl wants to see the alligator farm, please."

The figure of a large man came toward them, and when he saw Pansy, he stopped. "What was it you said?" he inquired of Pansy, and something in his voice made Pansy's eyes grow larger. Jordan watched Pansy's face carefully, saw the whites of her eyes glowing in the dim light.

"Sir, this little girl wants to see the alligator farm, please, sir." Jordan had never heard Pansy speaking so carefully. The man's entire face seemed to fit around a gigantic cigar that was stuck in the middle of his mouth, and while Jordan and Pansy watched, he seemed to reach some sort of decision and swiveled the cigar to the corner of his mouth.

"Twenty-five cents," he said at last.

Pansy fished around in her purse, handed him a quarter, and asked, "Is it safe for her to go see it alone? Another quarter would be a little rich for my blood. I mean, are the alligators in cages?"

The big man laughed as he took Pansy's quarter. "She'll be safe. Only reason we charge is to help with the cost of feeding live chickens to the 'gators."

Both Pansy and the big man seemed to relax a little. To Jordan, he said, "Just go through that door at the back, little lady, and you'll be at the alligator farm."

Jordan glanced at Pansy once again. "Go on," Pansy

urged her. "But don't be gone long. It's gonna be getting hot in that car."

"Okay," Jordan agreed, and she slowly walked the length of the narrow store, toward the door at the back. She put her hand on the door handle and hesitated a moment, feeling the rush of thrilled anticipation, before she opened it.

"Go on, honey," Pansy called to her. "Don't take long," she reminded Jordan again.

In the waiting car, Miss Amylee and Gertie sat in an uncomfortable silence, with neither of them looking at the other. Miss Amylee gazed out the open window at a barren cornfield, and Gertie studied her cuticles. So when Miss Amylee started talking, she startled Gertie.

"When I was expecting *my* first child," Miss Amylee began, "we were living up in the North Carolina mountains in an old farmhouse that was the best we could afford. My late husband was a country lawyer, and he didn't have much business to start with."

Gertie didn't know what to say, so she said nothing.

"I kept the house, worked the garden, canned fruits and vegetables against the coming winters. I also made quilts for us out of worn-out clothes and even chopped the firewood for our cookstove." She hesitated for a few moments before she added, "It was a hard life, but a good one."

Gertie still didn't know what to say, so once again, she remained silent.

"But at least I had me a wedding before I had a child," Miss Amylee said in a low voice. So at last, Gertie knew what Miss Amylee had been heading for, all along.

"Maybe I don't want me a wedding," Gertie grumbled.

"All depends on where he's gonna have me living. I don't want to live in no hot, dead little town like the one I come from."

"Well," Miss Amylee admitted, "maybe I just don't understand you young people."

"You're just like my grandmama," Gertie complained. "Got your minds set on one way of doing things and only one way."

"The right way," Miss Amylee whispered.

When Jordan opened the back door to the bait and Bible shop, she had no idea of what to expect, because deep down, she knew that nobody puts an alligator together the way she had imagined. But she was completely unprepared for what she saw: a small, fenced-in rectangle with a concrete floor and a washtub with rusty water in it buried in the middle. Beside the washtub, two small, dark alligators, asleep. Strewn around the pen were bloody white chicken feathers with flies crawling around on them. A strange, hot stench rose to meet Jordan's offended nose. She was about to turn around and go straight back to Pansy, but she hesitated just a moment too long, so that she suddenly could see an entirely different scene: a cool, sweet swamp, where the gnarled cypress trees grew out of the tea-colored water and healthy, young alligators rippled silently across the dampness.

Her vision was in such sharp contrast to what she was actually seeing that she stood motionless for long moments.

"Honey? You come on, now," Pansy called to her from the front door.

"I wish that for you," she said to the lethargic, captive alligators.

\*    \*    \*

When Pansy and Jordan returned to the car, both Miss Amylee and Gertie were sitting in a stony silence. Pansy noticed, but now her mind was set on trying to find Bill.

She drove on down the road, made several turns that supposedly would take her to this Highway 91. And after only a few miles, she saw a *construction ahead* sign and then a bit farther on, the big construction trucks.

# CHAPTER FIFTEEN

AUNT ROSE TRIED HER BEST to discourage Honey-Boy from walking into town again, but she succeeded for only two days. By the third day, his scratches had crusted over and the bruises on his face had lessened. But more than that: his smile had returned in full force, something that gladdened Aunt Rose's heart but that broke it at the same time.

"Santy Claus is coming tomorrow," he announced to her at breakfast on the day when she realized that she could restrain him no longer.

"Sure he is, honey," she answered, but at the same time she wondered at his ability to completely forget about having "fallen down." She wondered what really happened. Some of the young white boys were awful cruel, and she wondered if maybe they had taunted and hurt him, just for the fun of it. Just because he was black and completely innocent—a deadly combination, to her mind.

So as soon as she left to go to Miss May's, Honey-Boy left as well, walking along the weed-ridden sides of the road, grinning, and sometimes chuckling to himself. When he got to

Miss Sweetie-Pie's and knocked on the back door, Mary Lou opened the door and seemed genuinely happy to see him.

"Hey, Honey-Boy," she said, handing him his piece of pie. "We sure did miss you. Why didn't you come by for the last three days? You been sick?" He studied her face carefully and listened to her singsong words with interest.

"Fall down," he said, grinning. And then, to Mary Lou's delight, he added, "Santy Claus is coming tomorrow!"

"Sure, Honey-Boy," she said, laughing. Then she shaded her eyes and looked up into the blazing sky of a summer midmorning. "You really ought to wear a hat when it's this hot, Honey-Boy. Don't you think? Sun will make you sick."

Honey-Boy shaded his own eyes and looked up into the white-hot sky. "Hat," he repeated.

# CHAPTER SIXTEEN

PANSY PULLED THE CAR off onto the shoulder of the road and close to the first construction truck. When she got out, the blast of tar-acrid air almost took her breath away, and she staggered a little against the heat waves coming up off of the newly poured asphalt. She approached a worker leaning against the giant tire of a road scraper.

" 'Scuse me, sir," she shouted over the roar of machinery. The man turned his face to her, his eyes hidden by dark sunglasses.

"*Whatchuwant?*" he yelled over the noise, and Pansy backed up a step or two.

"I'm looking for somebody named Bill," she yelled.

"Bill *who?*" the man demanded. "We call each other by last names out here." He turned his back on Pansy and leaned again on the giant tire. Pansy walked back to the car. Gertie had gotten out and was standing behind the open car door, shading her eyes and looking for Bill.

"What's Bill's last name?" Pansy asked.

"Andersen," Gertie said. "With an *e*, not an *a*." Pansy

walked back to where the man still leaned against the tire. She stood behind him for a moment, looking over his shoulder at the flurry of mechanical activity going on. Men on giant machines that cranked and ground and roared great gushes of black smoke into the hot morning air. Some men working with rakes and some holding flags and signaling drivers so that the cars could go through on the one open lane.

"Sir?" Pansy yelled, and the man turned around again, his annoyance showing openly.

"Whutchu want this time?" he snarled.

"Last name is Andersen, with a *e*, not a *a*." The man seemed to find something about it amusing, and he let out a guffaw.

"Don't make no difference how it's spelled." And then, without a moment of hesitation, he cupped his hands around his mouth and yelled *Andersen!* at the top of his lungs, almost knocking Pansy over with the backward force of his yell. Then once again, with his neck veins bulging, he yelled *Andersen!*

*"Yo!"* came the answer, and Pansy watched while Bill disengaged himself from a long rake and started walking toward the man. When he glimpsed Pansy standing behind the man and Gertie standing beside the car, his step hesitated. But then he put his head down and came toward them as if he were wading through deep, brackish water.

"Somebody wants to see you," the man said, tossing his head backwards to indicate Pansy. "Don't be long or I'll dock your pay!"

"Yessir!" Bill answered, giving the man a wide berth and coming toward Pansy.

"I figured this was coming," Bill said over the roar of engines. He passed by Pansy and headed toward the car, with

Pansy following him. When he came to where Gertie was standing, he took off his steel helmet and held it in his hands. But all the trouble Gertie had taken to look nice for him was of no avail, for her face was red, swollen, and loaded with petulance. Under the fierce summer sun, her hair had gone limp and stringy, and rivulets of perspiration were running down her neck.

"I'm sorry, Gertie," Bill said, turning his helmet around and around in his hands. "I was trying as hard as I could to get enough money to bring you down here."

"No, you weren't." Gertie pouted. "You just went off and left me and you didn't mean to send for me at all."

"Listen, Gertie," he said, glancing in the car and seeing Miss Amylee and Jordan in the hot interior. "I can't afford to lose my pay, so you all take the key to my apartment and stay there and wait for me to get off work. We're only working half a day today, so I'll get there right after noon." He scribbled down an address and passed the key to Gertie. "It's not far," he added. "Go back down Highway Ninety-one, take a right at the second traffic light, and watch for the street number about the third block down." Then he hesitated and said, "It's kind of messed up, but . . ." And then there was nothing else he could say.

"Pansy, it's getting awful hot in this car," Miss Amylee said, and Jordan added an enthusiastic, "Amen!"

"Let's us go on, like Bill said. We got a lot to figure out."

Bill's apartment turned out to be an efficiency on the second floor of a concrete block building in a strip mall. It was flanked by a liquor store and a video rental store that advertised "adult films." The key was hard to turn in the door, and when they finally succeeded in getting it open, they were met with a blast of air just as hot, if not hotter, than outside.

"I gotta go to the bathroom!" Jordan yelped, gripping her knees together and bouncing up and down. Pansy looked around. There were only two doors, besides the front door, and the first one she opened was a closet. So she pointed to the other, and Jordan dashed in, slamming the door behind her.

Miss Amylee looked around at the kitchenette, and Gertie opened the refrigerator hopefully. It contained one unopened bottle of beer, half of a hardened doughnut, and a wedge of slightly dried-out cheese. Gertie grabbed the cheese and bit into it. Chewing, she addressed the others: "I gotta have me something—anything!—to eat. Else it's gonna hurt the baby."

Jordan came out of the bathroom, wiping her hands on her shorts.

"No towels," she said. "And the toilet paper's almost gone."

"Bathroom tissue," Miss Amylee corrected her, and when Jordan frowned in confusion, Miss Amylee explained: "A real lady always says 'bathroom tissue.' "

Pansy rolled her eyes at the ceiling. "Don't matter what it's called, if you don't have none," she said. Then, "Well, I saw a little grocery store down the street. You all stay here and turn on that fan. Just like an oven in here!"

With that, Pansy took her purse and left. Miss Amylee switched on a table fan that began sweeping the hot air back and forth across the room and sat down on the vinyl couch. Jordan sat beside her, though not touching, it was so hot. Gertie sat down on the small cot against the wall and continued eating the cheese, holding it in both hands, the way a mouse would do.

Jordan studied Gertie. Watched while Gertie's ears became longer and pointed. Saw the thin whiskers grow out of Gertie's cheeks and the eyes darken and grow beady. Jordan watched, utterly fascinated, as a gray, hairless tail curled out from under Gertie and draped itself bonelessly off the edge of the cot.

Jordan's scream split the room's hot air into lightning-struck fragments. Miss Amylee jumped and pressed a hand to her bosom, and Gertie jumped off the cot and dropped the remaining cheese onto the floor.

Jordan had been as shocked at the sound of her scream as Miss Amylee and Gertie had been, and she immediately put her hands over her face and burst into tears. She was only dimly aware of Miss Amylee's hand patting her back and Gertie yelling, "What? What?"

"She'll be okay," Miss Amylee assured Gertie. "I expect her blood sugar's low—she just needs food."

"*I* need it more than her," Gertie argued. "And besides, her screaming like that and scaring me so bad could hurt the baby!"

"Your getting startled won't hurt that baby," Miss Amylee said.

"Then what about that Crazy Honey-Boy of Aunt Rose's?" Gertie shot back. "Everybody knows how that mad sow scared her half to death and marked Crazy Honey-Boy forever and ever."

"Gertie, please don't bad-mouth Honey-Boy," Miss Amylee said in a well-modulated voice. *A real lady never raises her voice,* Jordan was thinking.

"What's going on here?" Pansy's voice cut across the hot room as she came in the door and put a bag of groceries on the kitchenette counter.

"What's going on here is that stinking Jordan's gone crazy!" Gertie huffed. "Gone crazy and just about scared us all out of our skins!"

Pansy went over and sat down beside Jordan, who still had her hands over her face. "You okay, honey?" Pansy asked, prying Jordan's hands away and brushing back the hair from her damp forehead. Jordan sighed miserably.

"I guess Peony should have packed the castor oil after all," she whispered.

"No, baby. No," Pansy assured her. "You don't need no castor oil. You just need some patience . . ." Here, Pansy shot a fierce glance at Gertie . . . "from folks who don't understand just how strong your imagination really is." Again, Pansy shot a withering glance at Gertie. "Let's have us some lunch," Pansy added. "That's gonna make all of us feel better."

Jordan, Miss Amylee, and Gertie all watched hungrily as Pansy began unloading things from the grocery bag: a loaf of white bread, a jar of mayonnaise, a pile of sliced bologna wrapped in butcher's paper, two ripe tomatoes, and a jar of sweet pickles. At the last, Pansy lifted out a roll of toilet paper and handed it to Jordan. "Please put this in the bathroom, Jordan," she asked.


Twenty minutes later, when they all sat around the tiny dinette table, completely sated by the good bologna and tomato sandwiches, Pansy belched softly.

" 'Scuse me," she said. Then she added, "Oh, I gotta go lie down a little bit." She went to the closet, rummaged around, and finally pulled out an old quilt.

"Come on, Jordan," she invited. "You and me on the floor." She turned to Miss Amylee, whose head had sunken down on her chest and touched her shoulder. "Come on, Miss Amylee. You lie down on the cot."

"What about *me*?" Gertie yelped.

"You get the couch," Pansy announced, and from the tone of her voice, Gertie knew not to argue with her. Soon, all were asleep, with the table fan squeaking pleasantly in its oscillations, sweeping warm air around the entire room.

Bill came home to a room filled with sleeping women and a sleeping child. He stood at the door, studying this small army of determined women, and he knew, instantly, that his fate was probably sealed. Still, he thought, it might not be so bad, being married to someone from such a wealthy family. He stepped carefully across the room toward Miss Amylee, noticing in his short trip that Gertie was snoring loudly, with her mouth hanging open and a thread of spittle on her chin. He reached over and touched Miss Amylee's shoulder most carefully.

"Excuse me?" he said in a soft voice. And never in a million years did he expect the reaction he got from this frail, elderly lady. Because as soon as he touched her shoulder, she shot up into a sitting position, her eyes wild, and mouth open, screaming, *"No,* Grandpa! *No! I didn't see anything!"*

With those piercing-scream words, the room seemed to explode around him, with Pansy and Jordan rising up off the quilt on the floor and Gertie snapping awake, with her hands over her stomach.

*"What?"* Pansy bellowed, as Bill backed quickly toward the door he had so recently entered.

"I'm sorry!" he yelled into the confusing explosion of women. "I'm sorry!" he repeated, holding out his hands in a manner a football player would use to stave off an approaching tackle.

*"What?"* Pansy bellowed again.

"Oh, what's going to happen to my baby," Gertie wailed, and Bill, still backing toward the door, stopped dead in his tracks while all of the color drained out of his face.

Pansy stopped yelling and studied him carefully.

"You didn't *know*!" she said, floating those amazing words out into the small, hot room.

"Baby?" Bill mouthed the incredible word, not once, but twice. "Baby?"

"Let's us go outside and talk," Pansy ordered, pushing past Bill and holding the door open for him. He backed right out of it, still repeating, senselessly, the word *"Baby?"*

"Sit yourself down on these steps with me," Pansy ordered. "We got some figuring we have to do."

# CHAPTER SEVENTEEN

Despite Aunt Rose's worries, Crazy Honey-Boy went right back to spending all day in town, as he had always done. He hung around at the Dairy Queen at lunchtime, and sure enough, some kind soul usually bought him a hamburger, and sometimes another bought ice cream for him. Then he went to Miss Sweetie-Pie's back door for his slice of pie and for telling a delighted Mary Lou that Santa Claus was coming tomorrow. After that, he stood around inside the post office for a while, enjoying the coolness of the air-conditioning. The townspeople who came into the post office smiled at him. "Hey, Honey-Boy," they said. "How you doing today?" And as always, he would grin and say, "Santy Claus is coming tomorrow!" And they would smile at the cheerful, excited words and at the beautiful anticipation in his eyes.

"Good old Aunt Rose," they would say later. "She does love that boy of hers. Shame about him being retarded." But others would say, "Isn't that something? That boy lives every day of his life in a child's Christmas eve. God must love him so much, to give him a lifetime of those kind of days." Someone new in town might say, "But oh! He's so strange-looking! Scares me half to death!" But those who had watched Honey-Boy grow up and amble around town for many years would have explained, "No . . . he's just like a child. Not a thing to be scared of about him!"

On Honey-Boy's way home, he often passed near Miss May's backyard, hoping to be able to wave at the man she sometimes hired to work in the yard. But no one was there that day. Nothing in the backyard except the laundry hanging out on the clothesline. And as he passed, he looked at the ladies' cotton bloomers hanging on the line. Bright pink flags hanging limp in the afternoon heat.

You really ought to wear a hat when it's this hot, Honey-Boy. Sun will make you sick.

He didn't even stop to wonder where he had heard those words. Silently, he passed on by the clothesline, rubbing his hand across the top of his head and thinking that tomorrow would be Christmas day and Santa Claus was coming!

# CHAPTER EIGHTEEN

"WE GOT US A SITUATION HERE," Pansy announced. Bill sat beside her on the steps, holding his head in his hands. "When I first found out you'd gone off and left Gertie, I was gonna find you and ask if you had *known* her."

"Known her?" he lifted his head and looked into Pansy's eyes with confusion.

"*Known* her—in the biblical sense."

Bill shook his head.

"Well, since she's pregnant, you *have* known her."

"Oh . . . uh, yes."

"So what I gotta ask now is this: Are you gonna do the right thing and marry her? Make an honest woman of her?"

"Oh, Lord!" Bill said with a terrible misery in his voice.

"Sure enough," Pansy answered. "You sure ain't gonna get no prize package with that one." Pansy motioned her head toward the apartment. "But I still believe you want to do right by her. That's your baby she's got in her, you know."

"I know. And . . . yes, I'm gonna do right by her."

"I'm right glad to hear it," Pansy said, letting out her

breath. Then she added, "Now, you seem to be a nice enough young man, and maybe you've gone and gotten yourself into more than you bargained for, but I tell you this: I want to see you and Gertie married with my own eyes. So we need to get it done fast, 'cause I gotta get Miss Amylee and Jordan on back home. You better think fast!"

Bill scratched the side of his head. "There's a guy on the road crew who's a preacher. I could call and ask him to do it."

"Then go call him now," Pansy directed, and Bill got up off the step and went back into the apartment. Pansy could hear the reluctance in his footsteps. *A good man,* Pansy was thinking. *A good man who's gone and messed up his life. 'Cause he deserves lots better'n her!*

When Pansy followed Bill back inside, he was on the telephone, and Gertie, Miss Amylee, and Jordan were perched around the hot room like wax figures with no breath in them.

"Thanks, Clay. We'll meet you there," Bill said into the phone. Then he turned to Pansy. "He'll marry us. Said to meet him at his church in an hour."

"Well, maybe I don't want to get married," Gertie whined.

Pansy glanced at Gertie and then, when she also glanced at Jordan, she resolved to choose her words wisely. "You *already* said yes, if you get my drift!" Gertie and Bill both blushed. They got her drift all right!

Within thirty minutes, they were ready to leave for the little church where Bill's buddy was a preacher only on Sunday mornings, but a road-crew worker the rest of the time. Gertie muttered once more about not wanting to "tie the knot."

"You just be grateful he's willing to do right by you," Pansy reminded her.

And while Bill struggled with his tie in front of the bathroom mirror, Gertie stood right beside him, "finger walking" up his arm and purring, "So what do you think about us going down to Panama City, Florida for our honeymoon?"

When Pansy overheard that, she had to bite her tongue to keep from saying, "Gertie, you silly fool! Will you ever be happy with what you have?" And the silent answer to that question, Pansy knew, was a resounding *no!* Bill murmured something about not having enough money for something like that.

When they were all ready, Gertie wanted to ride to the church in Bill's truck with him, but Pansy refused to let her do that.

"No! Gonna keep you right in my sight until that knot you don't want is tied good and tight," Pansy pronounced. "I'm not going to give you any little chance for more fornication!"

"Where is this church?" Miss Amylee asked, sounding a little upset. Pansy simply chalked it up to Miss Amylee's nightmare being interrupted by Bill's touching her on the shoulder, but she made a mental note to ask Miss Amylee about that later.

"Real close," Pansy assured her. "And after that, we can start in on trying to find that Jordan Creek." *One thing at a time!* she reminded herself. *And the next thing to get done is see Gertie married and respectable.* So Bill led the way to the church, and Pansy followed him, with Miss Amylee, Jordan, and Gertie all crammed into Mrs. Reverend Brown's big car.

Bill had been right about the church being nearby. They drove two blocks, turned left, and went down a hill where they could see a small church on the left-hand side, just before a bridge. The parking lot was small and gravel-covered, and when they all got out, a big man came out of the church and stood on the concrete stoop, waiting for them. His face was broad and open, and his soft smile was punctuated by a shiny gold tooth that glimmered behind his full lips from time to time. His skin was black and shiny, like satin, and the instant Pansy first saw this big man, her heart skipped a beat.

"Hey, Clay!" Bill called. And then he started making introductions: "Clay, this here is my fiancée, Gertie—and these folks are her family." Once again, Pansy failed to correct Bill, but not on purpose. Because her entire vision was filled to overflowing with the reverend—the most beautiful man she had ever seen! Bill continued: "Her grandmother, Miss Amylee, and this here little girl, Jordan, and their friend, Pansy." At each introduction, the big man smiled, bowed slightly, and nodded his head. But when it came to Pansy, he took in a quick breath, then stepped off the concrete stoop, exposing his highly polished shoes to the risk of dirt and dust, took her hand, and looked deeply into her eyes. "I am most happy to meet you, Pansy—what a beautiful name!" Pansy felt her face growing hot, but then she noticed Miss Amylee looking around the church grounds with a curious expression on her face.

"Thank you," Pansy managed to mumble, keeping the feeling of his warm hand as if his fingers had branded her palm. "Miss Amylee, you okay?"

"I . . . I just noticed that old chimney over there," Miss Amylee said. "This place feels so familiar to me!"

"They say there used to be a big old farmhouse there," the reverend explained to her, nodding his head toward the old solitary chimney seemingly rising right out of the undergrowth. "But the house was gone when I came to this church."

"Is . . . is that bridge down there . . . does it go over Jordan Creek?" Miss Amylee asked in something little more than a whisper.

"It does indeed," he answered, drawing his brows together and tilting his head toward her.

"Then . . . this must be it—my grandpapa's old farm place and Jordan Creek!" But then she hesitated. "But how can this be? My grandpapa's farm wasn't this close to the town. It was way out in the country."

"Well, I imagine the town has grown since you were a little girl, Miss Amylee," Pansy offered.

"More's the pity," Miss Amylee said, thinking of the strip mall and the ugly concrete building where Bill had an apartment. Then she turned to the reverend. "After we have a wedding, can we have a baptism?"

"Well, I don't see why not," he answered, smiling. "You wanting to get baptized, ma'am?" Even as he spoke, he was thinking that he'd never, ever, *touched* a white woman, much less dunked one in a creek.

"Not her," Pansy spoke up. "Me. But please let's get this wedding taken care of—these young folks' predicament has been weighing heavy on my heart."

"Predicament?" His forehead furrowed briefly and then cleared. "Oh." He restrained himself from glancing at Gertie's waistline. "Well, shall we go into the church?" he invited. But as Bill went in, he turned to the big man and said, "Clay, I'm sorry—I don't even know your first name." To Gertie, he explained, "We only use last names at work."

"My name is Isaiah," the big man said, in a way that made

the word *Isaiah* float out into the air all decorated with little curlicues. He turned a little, lifted his eyebrow, and glanced at Pansy yet again. And this time, Pansy smiled at him.

The inside of the small church was quite bare, with pews that looked as if they had been made out of old packing crates sitting in rows before an altar devoid of any decoration except for a plain wooden cross that looked as if it too had been nailed together out of cast-off wood. The reverend saw Pansy glancing around, and he explained, "We keep it simple here, Sister Pansy. We focus on the Lord alone."

"Yes," Pansy breathed, suddenly able to see something entirely more beautiful than a gold cross and fancy pews. "Yes." Out of the corner of her eye, Pansy saw Gertie once again finger walking up Bill's arm, whispering to him, and coyly tossing her head. *After him again about taking her off to Panama City for a honeymoon,* Pansy thought. And once again, a feeling of sadness swept through her. *A good man deserves better!*

"Miss Pearl?" the reverend called toward what appeared to be an office door off to the side. "Miss Pearl?" he repeated. In just a few moments a woman came out of the office. She was rotund and smiling, with skin a rich mahogany brown, and as she approached them, she waved both of her hands around in the air, as if she were drying freshly applied nail polish.

"Miss Pearl here will be the witness for this wedding," the reverend announced, putting his hand on Miss Pearl's shoulder. "She's the secretary for this church, and she performs many services—taking care of the records, singing in the choir on Sunday mornings, and coming at a moment's notice to help out, like today."

Murmured greetings and handshaking ensued. Then Miss

Pearl stepped to one side, while the reverend directed Miss Amylee, Jordan, and Pansy to the front pew. He then lined up Gertie and Bill right in front of the altar, briefly disappeared into the office, and came back out wearing a flowing black robe and carrying a Bible. The robe had a purple satin stole on it and the whole impression of his already huge frame was magnified by the robe. Pansy felt her heart starting to act like a terrified squirrel inside her chest. *Good Heavens!* she thought. *I didn't know I had those kind of feelings still left in me!*

"Dearly beloved," the reverend intoned, filling the inside of the little church with his rich, mahogany voice. And almost before Pansy could get herself calmed down and attentive, he was saying "I now pronounce you man and wife." Gertie let out a little cry and threw her arms around Bill's neck. Pansy let out a sigh of profound relief.

"Thanks, Clay," Bill said, shaking the reverend's hand. "When we get paid, I can give you a little something for doing this for us."

"Consider it to be a wedding present," the reverend said easily. "Besides, I think I may be the one who owes *you* something." He glanced at Pansy, who was talking with Miss Amylee and didn't notice.

Out in the yard, they all clapped and cheered as Gertie and Bill left in his truck. Jordan clapped the loudest of all, and she even hollered *"yay!"* Pansy knew that Jordan's elation was more for getting rid of Gertie than for the wedding itself, but she said nothing to Jordan. Instead, to the reverend she said, "I wish I'd thought to bring a little rice to throw at them."

"Rice is a symbol for fertility," the reverend whispered to Pansy. "And I think they're already taken care of, in that department!" Pansy was surprised to see a little sparkle in his eyes that she hadn't noticed before, and she immediately cast her eyes down to the gravel parking lot and hid her smile.

"And now, let's go back inside so we can talk. Miss Amylee and Miss Jordan can sit in the sanctuary, and we can go into my office and talk about this baptism."

Miss Pearl spoke up: "I'll stay with them, reverend."

"Thank you." He smiled and bowed slightly.

In the office, the reverend pointed out a chair for Pansy and settled himself into a large leather chair at his desk. He commented once again about Miss Pearl. "That good lady reminds me of my late wife," he said with a sad smile.

"You're a widower?" Pansy added, unnecessarily.

"Yes, for about a year," he answered, studying Pansy's face most intently. She let her full gaze meet his, and this time, she did not look away. He cleared his throat, and in a different tone, he went on. "Let's talk about baptism."

"Well, I guess the first thing you ought to know about me is that I killed a man," she said simply. Closing her eyes, she heard Isaiah Clay's sharp intake of breath and vowed to let that awful truth sink in before she went on. *Help me, Lord,* she begged silently. *Help me tell this big, beautiful man every single thing about me. And honestly!*

"How did that happen?" he asked, in a suddenly serious voice.

"Earl—Earlie—was my husband, and he'd beaten up on me every day we was married. Twelve long years I took those beatings 'cause that's how bad I wanted to have a man of my own." The truth of her own words surprised her. *Thank you, Jesus!* "Then one day I just couldn't take it no more. He came at me to knock me upside the head, just like always, and I

188

pushed him away. It was the very first time I'd ever tried to protect myself." She stumbled to a stop.

"Go on, sister," came the encouraging, mahogany words.

"Well, when I pushed him away from me, he fell. Hit his head on a big iron cookstove we had. And he died from that hit on his head. I went to prison for it, but not for very long. Everybody in town knew about Earlie beating up on me. I guess he must have bragged about it to other men. They told their wives, and the wives—most of 'em was maids—told the white women they worked for. And the white women told their husbands, who were lawyers and judges. Important men! I thought maybe one of them would help me, but the judge said that no matter what, a man was dead because of me, and I'd have to go to prison. Not for very long, but I would have to go . . . and that's where it happened."

"Where what happened, sister?"

She glanced at him uneasily. "Jesus Himself come calling on me. Said I was to get myself washed clean in the River Jordan and come to Him." Another sharp intake of breath from the reverend. "See, my last name is already Jordan, and after that visit, I changed my first name to River, just to remind myself of what Jesus said for me to do."

"The River Jordan . . . and you say that Jesus Christ Himself came to you?"

"He did that very thing," Pansy insisted.

"What did He look like, Pansy?" The reverend was obviously quite curious about the visitation, but his question held no hint of disbelief.

"Well, I didn't exactly see Him," Pansy confessed. "Just a light where there was no light, and I heard His voice. And His breath was like a perfume, only better. And at the last, I saw His hand."

"Hand?" the reverend questioned. Then he added, "What color was His hand, Pansy?"

"Color?" The question surprised Pansy, and she searched her memory—slowly, slowly, realizing that the hand had been no color at all. "It wasn't a color," she said, finally. "It was just a hand." Then she added, "And I saw a big angel who said she was going to help me."

The reverend nodded thoughtfully. Then, "go on," he prompted.

"When I got paroled, all I could think about was Jesus coming to visit me and telling me I should get baptized in the River Jordan. I got work taking care of Miss Amylee, and I meant to save up every penny I could, for getting to the River Jordan. But then I found out just how very far away the River Jordan really is. And Miss Amylee said that maybe we could find a Jordan Creek that used to run down behind her grandpapa's farm when she was a little girl, and . . ." Here, Pansy hesitated for a moment. "And I think that Jesus told me that Jordan Creek would be just fine for me to get washed clean in." Her voice stumbled to a stop. "When I found out I couldn't get to that River Jordan, I went ahead and took back my own name. Sure didn't wanna be called 'Creek.' "

The reverend almost smiled, clearly enjoying Pansy's animated recollections, but then he reminded himself of the gravity of the baptism he was about to conduct. He cleared his throat. "Are you sorry for what you did to your . . . late husband?" The voice was so kind, Pansy felt hot tears spring up in her eyes.

"I am sorry," she whispered. "Truth is, I should have left him a long time ago, before things got so bad between us."

"Have you repented of what you did?"

"Well, I mean never to do such a thing again, if that's what you mean," she said, sounding a little defensive. "Didn't go to hurt him none in the first place. Just wanted him to stop beating up on me."

"If you've repented, Pansy, then God has already forgotten your transgression. To Him, it was something that just never happened."

"Why, I never thought of such a thing," Pansy confessed. "That's wonderful! But are you sure?"

"Indeed I am, and it *is* wonderful," he almost shouted. Then he leaned forward in his chair and looked deep into Pansy's eyes. "Have you accepted Jesus as your personal savior?"

"Yes. In prison," she answered, thinking immediately of Lizzie—of her broken teeth and black eyes and her eternal question: "Have you accepted Jesus Christ as your personal Savior?" More broken teeth. More bruises. But she kept right on. And at the thought of Lizzie, tears filled Pansy's eyes. The reverend pulled a snowy white, carefully ironed handkerchief out of his pocket and held it out to her. She wiped her eyes but resisted the strong urge to blow her nose on that pristine handkerchief.

"So what are those tears about, sister?" he asked.

"About Lizzie—she was my friend in prison—and how hard she worked on me to get me to where I am today—or rather, where I hope I'll be," she amended.

"And where is that?"

"Baptized in Jordan Creek."

"Well, that's where we do all our baptizing, so let's do it. But first, let's pray."

191

"Lord," he intoned. "We come before you today thanking you for your Sacrifice. We can't truly understand what it must have felt like for You to hang on that cross . . . and all for *us*, Your children. We bring before You Sister Pansy, who is going to be baptized today. She has already repented of her . . . sin . . . and invited You into her heart, so please bless us as we perform this baptism for the washing away of all her sins. Help this good woman—this beautiful-hearted woman—to begin a new life this day, dedicated to Your service. Amen!"

*I am good?* Pansy was thinking. *I have a beautiful heart?*

The door of the office opened, and Jordan stood silhouetted in the glare of the late afternoon sunshine that was pouring into the sanctuary.

"Pansy?" she called. "Miss Pearl says there's something wrong with Miss Amylee and that I should come get you."

When they got into the sanctuary, they found Miss Amylee crying into her hands quietly, with Miss Pearl sitting close beside her and patting her back.

"What's wrong?" Pansy asked, kneeling before Miss Amylee. "You sick or something?"

"I don't know," Miss Amylee managed to say. "I don't know what's wrong. I'm scared!"

"Scared of what?" Pansy asked. Miss Amylee glanced up at the reverend. "Reverend Clay, you ever see any kind of . . . unusual animals around here?" Miss Pearl looked at him, alarmed.

"No, ma'am. Nothing except maybe a possum once in a while, one that's not had much luck getting across the road, usually. But no, no unusual animals. Why do you ask?"

"There's something around here; I'm sure of it." Miss

Amylee glanced toward the lone chimney that she could still see through the window. "That was my grandpapa's house, and I went there many times when I was a child."

"And did you see an unusual animal then?" he asked softly.

"Yes, I did!" Then a fresh bout of sobbing.

"Miss Amylee, let's get you something cold to drink. There's a refrigerator in the church kitchen, and I'll go see if there's some lemonade in there."

Pansy was using a cardboard fan to cool Miss Amylee, and Miss Pearl was still sitting close, patting Miss Amylee's shoulder while the reverend and Jordan went into the kitchen off to the side. There, they found some glasses and filled them with ice from the freezer. The reverend poured lemonade over the ice.

"Reverend, how can people get a baby when they aren't married?" Jordan asked, causing him to spill a little lemonade onto the table. He hesitated before he answered.

"Now that's something you ought to ask your mama about, Miss Jordan," and sighing in relief at the blessing of finding a way to sidestep such a troublesome question, he put the glasses onto a tray and went back into the sanctuary, with Jordan following him. Miss Amylee looked a little better—at least she had stopped crying. Miss Pearl had resumed what had apparently been their conversation prior to Miss Amylee's becoming upset: "So when they took out my gall bladder . . ." She stopped when she saw the reverend approaching, and while they all drank their lemonade, Pansy continued fanning Miss Amylee.

"You feeling better?" she asked anxiously.

"I'm sorry," the reverend said. "I should have known it was too hot, even in here, for you all to have to sit here for so long."

"It's not the heat," Miss Amylee said. "It's something else."

"What is it?" he asked.

"It's something evil," Miss Amylee said, and the sound of that word, spoken in a church, set all of their teeth on edge. Miss Pearl even forgot about her gall bladder story.

"In *here*?" the reverend asked, alarmed.

"No. Out there."

"Where?" Pansy asked.

"In the woods. By the creek. It almost *got* me when I was a little girl."

There was a long silence, and then the reverend spoke most carefully. "When you were a child, Miss Amylee, did you have an active imagination?"

"Yes." Miss Amylee shuddered, and Jordan looked at her as if she'd never seen her. Not really.

"Children often imagine frightful things, don't you think?" Again, the reverend was being very careful in what he said. "And maybe sometimes they imagine frightful things that they will remember forever as being real."

"I suppose so," Miss Amylee whispered, visibly calming.

"Perhaps that's what it is—simply a bad dream left over all these years."

"Maybe," Miss Amylee admitted.

"You feel good enough to sit here a little while longer and let Pansy and me get this baptism done? Jordan, do you want to wait here, or go to the creek with us?"

"I want to see Pansy get baptized," Jordan answered.

"Well, in that case, Miss Pearl, will you please stay for a little while longer and keep Miss Amylee here company?"

"I'll be glad to," Miss Pearl answered.

Pansy said, "That's good, 'cause we need to get on home as soon as possible."

"And where is home—if I may ask?" the reverend inquired in a casual way.

"Little town not far from Warrenton," Pansy answered.

"That so?" He seemed genuinely interested. "My mother and my aunt both live in Warrenton."

"That so?" Pansy echoed him.

"Why yes! Perhaps the next time I come up to see them, you will allow me to stop by and see you. . . ." He hesitated. . . . "You folks, as well?"

"That would be nice," Pansy said, noticing once again that strange feeling she had not known for so many years. Then, both the reverend and Pansy seemed to realize what was happening, and they turned their minds and hearts to the serious work that was at hand. The reverend cleared his throat. "If you go through that door on the right, you will be in the choir's robe room. There's always a white choir robe kept in there and a clean white towel to wrap around your head. If you need any help, I'm sure Miss Pearl here will be glad to assist you. And I'll go and get ready myself."

Pansy came out of the robe room wearing the thick, pristine white choir robe with flared shoulders and with the white towel wrapped around her head like a turban. The reverend came out of his office wearing an older robe and with his khaki slacks and tennis shoes showing beneath the hem. He had a somewhat worn but very clean blanket across his arm. "To keep you from getting chilled afterwards," he explained to Pansy. And so, while Miss Amylee and Miss Pearl stayed in the church, the Reverend Isaiah Clay, Pansy, and Jordan walked across the gravel parking lot, down the short hill behind the church, and to the edge of the warm, slow-moving creek. Jordan moved into the shade of a nearby tree and watched.

"I'll go in first," he said. "Then I'll help you."

With that, he waded right into the creek a few steps and, turning, he held out his hand to Pansy. At that incredible moment, Pansy realized that she would gladly have walked right into a lake of fire, if she had to, just to reach that hand.

Jordan smiled.

# CHAPTER NINETEEN

Bᴀᴄᴋ ɪɴ ᴛʜᴇɪʀ ᴏᴡɴ ʟɪᴛᴛʟᴇ ᴛᴏᴡɴ near Warrenton, the same blistering sun baked the asphalt streets into softness, and what little breeze had existed in the morning died down, leaving only withering heat and heavy, humid air.

Right after Honey-Boy had gotten his noontime piece of pie from Mary Lou at Miss Sweetie-Pie's Diner, dark, heavy clouds came up, stirring the hot air with even hotter air and sending townsfolk to peer through their windows at the darkening sky. Finally, after a few mutters of thunder, the clouds emptied themselves, and the cascading rain sent plumes of steam rising from the streets. Honey-Boy ran into the post office, from which vantage point he stood in unbelievably cool air-conditioned comfort and watched the conflagration of the storm. When it finally abated, the torrid sun came back out and once again began steaming and baking the sodden earth.

*You ought to wear a hat when it's this hot, Honey-Boy,* an unidentified voice whispered once again. And, for whatever reason, his mind flitted to the day before and to Miss May's neon-pink bloomers hanging on her clothesline. Without knowing why, Honey-Boy walked up the damp, steaming street, and then he cut over behind Miss May's house. Sure enough, the bloomers were still on the line, although they were soggy and dripping from the sudden downpour. Honey-Boy looked around to see if the yard man was there, but he wasn't.

So Honey-Boy walked over to the clothesline, unpinned a set of bloomers, wrung them out, and then stuck his head into them. He adjusted the bloomers until they were comfortable and cool on his hot scalp, rolling up the elastic waistline until the bloomers sat upon his head much like a winter hat. Then, smiling, he walked away toward the Dairy Queen.

As he passed the hardware store, three elderly men, who were sitting outside in the store's rocking chair display, looked up and then glanced at one another in alarm. In front of the bank, a lady came out and saw Honey-Boy walking along with ladies' bloomers on his head. She clutched a gloved hand to her chest and hurried away in the other direction, looking back in alarm. When Honey-Boy reached the Dairy Queen, word had already spread about what was happening, and the people inside were plastered against the windows, waiting to see the crazy black man who wore a white lady's drawers on his head.

In the sheriff's office, the phone rang and Miss May's hysterical voice came over the receiver. "Honey-Boy! Honey-Boy just stole my . . . unmentionables . . . right off the clothesline. I saw him myself!"

As Honey-Boy approached the Dairy Queen, Sheriff Amos pulled up between Honey-Boy and the Dairy Queen door.

"Hey, Honey-Boy," the sheriff called to him.

"Hey," Honey-Boy answered amicably. "Santy Claus is coming tomorrow." He grinned widely, totally oblivious to what was happening around him. Because once Honey-Boy took Miss May's bloomers and wore them on his head right down the middle of town, the people—even the ones who had known him all of their lives—saw him as a sexual creature. And worse, a sexual black man. Little did they know that in his heart and mind, he was still the same sweet child he had always been.

One of the ladies staring out of the window at the Dairy Queen touched the shoulder of the woman next to her and whispered something in her ear. The other woman put her hand over her mouth in shock. Then she whispered back, "I think you're right. That *is* a bulge in his pants! Oh, my Lord!"

"Come on, Honey-Boy, and let me give you a ride home," the sheriff said, taking one of those massive arms in a gentle grip.

"Ice cream?" Honey-Boy asked hopefully.

"Not today, Honey-Boy. Not today." With that, Amos opened the passenger door to his cruiser and settled a grinning Honey-Boy into the seat. The people up and down the street and the ones peering from behind the glass of the Dairy Queen sighed collectively in relief. Honey-Boy smiled and waved his fingers at them as the sheriff drove him away.

When the sheriff pulled his car into Aunt Rose's small backyard, she heard the engine and came out onto the back porch, wiping her hands on her apron, but when she saw him go around to the passenger side and open the door, she almost fainted. There was Honey-Boy—*her Honey-Boy!*—sitting in the sheriff's car and wearing a pair of Miss May's bloomers on his head!

"What on earth!" Aunt Rose sputtered as the sheriff took Honey-Boy's arm and helped him out of the car. "Take that off your head!" she yelled at Honey-Boy.

"I left it on him so you could see for yourself," the sheriff explained, reaching up and sliding the bloomers off Honey-Boy's head. Honey-Boy rubbed his scalp and grinned at the ground. Aunt Rose came down the steps and held out her hand to the sheriff.

"I know these bloomers," she said. "Miss May's. Washed 'em myself." The sheriff handed them to Aunt Rose.

"We got us a problem, Aunt Rose," he whispered. "We gotta talk."

While Honey-Boy was settled in his room with a comic book, Aunt Rose came back into the kitchen, sat down at the table with the sheriff, and folded her hands on the tabletop as if she were saying a prayer.

"How come him to do such a thing?" Amos asked quietly.

"I don't know," Aunt Rose answered truthfully. "He's never taken anything before."

"Well, it's more than just taking," he said softly. "You know that, don't you?" His eyes were reluctant to meet her own, and when he glanced at her, he was glad that she was still looking only at her own hands folded neatly on the table.

"I know," she admitted.

"Folks are gonna be awful upset about this kind of thing, Aunt Rose. Now they all know Honey-Boy, and they all love you, but a fully grown black man walking through town with a white woman's underwear on his head is awful shocking!" He hesitated. "I'm afraid some of the younger menfolks might be even more upset than the ladies. Do you understand me?"

She nodded, because she did understand. She had understood for all the years that Honey-Boy had been old enough to move around alone that a day like this could come. *Would* come. And here it was.

"We got us some hotheaded youngsters too. I expect that some of them are those skinheads you hear about, but I haven't any proof of that," the sheriff added. "I think Honey-Boy better not come to town anymore." The sheriff's voice was tight with the pain he knew he was inflicting upon the revered Aunt Rose. "Keep him at home. Keep him safe."

"Thank you, Sheriff," Aunt Rose whispered. "Thank you for bringing him home."

"I'll do everything I can to calm down folks," he assured her. "You just find a way to keep him out of town."

After the sheriff left, Aunt Rose remained sitting at the table for a long time, studying her hands. *Keep Honey-Boy from going to town? How? How do I do that?*

"Sheriff's going to try to calm folks down? How's he gonna do that?" she whispered to her hands, and suddenly, she thought she saw bright orange flames reflected in her kitchen window. She jerked her head toward the window. No flames. Just the crisp green leaves of the crepe myrtle tree outside plastered against a sizzling, white-hot August sky. Behind her, Honey-Boy ambled into the kitchen and lifted a pot lid hopefully.

"Come here and sit down, baby," she said, and he did, grinning at her and then opening his mouth just like a baby bird and pointing his finger at it. Aunt Rose got up, fetched a cold biscuit for him, sat back down, and watched while Honey-Boy, still grinning, stuffed it into his mouth. She waited patiently as he chewed and finally swallowed. Then she cleared her throat.

"Honey-Boy, listen real good to your mama," she started.

"How come you to take Miss May's bloomers?" She pointed to the folded pink bloomers resting on the kitchen counter. His eyes shifted to the bloomers and then back to Aunt Rose. Slowly, he smiled and reached up to rub his hand across the top of his head.

"Yes, I know," she said wearily. "You put them on your head. But why?"

His beaming smile never stopped, but a quizzical line formed between his eyebrows. Aunt Rose rubbed her forehead and closed her eyes.

"I don't want you to go to town anymore," she announced, and she waited a moment before she glanced warily at Honey-Boy. He was still smiling brightly. "But Santy Claus . . ." he started to say, but he didn't finish, because Aunt Rose's face bore the most horrified expression anyone could imagine. It registered to Honey-Boy simply as something he'd never seen in her face before.

*Oh, my Lord! I know how to stop him from going to town!* She felt fire-hot tears burning the back of her eyes. *No! I can't do that!* she screamed silently. Across the table, Honey-Boy tilted his head at her and drew his eyebrows together. But the smile still stayed. She stood up quite suddenly, pushing all of that terrible knowledge out of her mind. "Let's have us some supper," she announced, going to the refrigerator and taking out some black-eyed peas to warm up and have with fresh cornbread. Honey-Boy sat quietly at the table while Aunt Rose went into a flurry of activity. *I'm gonna pretend that this is an evening like any other,* she whispered silently to herself. *Just like always, I'm fixing our supper, and if I can just do the usual things, everything will be all right.*

\*　　　\*　　　\*

While they ate, she watched him closer than she had ever done in her entire life, studying the way his jaw muscles bulged and the sinews in his temples rippled as he chewed great chunks of buttered cornbread. She gazed at the perfect moons of his fingernails as if she had never seen them before. His thick wrists, and his strong arms bulging with healthy, young muscles. *Who would you have been?* she wondered, *if you hadn't gotten marked by that old sow?*

When he finished eating, he smiled at her and turned his innocent eyes upon her. Then, involuntarily, the task that was surely ahead of her intruded. *Not right, for a mama to kill her own son! And a killing this will surely be! 'Cause I've lived in this old world long enough to know there's more than one way to kill somebody. Take a man who beats up on a woman, like old Earlie did to Pansy. Why, he killed her a thousand times before she pushed him away. Killed her over and over again. Or a man who turns cold and distant on a woman for no reason, and he watches her die, little by little, right in front of his eyes. And he don't care. Don't lift a finger to save her! But a mama killing her own son that way? Not right! But a killing is what it's gonna take to save him. Kill his joy to save his life!*

"Honey-Boy," she started out, feeling her stomach lurch in alarm. "Listen real good to me now." She waited until the innocent, warm eyes were securely locked with her own. "Honey-Boy, I have to tell you something that you won't like."

*How can I do it? How can I take away the only world he's ever lived in? The world of glad news he goes into town every day to tell folks about? But I gotta remember this: he's gonna die anyway! Either at the hands of some devil-filled, hotheaded people in town or by . . . my own hand . . . my own voice. Bet-*

*ter to let it come from me. From somebody who loves him! Help me, Jesus!*

"Honey-Boy, Santa Claus isn't coming tomorrow." She let the first terrible words float out into the hot air of the little kitchen. "He isn't ever going to come again." She glanced at the face—the face that now was totally blank. He started to say his typical words: "Santy Claus is—"

*"No!"* Aunt Rose insisted. "*No,* he's *not* coming! Do you hear me? He's not real! I made him up!" Once again, her stomach lurched in revulsion at her own words, and she watched with the heaviest heart she had ever felt, while the smile on Honey-Boy's face fell into an open-mouthed, silent *no!*

And simply because she didn't know what you were supposed to do after you've murdered your own son's happiness, she got up from the table and went to the sink. As she ran the water for washing the dishes, her tears fell into the soap suds. She turned back to the table, and watched Honey-Boy sitting there, alone. All the hope and all the joy had gone from him fully.

The "Honey-Boy incident," as it was called, was the main topic of conversation among the townspeople for many days, but it was almost a week before anyone heard about what method Aunt Rose had used to keep Honey-Boy from going to town. Most of the people in town missed Honey-Boy's childlike anticipation and his daily, joyous announcements about Santa Claus coming tomorrow, and they were horrified that Aunt Rose had to do what she did to her own son. But some of the people—those who were so frightened by what they called his "blossoming sexuality"—breathed a sigh of relief.

"Who'd have thought it?" those ladies whispered to each

other in the corners of front porches. "I always believed that he was just a child in his mind and would always stay that way forever," they murmured. "But you never know," others confirmed quietly. "You just never do know about those kinds of . . . feelings *grown men* can get! And he was definitely a grown man!"

When Mary Lou, at Miss Sweetie-Pie's heard about it, she burst into tears, and no one could console her.

# CHAPTER TWENTY

Pansy STEPPED DOWN into the muddy, bathwater-warm creek, her bare feet touching mud, pebbles, and submerged grass she couldn't see. The reverend's hand was stretched out toward her, and when she took it, she felt the warm, strong fingers of a good man and the hardened palm of a construction worker. She took a short breath and glanced up into his face, studied the bottomless brown eyes and the strong, kind line of the jaw. Together, they walked out to where the creek was deep enough for her to be submerged.

"Do like this, Pansy—put your hands one over the other under your chin, like this." He demonstrated, crossing his large hands over each other and placing them high on his chest—just under his chin. The sight of those large hands suddenly made Pansy catch her breath. She could have looked at them forever, at the smoothness of his skin on the back of his fingers and the rich, bulging veins.

"You okay, sister?" he inquired.

"I'm all right," Pansy breathed.

"I'll do everything. All you have to do is hold your breath

for a little minute and let me lean you backwards." Somehow the image of Earlie's face appeared in Pansy's imagination. His angry face and the cold, hard fists and the sneers and the name-calling, and for a moment, she wondered, *Can I really let a man . . . any man . . . put me under the water and then trust him to bring me up again? Not drown me? Not smile as he watches me die?*

"Are you sure you're okay?" the reverend asked her again, and when she looked at his face, the images of Earlie's face and his fists and his cruel words vanished, and nothing was left in her field of vision except this beautiful, beautiful, smiling man.

"I'm ready," she whispered. He gently placed one strong hand on the back of her neck and the other over her own folded hands under her chin.

"Pansy, I baptize you in the name of the Father, and of the Son, and of the Holy Ghost," he intoned in his deep baritone, his golden words filling the humid summer air under the canopy of trees lining the creek. Immediately, he leaned her backwards, pushing gently on her folded hands and holding her firmly be-hind the neck. When the water closed over her face and the coolness of it prickled her sun-warmed scalp, she briefly opened her eyes to see gray water, bubbles, and above the bubbles, his broad, dark face. As quickly as he had put her under, he brought her up again, his arms strong and comforting. Pansy closed her eyes, thrust her streaming face toward Heaven, and raised up both of her arms. She stood that way for a long moment, think-ing about Jesus Himself really wanting her. About His visit to her in jail. About Lizzie and her broken teeth and black eyes. And especially about this beautiful man who had just baptized her. Had done this wonderful thing for her!

"You all right, sister?" he whispered yet again.

"I couldn't be any better, praise Jesus!" she answered most truthfully. He took her elbow and guided her to the creek bank where he shook out the blanket and wrapped it around her. Jordan, still standing in the shade, burst into applause, and Pansy and the reverend grinned at her.

"Hooray!" Jordan shouted. "I wish we had creek baptizing in *my* church. But all we do is get sprinkled."

"Reverend Clay?" Miss Pearl called from the top of the hill.

"Yes, Miss Pearl?"

"I would come on down there," Miss Pearl explained. "But my arthritis is so bad."

"So what is it?"

"Mrs. Wilkins phoned and said to tell you that Mr. Wilkins has just been taken to the hospital, and she wants you to meet her there," Miss Pearl yelled. "Right away. She sounds awful upset," she added.

"You go right on along, Reverend Clay," Pansy urged. "We've taken up way too much of your time already."

"No." He smiled. "That isn't possible. Now, Pansy, I have to go be a shepherd to my flock." Incredibly, he reached out and took her hand, and the warmth of his skin once again almost blistered her palm. "But when you go back to the church to change, I'd appreciate it so much if you'd be willing to write your phone number or your address down and put it on my desk. Will you do that, please?" He pressed her hand earnestly, looking deep into her eyes.

"I . . . will," Pansy assured him, not drawing her hand away. "You go along now, and thank you." At last, she found the strength to lift her hand away from his, but at the moment she accomplished this great feat, her hand yearned to touch his again. Hungered for it!

To Jordan, she said, "You go right along too, Jordan. Miss Pearl may want to go to the hospital with the reverend, and you need to stay with Miss Amylee. I'm coming along, but I need a little quiet moment to myself, please."

"Okay," Jordan agreed, and off she went, skipping up the hill just behind the reverend. When he reached the top, he stopped, turned, and slowly raised a hand toward Pansy—almost a benediction in itself. Pansy nodded to him and then pulled the blanket closer around her shoulders, enjoying the feeling of being a little bit cool, for a change. As she gathered the blanket around her shoulders, she turned to the creek and started trying to gather about her all that had happened within the last couple of hours. Remembering how she felt the first time she fixed her eyes on the Reverend Clay—*Isaiah!*—looking into his eyes, his deep, kind eyes. Feeling his strong hands lifting her up out of the water. Lifting her up with her sins forgiven. Forgotten! Her prayer arose as naturally as her breath:

*Thank You!*

After a few minutes, Pansy heard a car engine start up, and she saw the reverend driving away in a hurry with Miss Pearl in the passenger's seat. And the very next thing she saw was Gertie stomping down the side of the highway with a rigid and determined stride, then heading down the hill to the creek, with her face in a terrible pout. It was almost too much for Pansy to comprehend.

"What on earth!" Pansy called to her. Gertie stomped right up to Pansy, jutting her belligerent chin right into Pansy's face.

"He isn't gonna take me to Panama City!" Gertie spat, as if they were the most terrible words she had ever spoken.

"What?"

"I said, he isn't gonna take me—"

"I heard that much," Pansy interrupted her. "Honey, maybe he just can't afford it . . . right now, at least, and what are you doing back here?"

"I've left him," Gertie said. "I ain't gonna live here and never get to go anywhere and do exciting things!" Her pouting face was a brilliant red, infuriated mask, and Pansy could do little other than to stand there with her mouth hanging open. "I'm leaving him, just the way he left me!" Gertie added.

"But Gertie!" Pansy couldn't seem to find any words.

"I'm not gonna spend my life in some teensy little apartment in some hot, dead little town!"

Pansy reached out to put her hand on Gertie's arm. "Surely you don't mean that!"

"I do mean it," Gertie insisted, batting Pansy's hand away viciously. "I want to go somewhere and do something, and this isn't it! You gotta take me to Atlanta! That's where I want to go. It's the biggest city I know about."

"Atlanta? Who do you know in Atlanta?" Pansy asked, still struggling to keep up with what was going on in Gertie's mind.

"Nobody! And that's okay. I just want to go live in the biggest city I can find," Gertie insisted.

"How you gonna take care of yourself and that little baby you're carrying?" Pansy said, with an *ah-ha!* tone in her voice.

"I'll find a way," Gertie said. "And besides, you have to take me, because this is all *your* fault!" Gertie shouted suddenly.

"*My* fault?" Pansy shouted back. "*My* fault when you're the one called me and begged me to help you? And I'm the one borrowed Mrs. Reverend Brown's car and went and got you and then drove you all the way down here?"

"Yes!" Gertie yelled. "You're the one that made me marry him!"

"Well, you can fuss and fume and spit and spat all you want, and you can even blame me instead of yourself," Pansy shouted. "But I'm certainly not gonna take you to Atlanta! I swear, Gertie, you're crazy! Just plain crazy!"

At those words, Gertie howled like an animal, reached out and pushed Pansy backwards *hard*. Pansy took a few stumbling steps, her mouth hanging open in shock and surprise, but before she could even fully realize what was happening, Gertie ran up and pushed her again, even harder. Pansy's feet went out from under her, and she sat down on the hard ground, with the breath momentarily knocked out of her. But then, as she looked up into that swollen, furious face towering over her, something in her seemed to click out a terrible message: No! Nobody's ever going to hurt me again! Nobody's going to beat up on me!

Pansy came up with her fists clenched in front of her face, and she was certainly ready when Gertie came at her yet again, crying and furious. To Pansy's great credit, she resisted striking out with the big fists, and instead, she grabbed a double handful of hair on either side of Gertie's head. Pansy grunted from the stomach punches, the furious kicks aimed at her shins, and Gertie's spine-chilling screams of rage and helplessness. For long minutes, Pansy drag danced the kicking, screaming Gertie to the edge of the creek, and letting out a great shout of her own—*"yes!"*— threw Gertie right into the water and watched with a deeply satisfied smirk as it closed over Gertie's head. Gertie came up out of the water, sputtering and screaming and crying.

"You!" Gertie spat creek water and pointed an accusing finger at Pansy. "You stinking black *nig*—"

*"Shut up!"* Pansy bellowed, startling all the humid air above the creek. "You say that word, and I'm gonna come in there and sit on your stinking face!" With all the screaming and the sputtering Gertie and Pansy were doing at each other, neither one of them heard Bill come running down the hill until he shouted, "Hey! What's going on here?" He ran straight into the creek, pulled Gertie to her feet, and then managed to duck as she swung at him. Struggling, he finally managed to pin Gertie's arms to her sides and in that strange hug, he walked her up onto the bank.

"Took me a little minute to figure out where she'd go," Bill said to Pansy, breathing hard. Gertie had stopped struggling in his iron embrace, and she simply stood with her head down, still blubbering softly. "But what's going on here?" he asked again.

"I think you know," Pansy said.

"Oh . . ." Bill loosened his grip on Gertie and turned her to face him.

"Gertie, I just don't have the money for a real honeymoon . . . right now." He glanced uneasily at Pansy before he went on. "But I'm gonna take you to Panama City, just as soon as we can save up for it." Again, he glanced at Pansy, who nodded her head. Gertie jerked away from him and swung at him once more. Again, he ducked away from her fist and clamped her arms against her sides. She stopped, glum and silent as a stone.

"You see what you're up against, don't you?" Pansy asked.

"I do," he said, after having said it only an hour or so before, and in the church, and standing in front of the altar.

"Well, you'll have to take a firm hand with her," Pansy said, deciding right at that very moment not to say anything to him about Gertie wanting to go to Atlanta. "Now I don't mean that you should ever be rough with her. Don't you *never, ever* raise your hand in anger against her! I myself been on the receiving end of that kind of thing, and nobody should have to live like that—being treated worse than a dumb animal. One that don't have no feelings, don't have no love to give, don't have nothing a man wants . . . except for one thing!" *Nobody will ever do that to me again!*

"And you," Pansy addressed Gertie, resisting the strong urge to slap that silly face. "You always bellowing about wanting to go somewhere—well, this is your somewhere. Here. With Bill. And you always wanted to do something—well, you got something to do now—being this man's wife." After a hesitation, Pansy added, "And a better man than you deserve! And you got yourself another job gonna start in a few months being a mama. So you work on being a better mama than your own mama was to you," Pansy admonished. "I imagine the Reverend Clay is gonna keep an eye on you, so you better learn how to do things right, for the very first time in your life!" At the last, Pansy said to Bill, "Just be firm, but don't be mean."

"I can do that," Bill answered. "Now come on, Gertie—we're going home."

Pansy watched while Bill and a somewhat subdued Gertie walked up the hill, one of his arms around her shoulder and the other holding her wrists together in front of her, just in case she took a notion to swing at him again. When they were gone, Pansy turned back to face the creek, closed her eyes, and lifted her face toward heaven.

"Lord, please forgive me! Here I haven't been baptized more'n fifteen minutes, and I already done throwed a pregnant white girl in the creek! I'm sorry. Please help that good man, Bill. Why, if Gertie had been with somebody like my old Earlie for a single day of her life, she'd appreciate having such a good man." Pansy's words conjured up an image of Isaiah Clay, and she hurriedly finished her prayer. "I'll try to do better! And thank you!" When Pansy at last started up the hill toward the church, she thought she heard Someone laughing. A happy, delighted chuckle.

In the church, Jordan rushed away from the window where she had spent long minutes delighting in watching the fantastic altercation between Gertie and Pansy and when Pansy came in, Jordan was sitting with an innocent and slightly bored expression, fanning herself with a cardboard fan. Miss Amylee was standing at a window on the other side of the church, looking out at the lone chimney that used to be a part of her grandfather's house. Pansy touched Jordan's arm.

"Soon as I get my clothes changed, we'll be on our way," she whispered, so as not to disturb Miss Amylee, who was talking to herself under her breath. "We gotta get you and Miss Amylee back home."

"I like what you did to Gertie," Jordan offered.

"You saw us?" Pansy asked.

"Well, sure," Jordan answered. "Couldn't help but see you, after hearing all that yelling and hollering going on."

Pansy glanced over at Miss Amylee, who was still standing at the window, muttering under her breath.

"Miss Amylee watch us too?" Pansy asked.

"No," Jordan said. "She didn't seem to notice."

"We gotta get her home," Pansy said, and she went into the robing room to change back into her clothes. After she towel-dried her hair as well as she could, she stepped into the Reverend Isaiah Clay's office and wrote her name and phone number on a piece of paper, as he had asked her to do. She resisted the urge to draw a heart underneath the phone number, but her eyes fell upon the large leather chair, and without thinking, she sat down in it, noticing its pleasant creak. She leaned back in the chair. *Something to lean on that won't let you fall.* And she realized at that moment that she really didn't want to leave his office, his chair . . . him. But they had been gone from home for far too long, and they all had obligations. Pansy's was to get Miss Amylee and Jordan home safely.

When Pansy reluctantly left Reverend Clay's office and came back into the church, Miss Amylee was still talking, only louder than before. Jordan was leaning on one of the pews, watching Miss Amylee and listening to her.

"It's time for us to get on home," Pansy said. But neither Miss Amylee nor Jordan seemed to notice Pansy or hear her. Miss Amylee was saying to no one in particular, "Grandpapa got me in a nice, clean dress for church and told me it would make God real happy if I stayed clean until we could get there. And then he said that if I messed up my dress, the *beast* would get me!"

Pansy didn't notice Jordan's eyes glazing over, and Miss Amylee went on in her reverie: "And all I wanted to do was throw a few pebbles into the creek, while Grandpapa got himself ready for church. I didn't mean to fall in, but I did, and when I crawled out, I heard . . . something . . . coming through the bushes on the other side of the creek, and I knew it was the beast Grandpapa warned me about!" Her vacant blue eyes had taken on a hue of childish terror. "I ran and ran, and I could hear it behind me, and I could smell its sour hair!"

Pansy waited before she spoke very calmly to Miss Amylee. "You know, when some folks talk about the *beast*, it's the devil they're talking about. Maybe that's what your grandpapa meant."

"No!" Miss Amylee insisted. "It was truly some kind of a terrible beast, and it almost got me!"

"Not a beast." Jordan's low voice surprised both Pansy and Miss Amylee.

"What?" Pansy asked.

"Not a beast," Jordan repeated, now absorbed in watching in her imagination as the little girl, Amylee, fell into the creek. Jordan heard the bubbling water through little Amylee's ears, and she felt the icy shock and the wetness of the creek on Amylee's skin. *The fear!* She watched the bushes on the other side of the creek and heard something rustling in them. She repeated: "Not beast." Slowly, she began smiling, as she watched a deer come out of the bushes and the shadows, a deer startled by the sound of little Amylee falling into the water.

"It's a deer!" Jordan cried joyously. "That's what it is—a deer!"

Miss Amylee had turned to face Jordan. "A deer?"

"Sure! I'm looking right at it!"

Miss Amylee let out a short, uncertain laugh. "A deer? That's what I've been afraid of all my life? A *deer?*" She gave a short, incredulous chuckle, as her eyebrows shot up. "Well, what do you know about that!"

Pansy asked, "Miss Amylee, did your grandpapa get real mad at you for falling into the creek?"

"No, come to think of it, he didn't. He just said 'I see the beast almost got you!' Then he laughed, as a matter of fact."

Miss Amylee smiled and shook her head. "Oh, how did I let things get so twisted up? And then leave them that way for so long?"

"Then he probably *did* mean the devil," Pansy said. "That if you disobey, you're letting the devil take over, instead of God."

"Yes," Miss Amylee said. "That certainly would explain it."

"I wish you could see that deer," Jordan mused. "It's so fine and delicate, and he has such tiny hooves and beautiful, dark eyes." Miss Amylee studied Jordan carefully. "I think I can see it, Jordan."

"Well, we've had ourselves a miracle, sure enough," Pansy breathed. She could simply look at Miss Amylee and see the weight lifted off of her thin shoulders—see a healthy-looking bloom coming into her faded cheeks.

"Thank you, Jordan," Pansy said. "You being such a dreamy little thing has surely made a miracle!" Then Pansy gazed past Miss Amylee's shoulder and stared for the last time at the lone chimney jutting up in the late afternoon sun, and while she watched, heavy rain clouds scudded across the sky and shut out the sun.

"We better get on the road," Pansy said. "I gotta get you folks home safe and sound."

# CHAPTER TWENTY-ONE

PANSY DROVE OUT of the gravel parking lot and headed Mrs. Reverend Brown's car north. In the passenger's seat, Miss Amylee fell almost at once into a deep, peaceful sleep, but Jordan leaned against the back of Pansy's seat, pensive and thoughtful. Pansy was thinking of the small church and the big, beautiful man in it. *I will see him again. I don't know when, and I don't know where, and I don't know how, but I will see him again! I know it for a fact—so thank You, Jesus!*

Jordan was watching her carefully. "You're really happy about Miss Amylee, aren't you?" she asked.

"Yes, child. Maybe now Miss Amylee won't be so sad all the time. I think that imagination of yours is a great gift!"

"Gift?" Jordan had never thought of such a thing at all. For her, it always had been an affliction she had to suffer—complete with all the pinching of her own legs and the countless doses of castor oil to try to banish it. But then she considered that maybe Pansy was right. Maybe it really was a gift. A troublesome one, perhaps, but a gift nonetheless.

"A gift," Jordan repeated. Not a question this time, but a simple statement.

Then, right out of the blue, Jordan asked Pansy, "You really liked Reverend Clay, didn't you?"

"Sure did," Pansy breathed. "And I still do."

"Will you keep on liking him, even if you find out he isn't real?"

Jordan's innocent question floated high above Pansy's head for the briefest moment before it plunged like a devouring hawk straight into her heart. Her mouth fell open and she stared in the rearview mirror at Jordan's completely passive face.

*What on earth do you mean, not real?* The words screamed to be spoken, but Pansy's mouth was still hanging open. Mute.

"I mean," Jordan went on, as if she really had heard Pansy's silent question. "I know you were expecting a *woman* angel. But . . ."

The first word exploded out of Pansy's mouth: *"What?"*

Jordan jumped and then stammered, "You know . . . the angel with the gold tooth. You're the one who told us all about that, and even though Jesus decided to send a *man* angel, I wondered if you would talk with him . . . Reverend Clay . . . about him maybe being that angel."

"Oh, my Lord!" Pansy breathed. And the images that tried to crowd all at once into her head were all of the Reverend Clay—his aroma, the shine of his skin, the warmth of his hand, his gold tooth! *But I'm sure it was a woman angel I saw that night in prison,* Pansy argued with herself. *At least, I think it was a woman.*

"Do you still like him?" Jordan asked again.

"Listen, honey, do be quiet for a little minute and let me think, please."

219

"Okay," Jordan agreed, sitting back and watching the dark countryside go past the car windows. "I'm sorry if you're upset," Jordan added, but Pansy just waved her words away over her shoulder. Soon, Jordan stretched out on the backseat and fell asleep without getting an answer to her question or a response to her apology.

Pansy, now alone with her thoughts, stared relentlessly at the road ahead of her, not even realizing that she had turned on the wipers when the fat, warm raindrops started plopping against the windshield. Raindrops that seemed to be falling from Heaven to echo the tears of frustration and sorrow and confusion inside of her.

*Could it be?* she argued with herself. *Could it be he was the angel Jesus sent to me, and like a fool, I went and fell in love with him? Why, people can't fall in love with angels!* But then, she found her mind racing over details she hadn't considered before. His name, for one thing: *Isaiah Clay.* Isaiah, the prophet from the Old Testament! And "Clay" for the human body? The clay vessel? The Potter's clay? *And if I turned this car around right now, and drove straight back down this same road, would that little church even be there? Did I have a dream? Is there something wrong with me? Am I losing my mind?*

Her astonishing musings brought a feeling of a grief more terrible than any she had ever known. Suppose he wasn't a mortal man, after all? How could she live without him? Without the possibility of having that big, kind, good-smelling man in her hopes and dreams? The twin beams of the headlights shone down upon the blacktop highway, and tree frogs chirped on either side of the sad, dark roadway. *But he has to be a man,* she argued. *Else, how would Bill know him from the*

*highway crew? And what about Miss Pearl—she could see him.
Pearl . . . oh my Lord! Pearly gates?*

Fat tears loomed in Pansy's eyes. Tears of sorrow and of joy,
of a supreme happiness that perhaps would bring the deepest
sadness she had ever known. *Was it all a dream? Something
that didn't happen?*

"I'm coming home, Mama," she spoke softly into the darkness. "Coming home from a place that maybe I only dreamed."

When they finally reached Miss Amylee's house, dawn was
just breaking, and Pansy felt completely worn out—more from
wondering about Isaiah Clay and grieving at the possibility of
his not being real than from driving all night long. That long
drive through more than one kind of dark!

As soon as Miss Amylee and Jordan were safely settled in-
doors, Pansy said to them, "Now you all just wait right here,
while I take Mrs. Reverend Brown's car back."

"Aren't you too tired for that right now?" Miss Amylee
asked.

"Yes, I am too tired," Pansy confessed. "But it has to be
done, and I'll feel better when I've gone ahead and done it."
She didn't add that she was anxious to ask the Reverend
Brown to do some snooping for her—find out something
about the Reverend Isaiah Clay, because she figured that there
had to be some kind of a registry of ministers or something like
that, and she would ask him about it—but without dropping a
single hint of what she truly feared—that he didn't exist at all,
that he had simply been a heavenly apparition.

The two-block drive to Reverend Brown's house felt longer
than the nightlong drive Pansy had just completed, because
she knew that, once she handed the car keys to the reverend,

her last connection to Isaiah Clay would have been lost, and that was the loneliest feeling she'd ever had. So that when she finally pulled the car into the driveway of the Brown residence, she sat there for long moments before she even turned off the engine.

While she was sitting there, Reverend Brown came to the front door, wearing a robe over his pajamas and holding a coffee mug.

"Come on in, Sister Pansy," he called. "Let me fix you a cup of coffee while you tell me about your trip." Pansy went inside and sat down on the couch. Soon, the Reverend Brown came out of the kitchen and held out a mug to her.

"Excuse me just a moment," he said, disappearing into the back part of the house. Pansy sat all alone on the Reverend Brown's couch, holding the mug in her hands and trying to breathe normally. Her heart was thudding against her ribs as hard as if she'd just finished a long run. *Maybe it has been a long run,* Pansy thought. *What all I've been through—with Earlie and then going to prison, and I thought it would all change, once Jesus came to me right in my cell. But maybe things changed in a way I didn't think about. In a way I don't want. Help me, Jesus!*

When Reverend Brown came back into the living room, he was wearing well-ironed khaki pants and a clean shirt, and his hair had been combed. He emanated a warm, soapy aroma.

"Forgive me, Pansy . . . uh . . . River, but you seem bothered by something. Did the trip go okay?"

"The name is Pansy, Reverend. I took back my old name, once I found out how far away the real River Jordan is—all the way across the ocean."

"So you've given up on that?" he asked, smiling.

Pansy was a little puzzled at his smile. Was he trying not to laugh at her? She decided to ignore it.

"Yes, but I did get myself baptized in a Jordan Creek Miss Amylee remembered from her childhood." As she spoke, the Reverend Isaiah Clay's face appeared in the brimming coffee, complete with the signature angel mark, the gold tooth. She used the tip of her finger to stir away the image, reluctantly.

"So you did get baptized?"

"I did."

"Well, I could have done that for you," he said, and Pansy noticed the slightly offended tone in his voice.

"I wanted at least to get part of the name right, what Jesus told me to do," she explained.

"Oh . . . and you all found Gertie's . . . friend?"

"We did, and I got them to tie the knot. But maybe that wasn't the right thing to do."

"Sure it was," he said easily. "Leastwise now that little baby will have a mama and a daddy."

"Well, a daddy, at least," Pansy agreed. "I don't think Gertie is going to make any better a mama than the one she had."

"You're still looking pained, sister. Is something else bothering you?"

"Well, I think Bill's a nice young man, and he probably deserves someone better than Gertie." The Reverend Brown continued to stare at her, slowly twirling his thumbs around each other, as a gesture to let her know that he would wait patiently until whatever was really bothering her came to the surface.

Finally, she found the words. "There's something I need you to do for me."

"Name it, Pansy. Get it off your chest."

"Well, could you do a little bit of snooping for me?"

He looked surprised and perhaps a little offended.

Pansy hesitated. "Not anything bad," she added hastily, although she wasn't sure that was a true statement at all. It was sure enough going to be bad if he found out that Isaiah Clay didn't even exist. Not only would Pansy have lost the only man she ever met who was genuinely kind, but Reverend Brown would have all kinds of questions, perhaps even about her sanity. "The preacher who married Gertie and Bill and who baptized me. His name is . . . Isaiah Clay." She stumbled to a stop.

"What about him?" Again the slightly amused expression came into Reverend Brown's face.

"Can you find out anything about him?" She didn't add *find out if he's real!*

But the Reverend Brown laughed heartily. "Don't need to snoop to do that for you, sister. I know him well. His mama and aunt live near here. Fine man! Fine, fine man!"

Man! Was there ever so beautiful a word? Man! A flesh-and-blood man!

The Reverend Brown continued, "Why, Sister Pansy! What joy has spread across your face! Has your heart possibly reached out to Isaiah? That would sure enough be a blessing! It's been well over a year since he lost his beloved Iris."

"Iris?"

"His late wife. Lovely woman! Lovely woman!"

Pansy thought for a moment before she said, "Yes, she would have been lovely! And lucky too."

"If your heart is truly reaching out for his, perhaps—at last!—you will be lucky too." Pansy tried to hide her smile, but the flood of relief and joy surging through her was almost more than she could bear. Insanely, Reverend Brown's descriptions of Isaiah and Iris interchanged themselves with what Reverend Isaiah Clay had said about Pansy in his prayer:

*Fine man! Fine man! loses Lovely Woman. Lovely Woman*
*Heart-is-Beautiful Pansy loses a loser!*
*Fine man! Fine man! meets Heart-is-beautiful woman*
*Heart-is-beautiful woman meets Fine Man! Fine man!*
*How perfect!*

Smiling, the Reverend Brown watched Pansy and gave a little prayer of silent gratitude.

"I need to get home," Pansy stammered at last. "Thank you for letting us use Mrs. Reverend Brown's car." Reverend Brown said not another word, but he just smiled and smiled.

Pansy's short walk back to Miss Amylee's was the kind of thing she had only heard about in songs on the radio—how her feet seemed to float right above the ground, and all of the earth—the birds singing and the breeze blowing through the pine trees—seemed to be singing with her: *He is real! He is an honest-to-goodness man! A fine man! And he said I had a beautiful heart! Has the world ever been more beautiful? Has life ever been so wonderful?*

Pansy was in such a glowing, giddy state that she was halfway across Miss Amylee's front yard before she saw a car parked under the portico. A strange car, yes—but something vaguely familiar about it.

She came through the front door and into a living room that was filled to the brim with the very real presence of Reverend Isaiah Clay! *Fine Man* himself, in the flesh—big, kind, wonderful, and smelling of minty toothpaste.

"What are *you* doing *here*?" she asked, stupidly.

He smiled, flashing the gold tooth that had caused such confusion.

"I drove all night," he said.

"But how did you find this house?" Pansy was filled with a delicious curiosity. She wanted to know everything: did he stop for coffee? Did he put cream and sugar in the coffee? *Why* would he drive all night long?

"Actually, I phoned Reverend Brown when I got as far as Macon." He stifled a laugh. "Waked him up long before dawn, just to find out how to get to Miss Amylee's house."

Pansy saw Jordan's head appear around the door to the dining room, and once Jordan's and Pansy's eyes met, Jordan walked easily into the living room to stand with Pansy and Isaiah and to glance at him with open curiosity.

"I'm so glad he came!" she said simply to Pansy. "Aren't you?" And then Jordan silently mouthed the words, *He's real!*

"Oh, yes," Pansy answered, and suddenly feeling timid, she asked, "Where's Miss Amylee?" The question was more to take the attention off herself than to really wonder.

"She's taking a nap. Said she was tired from the trip."

"Well, I expect so," Pansy said. "Come on in the kitchen, and I'll make us a nice, big breakfast. You haven't eaten, have you?" she asked Isaiah.

"No, indeed," he said, beaming. "And I would certainly love a good, home-cooked breakfast!"

Pansy set about fixing the best breakfast she'd ever cooked, and the whole time, the Reverend Clay sat at the kitchen table, looking big and so sweet in the chair, and he watched her with a smile and a lifted eyebrow—a most interesting gesture. As Pansy cooked, she glanced at him from time to time and won-

226

dered how she could experience such a new feeling, almost like a young girl!

When breakfast was cooked, they all ate silently, exchanging glances and smiles from time to time. Pansy watched with pleasure as the good reverend wolfed down the over-easy eggs, fragrant sausage, buttered grits, and high, light biscuits with obvious relish. When finally he sighed, leaned back, and placed his hand on his chest, Pansy said to Jordan, "Honey, would you give the reverend here and me a little minute of privacy, please."

"I'll go watch TV," Jordan said, giving Pansy and the reverend a small, happy glance.

When they were alone in the kitchen, Pansy asked him, straight out, "And why are you here?" It was the identical question she had first asked when she came into the living room and saw him there. She held her breath, almost willing her ears to hear the answer she so desperately wanted, and while she waited, she studied her hands, folded on the table.

"I had to see you again," he explained. "I couldn't stand by and have you just drive away from me. I *had* to come!"

"You're missing work," she stated, unable to acknowledge, right away, the intensity of his words.

"I know."

"They'll dock your pay."

"I know."

"Folks in your church will wonder where you are."

"I know."

Finally, Pansy could think of nothing else to tell him about how much it had cost him to travel all those many miles. *For her!* She waited for long minutes before she looked up and into his deep, brown eyes. In those eyes, she could almost see her own reflection.

"When I got back from the hospital," he began explaining, "I went straight to the church, hoping against hope you all would still be there. And I couldn't stop thinking about you. Then I started thinking about how you and Jordan and Miss Amylee were all alone and driving in the dark, and I just got into my car and started following you. Figured if you all had car trouble or anything like that, I'd be coming along right behind you, and I could help you out."

Here, he hesitated and gazed at his hands for a long moment before he continued: "And it was much more than just wanting to know that you got home safe and sound—I had to see you again. I had to *know*. Do you understand what I'm saying?"

Pansy sat silently for several moments and with her eyes closed, letting the sweetness of his words sink deep into herself. Then she finally looked back at him and smiled. "Well, praise Jesus," she said at last.

"Amen!" the reverend shouted happily. Then he pushed his chair back from the table, took Pansy's hand and drew her upwards to stand face-to-face with him. "Now I have to go right on back home. But when I come again, I'd like to take you to meet my mother and my aunt. Would you agree to that?"

"I would," she murmured. "You have to go so soon?"

"Unfortunately, yes. Our little church is growing, and pretty soon, I'll be able to give up the construction work and just be a full-time minister to that wonderful flock. But until then, I do have to keep my job."

"I hope you'll be able to come again soon," she offered.

"I will. I promise."

\* \* \*

"Yoo-hoo!" came the call from the living room. "Yoo-hoo, Pansy? You all okay?"

"In the kitchen," Pansy called back. She took Isaiah's hand and led him toward the dining room. Peony came walking rapidly through the dining room, carrying her suitcase and already talking to Pansy. "I just got back, and I saw that car in you-all's portico and . . ." Spotting the strange, big man who was holding Pansy's hand, an astonished Peony stumbled to an abrupt silence.

Pansy murmured, "Peony, this is the Reverend Isaiah Clay. Isaiah, this is my sister, Peony."

But neither Pansy nor Isaiah looked directly at Peony, because they were too wrapped up in looking at each other.

"What?" Peony bellowed, making both Pansy and Isaiah jump.

*"What?"* she bellowed again.

"I said—" Pansy started, but Peony cut her off.

"I *know* what you said!" Peony put down her suitcase and tossed her purse onto the dining room table. Then, scowling at the big man, she thought better of where she'd put her purse. While he watched in benevolent amusement, Peony grabbed the purse and tucked it protectively under her arm.

"Peony, this is Isaiah," Pansy tried again. "Isaiah, this is Peony."

"How do you do?" Isaiah crooned, stepping forward and extending his hand warmly. Peony recoiled as if the hand held a poisonous serpent, and she turned to the side, so that the arm clutching her purse was a few inches farther away from him.

"Why, Peony!" Pansy said. "What's wrong with you?"

"No!" Peony snarled. "What's wrong with *you*?"

Isaiah lowered his hand and retreated, smiling.

"Nothing's wrong with me," Pansy protested. "In fact, maybe for the first time in my life, everything's right!"

Isaiah cleared his throat. "Why don't I go ahead so you two can speak more comfortably," he suggested. "I really need to leave anyway, and Peony and I can perhaps get to know each other another time."

"I know you need to leave," Pansy said. "Sister, I'll be right back."

"I hope you feel better," Isaiah spoke softly to Peony, but she clutched her purse and waved his words away with the back of her hand, her restrained fury heating up the room.

"She'll be better soon," Pansy assured him, as they walked toward the front porch. Jordan was still sitting in front of the television. " 'Bye, Reverend Clay," she called.

"Good-bye to you, Miss Jordan," he answered. Pansy nodded her head toward the dining room. "Jordan, please go sit with Peony while I walk Reverend Clay out to his car."

"Sure," Jordan agreed. "I wanted to go to her right away, but her getting so upset kind of scared me."

When the Reverend Isaiah Clay waved and drove away from Miss Amylee's house, Pansy thought that no house could be more beautiful than this one, which had held his richness and goodness, if only for a brief time.

And then Pansy knew that she had to go back inside now and deal with Peony. It wasn't going to be easy!


"I just don't believe it!" Peony growled, the instant Pansy came back into the house.

"Let's go into the kitchen," Pansy suggested, not objecting when she noticed Jordan following right along.

Peony scowled. "You gonna let this child hear what we're gonna be saying to each other?"

Pansy studied Jordan's face for a long moment before she said, "And what kind of things are we gonna say?"

"We're gonna talk about *men*!" Peony sputtered.

"Well, then," Pansy pronounced. "I think Jordan here should listen. She's gonna be a woman one of these days, and she needs to know what goes on between a man and a woman."

"Why, I never . . . !" Peony fumed.

"Or would you rather she got all her information from watching Mr. Franklin and Miss Alice?" Pansy added.

Jordan listened without speaking, but she was remembering her own daddy and the warmth that shone from his eyes whenever he looked at her or her mother. So maybe Jordan already knew more about men than Pansy realized.

Peony thought over Pansy's words worriedly, and then she suddenly relented.

"Fine!" she said. "But I got plenty to say to you, Pansy, and I'm not gonna pull any punches!"


When they went into the kitchen, Peony looked at the breakfast dishes and harrumphed. "You cooked breakfast for . . . for *him*?"

"Yes," Pansy answered, as she made quick work of clearing the table.

Peony glanced uneasily at Jordan. "Did he stay the night?" She floated the question out easily into the warm kitchen air.

Pansy stopped wiping down the table and glared at Peony. "No, he most certainly did not!"

"Sit down!" Peony barked, and both Jordan and Pansy obeyed without thinking. Jordan crossed her arms on the table and rested her chin on them, her eyes easily shifting back and forth between the two women. Pansy sat ramrod straight, with her shoulders squared.

"Who is he? Where did he come from? How did you meet him?" Peony's questions came in rapid-fire succession.

So Pansy patiently told her the whole story, adding at the end, "And Reverend Brown himself said that Isaiah is a fine man!" As Pansy told the story, Peony's shoulders began to relax, and she leaned forward, consuming every word. When the story was done, they all sat in silence.

Peony stared at her sister with the saddest eyes Jordan had ever seen. "Lord help us!" Peony finally breathed. "You're *in love* with him!" It was a small pronouncement, but one that had the bitter sound of possible devastation in it.

Pansy said not a word, but she stared at Peony with glistening, shining eyes. Peony sighed again. "You're willing to do this?" she asked. "Willing to give another . . . man . . ." She fairly spat the word. "Give him the chance of hurting you?"

"I am," Pansy whispered. "And he won't!"

Peony shook her head and let out a couple of soft grunts.

"It'll be okay," Pansy crooned.

"Oh, I hope so," Peony said. "I surely do hope so."

"Let me fix you some breakfast," Pansy offered, and that's how Jordan knew that the conversation was over. While Pansy cooked some eggs and sausage for Peony, Jordan sat quietly, watching Peony, who was staring at her hands, her lips moving but no sound coming from them. And Jordan was thinking about men and women and what they could do *to* . . . or *for* . . . each other. She was thinking of Pansy and Earlie, Peony and Willie, Alice and Franklin, Gertie and Bill, and now Isaiah and Pansy. Jordan's daddy's smiling face suddenly entered her field of vision, and Jordan knew that when it came to be time for her to fall in love and to marry, she would find someone exactly like her daddy—gentle, smiling, and kind, like Bill or like the Reverend Isaiah Clay. And for anyone like Mr. Franklin or old Earlie or Peony's Willie, she would cast her utter contempt upon them—cast it until they stumbled backwards and finally plunged off the high cliff of her own esteem! In that moment, Jordan knew that she deserved better than they could have offered, and that she would *have* better. How she knew it, she didn't know, but it was definitely true, and that was enough. Pansy had certainly been right. It had been good for Jordan to hear them talk about men and women.

After Peony left, Miss Amylee waked up, so Pansy, uncomplaining, made breakfast yet again. Miss Amylee looked bright and rested, and right in the middle of having her good breakfast, she put down her fork, rested her chin on her hand, and smiled at Jordan. "It was a deer!" she said.

Pansy was standing at the sink, and she didn't hear Miss Amylee. She was busy looking at the smiling face of the Reverent Isaiah Clay looking back at her from the soapy water. And when she picked up the very cup from which he had been drinking his coffee, she briefly touched the rim with her own lips.

Jordan, being still a child, did not realize what had happened that simple morning around a simple kitchen table, and she could not have put the right words to it at all. But later in her life, she would be able to express it, and it is this: *all human beings, no matter their gender or their race, or their age, deserve to be treated with affection, if possible. Or simply with respect, if affection is not possible. We owe it to each other, every single one of us; we are admonished to accomplish it, and accomplishing it will bring the victory that is our great inheritance!*

Alice and Franklin returned from their trip to Savannah the next day, and right away, Jordan knew that Peony had been wrong when she said that things would probably be better after their trip. Quite the opposite was true—Franklin seemed more highly-strung than ever and Alice more sweeping in her gestures of submission and subservience to him. But one good thing happened, as well: Alice and Franklin got so caught up in themselves that they seemed to forget about Jordan. And she didn't mind that one little bit, because she had resolved to tune in to her Gift, whether they liked it or not. No more pinching her own legs, and as for the castor oil problem, Peony and Pansy had worked that out between themselves, though it had to remain the darkest of secrets. If Alice or Franklin had learned about it, they would have fired Peony right on the spot—and heaven only knows!—Mr. Franklin probably would have pitched her right over the porch railing himself! But they never did find out about the plan, which was this: whenever Alice ordered a dose of oil for Jordan, Peony made sure they were alone in the kitchen, and she poured some castor oil right down the sink so the level in the bottle would go down, and gave Jordan a "dose" of tap water in a spoon.

"You've got such a good imagination, you just *pretend* it's castor oil," Peony always whispered to Jordan. "Do you just as much good as the real thing."

\*     \*     \*

So that on the last day of summer vacation, Jordan once again sat by the fish pool, thinking. She well knew that, for her first school assignment, she would have to write a composition about her summer, and she was pondering about the several stories she could tell: Gertie and Bill, perhaps? No. She wouldn't want to write about Gertie getting herself a baby before she got a husband. About Honey-Boy? No. That was not something to write about. For one thing, it was too sad, and also, there was something about the way grown-ups talked that made her think there must be something dirty about what happened. Something that she just didn't understand. About Miss Amylee and the "beast"? No. Again, a sad story, albeit with a happier ending, but one that was better left unsaid. About Pansy and the Reverend Isaiah Clay? Yes! That was it.

She would write about how he came to visit Pansy again and again and how he took her to meet his mother and aunt. About the many phone calls back and forth, and the happiness in Pansy's voice and her laugh, and even in the way she walked. Jordan had only to close her eyes for a moment to be able to smell the wedding flowers and hear the swishing of Pansy's beautiful dress and watch as the Reverend Isaiah Clay and Pansy Jordan walked up an aisle toward a beaming Reverend Brown.

She was thinking that everything had changed so much for all of them, just because of that kindness Pansy tried to do for Gertie. Gertie had herself a husband, even if maybe she didn't want one. Miss Amylee found out that the "beast" she'd been so scared of all her life was really something quite beautiful and fragile, and of course, Pansy's entire life had been changed, most beautifully. But Jordan couldn't quite put her finger on what had changed for *her*. Something . . . but what? Maybe something as simple as the deep, delicious joy she felt when she watched Pansy toss that stinking Gertie right into the creek! Yes—maybe that was it, and whatever it *meant* really didn't matter. She would find out about that later. She was sure of it.

But maybe she also learned the most from the alligator farm—learned from those poor, lethargic creatures confined in a pen and with nothing to swim in except a tub of stagnant tap water. Because when Jordan sat at the dining table with her mother and stepfather, she became like those captive reptiles: she went all quiet and remote, eating every bite of her dinner and remembering that, once they all left the table, she would be free to go into the kitchen with Peony, and then she would be alive and bright green and free to enjoy sweet, flowing swamp water. That was the way life was supposed to be lived, and Jordan knew that her love of natural freedom of spirit was what she would always have. Forever.

By the pool, Jordan looked all around her—at the azaleas, devoid now of blooms, and high above her head, where all the healthy green leaves on the trees were rich and vivid. But in autumn, the leaves on the trees would turn gold and red and yellow, and some would fall into the fish pool, to provide colors matching the iridescent colors of the fish. On the surface of the water, Jordan could see the reflected faces of everyone who had been in her summertime. Some of the faces were smiling— Miss Amylee's and Pansy's and Reverend Clay's. Some were sad—Aunt Rose's and Honey-Boy's. Some were without any expression at all—her mother and stepfather. But in all of it, somehow a deep, strange peacefulness.

"Jordan?" Peony called. "You out there? Come on in here

a little minute, sugar. Your mama wants you to have a little dose of castor oil, just in case."

Jordan glanced back into the pool and saw her own smiling face before she scampered toward Peony's voice.

# POSTLOGUE

WELL, *who would have believed that so many things could happen in such a short time? From the day I pushed poor old Earlie away from me and—even though I didn't mean to— caused him to die, right up until the day I married the Reverend Isaiah Clay, was less than four years, including my prison time.*

*So somewhere, somehow, that big old angel woman I saw in prison must have been around. I never did spot her myself, but I'm sure she was around, helping everybody to be in the right place at the right time. That's how perfectly it all seemed to work out. All except for Honey-Boy and Mama, that is. But even they seem to be doing better now. Honey-Boy is still trying to find another world to be comfortable in, but he is pleasant and quiet, just as he always was, unless he started in to telling folks about Santa Claus. Well . . .*

*Now, of course, we had to find somebody else to stay with Miss Amylee so I could go and live with Isaiah, as a proper wife, but since old Miss May finally got so confused and upset that she had to go live in an old folks' home, that freed Petunia to help with Miss Amylee. Petunia came and we overlapped for a few weeks, to give Miss Amylee time to get to know her. They seem to get along right well, so I never did feel guilty about getting married and moving away.*

*But I had been right in thinking Gertie wouldn't stay with Bill. Right after the baby came, she ran off, and even though he tried, he never did find her. But oh, that little baby! What an adorable little girl! Bill got himself a carpentering job—a noble profession indeed!—so he doesn't have to move around with road crews anymore. He comes to our church every single Sunday morning and brings the baby with him. Sometimes, I get to hold her. I look down into that beautiful, innocent face, and part of me is sad—because I know that life is going to wound her, just the way it wounds everybody. But I'll do the best I can for her, and between Bill and me and Isaiah, we can teach her how to be strong. Now, Gertie ran off so fast, she didn't even name that little baby, but Bill named her after his own mama, Sue Ann, and he's just the best duddy in the world. Don't know what on earth he will tell her when she's old enough to ask, but he doesn't have to worry about that for a little while. I told Bill that when Sue Ann is old enough, I want to tell her about the day I threw her mama into Jordan Creek. But I'll change the story around so that it's Gertie who throws me in the creek, because that little girl is going to need to hear stories about how her mama was good and strong and beautiful. And goodness knows, those are few and far between. But I think I can make up some stories that will make her like her mama—and herself.*

*Peony and I whipped up a plan for sparing little Jordan that awful castor oil, and after that, Jordan was lots happier. Mr. Franklin and Miss Alice are still together, but goodness knows why! He just gets more and more particular, for my mind. But they are more forgiving of letting Jordan spend time with Miss Amylee. So that's a good thing.*

*I wrote a long letter to Lizzie, telling her about my amazing year and, at last, thanking her for leading me to Jesus. I haven't gotten a letter back yet, but when I do, I expect she'll be up to the same old tricks—trying to get folks to ask Jesus to come into their hearts and getting her black eyes and bloody nose for it.*

*And now that I'm a preacher's wife, I got me no choice about whether to be good or not. Because a lot of folks look up to me and depend upon me, and I always try to do the best I can for them. I used to think of old Earlie sometimes and maybe feel bad about what happened to him. But then Isaiah always reminds me that I don't have to ever worry about my past sins, once I got my-self baptized. He says that when he lowered me into the water, all my old sins died. And that when he lifted me up, I was a res-urrected creature—a new person, so that as far as God is con-cerned, my old sins were as far as the East is from the West.*

*Well, that's exactly how I feel about where I started and where I ended—in the strong, kind arms of a good man who thinks I'm good-hearted and capable. A man who respects me and who leads me into respecting myself.*

*As far as the East is from the West. Yes! Thank You, Jesus!*

# ACKNOWLEDGMENTS

I am grateful to:

Harvey Klinger for his expert guidance and endless patience.

Carole Baron for the brilliant editing that always makes the story better than it was.

Amy Hughes, for being my fellow Southerner at Dutton. Yes, Amy, Tennessee is truly beautiful.

Friends and family for their continuing support and encouragement. I am blessed!

I also want to thank Pansy Jordan for so unexpectedly falling in love with the Reverend Isaiah Clay. Despite my initial, stringent objection, you knew what you were doing, and I was wrong in trying to stop that great love you needed to express.

Finally, as always, my eternal question: *Did I tell this story right, Mama?*